CAFFEINE NIGHTS PUBLISHING

SHAUN HUTSON

DEADHEAD

Fiction to die for...

Published by Caffeine Nights Publishing 2023

Copyright © Shaun Hutson 2023
First published in Great Britain
by Little, Brown and Company in 1993
and by Warner Books in 1994
Reprinted 1994,1995,1998,1999

Shaun Hutson has asserted his rights under the Copyright, Designs and Patents Act 1998 to be identified as the author of this work.

CONDITIONS OF SALE

All rights reserved. No part of this publication may be reproduced, stored in a retrieval system, or transmitted in any form or by any means, electronic, mechanical, photocopying, scanning, recording or otherwise, without the prior permission of the publisher.

This book has been sold subject to the condition that it shall not, by way of trade or otherwise, be lent, resold, hired out, or otherwise circulated without the publisher's prior consent in any form of binding or cover other than that in which it is published and without a similar condition including this condition being imposed on the subsequent purchaser.
All characters in this publication are fictitious and any resemblance to real persons, living or dead is purely coincidental.

Published in Great Britain by
Caffeine Nights Publishing
Amity House
71 Buckthorne Road
Minster on Sea
Isle of Sheppey
ME12 3RD

caffeinenightsbooks.com

British Library Cataloguing in Publication Data.
A CIP catalogue record for this book is available from the British Library
ISBN: 978-1-913200-12-1

Everything else by
Default, Luck and Accident

As ever and always, this book is for my daughter.

ASSASSIN
BODY COUNT
BREEDING GROUND
CAPTIVES
CHASE
COMPULSION
DEADHEAD
DEATHDAY
DYING WORDS
EPITAPH
EREBUS
EXIT WOUNDS
HEATHEN
HELL TO PAY
HYBRID
KNIFE EDGE
LAST RITES
LUCY'S CHILD
MONOLITH
NECESSARY EVIL
NEMESIS
PROGENY
PURITY
RELICS
RENEGADES
SHADOWS
SLUGS
SPAWN
STOLEN ANGELS
TESTAMENT
THE SKULL
TWISTED SOULS
UNMARKED GRAVES
VICTIMS
WARHOL'S PROPHECY
WHITE GHOST

Hammer Novelizations
TWINS OF EVIL
X THE UNKNOWN
THE REVENGE OF FRANKENSTEIN

ACKNOWLEDGEMENTS

DEADHEAD was first written and published in 1993 (and yes, I did have to check my website again to be sure…thank you Graeme…) so I just thought I'd add some new acknowledgements to…er…supplement the originals.

I'm thanking the usual suspects starting with my publisher Darren Laws who continues to be supportive and incredibly well organised when it comes to my books. Thanks, mate. Huge thanks to him and everyone else at Caffeine Nights.

Many thanks too to my agent Meg Davis whose expertise is a constant relief.

I'd also very much like to thank Marc Falvo at *Editions Faut de Frappe*. The first of many projects, I hope.

The usual nods to Emma Dark, Michael Knight, Matt Shaw, Graeme Sayer and anyone else I've forgotten but who should know why they're here anyway.

Thanks also to Claire, Monroe, Dani, Belinda, Bruce, Dave, Adrian, Steve, Janick, Nicko and Mr Rod Smallwood.

Obvious and heartfelt thanks to my daughter, Kelly.

And, as ever and most importantly, to you lot out there. My readers. Old and new. I honestly don't think you have any idea how much I appreciate your support and loyalty. Just take each book as another thank you from me. Deal?

Shaun Hutson

DEADHEAD

Deadhead was written in about four or five months in 1992 and was the second novel I did that people started labelling something other than "horror." That's the problem in this business or any business which includes a modicum of creativity. People get nervous if they can't drop a product into a handy pigeonhole and they get even more nervous when they can't drop it into a pigeon hole that they've already shovelled your other work into.

Publishers get nervous because they think that the "horror" writer they signed is choosing to branch out. Marketing people get nervous because they can't use the same campaigns they've been recycling for the last five years and readers get nervous because they think a writer they've previously loved has left them behind for new pastures.

None of these was true of either myself or Deadhead. It was merely that I wanted to write that kind of novel at that time. I never consciously sat down and thought "fuck it, I'm not doing horror any more." Why would I do that? Horror novels and being a horror writer had bought me a beautiful house, given me a fabulous career, paid for Season tickets at Anfield and funded Christ knows how many exotic holidays etc. etc. I never, ever wanted to stop writing horror. As far as I'm concerned, I never did. But, just because Deadhead and White Ghost (I think I got away with that one because Sean Doyle was in it), didn't contain resurrected Celtic Gods, undead gangsters, vampires, reanimated foetuses or flesh-eating slugs, people thought I was abandoning the horror genre.

Now, it might just be me but if anyone can dismiss a story about a private detective dying of cancer trying to rescue a young daughter who has been kidnapped by a gang who make pornographic snuff movies as anything other than horror then our definitions of that word are at cross purposes!

But the most important factor was how I myself felt about the genre and about horror in general. I'd loved it as a kid. I loved it as I grew older and as I wrote. Yes, I'd written in other genres under pseudonyms (war, westerns, non-fiction) but horror is where I feel most comfortable despite my occasional claim that "they're all books, it doesn't matter about the genre."

I believed that then and still do. I never ever objected to being labelled as a horror writer despite the fact that the genre and many who worked within it were never taken as seriously by the publishing business as writers working in more...ahem.. 'worthy' genres. Fuck that. Horror fans are the most loyal, most supportive and most dedicated of the lot. I've got readers who are still with me who were reading me in the 80's!!! You don't get much more loyal than that.

Deadhead was also the first book where a publisher actually questioned my penchant of having less than happy endings. One particular meeting led to me being called the "literary equivalent of a football hooligan" (the fact that I'd kicked a waste bin through a window probably didn't help) and my manager telling them, "You don't sign Iron Maiden and get them to record 'Moon River.'"

So, Deadhead had a somewhat chequered existence, but I still look on it with a great deal of affection. However, it was the second book of mine to be banned! The first one was Chainsaw Terror which I did as Nick Blake and which was banned by the huge wholesaler Bookwise, but this one was banned by W.H. Smith. I suppose the subject matter tipped them over the edge. Despite that, it sold well, and it was very well reviewed including a cracker from Julian Lloyd Webber who was a big fan. In fact, he even invited me to play in a celebrity cricket match because he wanted to meet me!!! Me, a fucking celebrity...the irony.

I must just tell you that Deadhead was actually inspired by a Western. Namely, The Shootist, John Wayne's last film. In that particular picture, Wayne played a gunfighter who's dying of terminal cancer, and he decides to provoke a gun fight with old adversaries so he can die in a hail of bullets rather than succumb to the insidious onslaught of the disease.

That film fascinated me, and the novel (by Glendon Swarthout) contains one of the most brilliant descriptions of a shootout I've ever read. So, it was something of an inspiration on both counts.

So, for those of you reading it for the first time then enjoy the cocktail of snuff movies, porn, cancer and extreme violence and for those of you coming back to it I hope you enjoy it again. Although maybe 'enjoy' is the wrong word but you know what I mean.

One of the characters in Deadhead is searching for his sister who has run away from Ireland to London to become a prostitute and in order to track her down he rings or visits a number of places that cater for that kind of thing. In order to make it more believable I actually rang many of these 'establishments' myself for added realism and colour. That was fun trying to explain that to the wife!! But I'm nothing if not dedicated. I'd worked briefly in a porno book shop in Soho while researching Captives three years earlier so this was a bit easier.

Right, enough of this. Get stuck in to the book that many say contains the bloodiest and most violent ending I've ever done. Horror? You make your minds up.

Shaun Hutson 2023

'Deadhead is a fantastic read, a real page-turner that would enliven any journey'

Daily Express

Phillip moved towards three bags bundled together at the top of a flight of stairs leading down to a basement flat...

Further up the street his colleagues were collecting bags, waiting until the wagon drew nearer before hurling them inside. Phillip decided he needed help with these three.

Besides, the smell was appalling.

He reached for the third.

The top of the black bag tore as he pulled it, the plastic ripping, the bag toppling over.

Flies swarmed from inside, a cloud of parasites buzzing madly around Phillip and the stinking contents of the bag. There were more maggots, too, flooding out across the pavement.

In amongst it all was a shape Phillip did not instantly recognize.

It was bent double, the skin mottled blue and grey where it wasn't covered in blood.

He smelled an odour so rank, so fetid that it was all he could do not to vomit.

Then he saw the head as it sagged forward, cracking hard against the pavement. One sightless eye gazed up at him. The other had gone; the socket was now filled with hundreds of writhing maggots.

The body of Maria Jenkins lay at his feet.

'Terrible experiences make one wonder whether he who experiences them is not something terrible.'
Nietzsche

Part One

'Boys and girls come out to play, the moon doth shine as bright as day.
>The Oxford Dictionary of Nursery Rhymes

'Men fear Death, as children fear to go in the dark.

One

Robert Slattery felt as if someone had wrapped him in hot bandages. The moisture trickled down his back, beading between his shoulder blades as he walked, coursing down his spine, soaking into his T-shirt.

Although he wore only a thin top, shorts and trainers, he found the heat almost unbearable. The onset of evening had brought a respite from the blazing sun, but the searing heat had been replaced by a cloying humidity that seemed to blanket everything like a heated shroud.

The ground was cracked and dry, the grass brown and dying. The earth itself had split and yawned in places. Wounds in the dirt gaped like thirsty mouths, waiting for the rain which showed no signs of falling.

The entire country had been gripped by the heatwave for more than a month now. Less than an inch of rain had fallen and most of that had been in one massive deluge three weeks ago. Since then there had been nothing but unrelenting heat.

Slattery hated the heat. It was so bloody undignified walking around in a shirt which stuck to your back after only a few minutes. He'd dug out every single black or white shirt he possessed since the heatwave began. To wear red or blue would have meant risking those dreaded dark rings of sweat beneath the arms. Even the strongest anti-perspirant seemed helpless against the onslaught. He drew a hand through his hair and felt perspiration on his forehead.

As he walked slowly across Clapham Common he glanced to his right and left at the other souls who had ventured out into the sickly humid evening.

There were kids kicking a football around, shouting and dashing back and forth as if unaware of the temperature.

On a park bench nearby a couple in their early twenties were kissing passionately, limbs entwined like mating squids. Slattery smiled to himself as he passed, trying not to look too closely but unable to ignore the fact that the girl was particularly attractive; her cut-off denim shorts displayed a fine pair of tanned legs.

He wandered on, glancing down at his dog. It was, after all, the reason he was on the Common this evening. Slattery tossed a small rubber ball he pulled from his pocket and watched as the smooth-haired mongrel went chasing after it. The ball bounced close to a man sitting on one of the wrought-iron benches. He glanced irritably across and Slattery raised a hand in apology. The dog scuttled beneath the bench to retrieve the ball, apparently oblivious of the seat's occupant, and loped back towards Bob, the ball held in its jaws.

Perhaps he was feeling the heat too, Slattery thought, as he pulled it from the dog's jaws and threw it again, this time towards the trees.

The dog set off and caught the ball, returning it once more.

Clouds of midges circled around the tops of bushes like millions of animated cinders stirred by an invisible breeze. He watched them for a moment as he strolled on, feeling the perspiration soaking even more deeply into his T-shirt.

His dog looked up at him as if it expected the ball to be thrown but didn't really relish the prospect of retrieving it. He exhaled deeply, then sucked in a lungful of the dry air. There wasn't a breath of wind. The sinking sun bled across the sky but, despite the dark blue clouds gathering, the approaching night promised no respite from the heat.

Slattery threw the ball again and the dog loped off after it, disappearing into the bushes.

While he waited for the animal to return, he leant against a water fountain that looked as cracked and dry as the parched earth. He pressed the knob but no water came out. All he heard was a low gurgling sound.

From behind him there was a shout; he turned to see the kids who'd been playing football jumping around excitedly. He smiled to himself. Obviously a goal had been scored. Either that or someone had heard there was going to be a rain shower. He grinned and looked towards the bushes, waiting for his dog to reappear.

'Come on, Sam,' he muttered to himself, wiping perspiration from his forehead.

Then he heard the barking.

He frowned and set off towards the bushes. Perhaps Sam had found a bitch in there, he mused. Dirty little sod.

The barking continued.

There were other dogs on the Common and one or two were looking in his direction. He just hoped he didn't find himself surrounded by a pack of them.

He pushed his way through the bushes and caught sight of his own dog standing a few feet away.

He muttered as stinging nettles prickled his calves. Flies and wasps buzzed around him irritably.

The dog was standing perfectly still, only its head moving as it barked loudly.

'What's wrong with you?' Slattery asked, brushing leaves from his T-shirt.

Then he noticed the stench, a smell like rotting meat only more pungent. It was so strong he felt his stomach somersault.

'Shit,' he muttered, covering his mouth, glancing first at his dog then at the swarm of flies that hovered around the object in front of him.

It took him only a second to realize what it was.

'Oh, Jesus Ch . . .'

Slattery never managed the last word.

He turned away and vomited violently.

The dog continued to bark.

Two

'So you're satisfied that the woman in the photos is your wife?'

Nick Ryan took a final drag on his cigarette and ground it out in the ashtray on his desk. With the phone wedged between his shoulder and his ear he reached for the packet of Dunhill, took out another cigarette, and lit up again, drawing deeply.

The voice on the other end of the line was hesitant.

'I suppose so,' Eric Johnson told him.

'Either it is or it isn't, Mr Johnson' Ryan said, blowing out a stream of smoke.

'This isn't easy for me, you know.'

Ryan raised his eyebrows and glanced at his watch.

'I'm sure it's not,' he said, trying to inject a note of sympathy into his voice. 'But you should recognise your own wife.' As he spoke, Ryan flicked through the dozen black-and-whites. They showed a woman in her late thirties getting into and out of a car with a man. Others showed her walking with the same man. Some had been taken in a crowded street, others in a park.

In one of them the couple was kissing.

'It's a bit of a shock' Johnson told him. 'I mean, I suspected her of having an affair, I know, but...' The sentence trailed off.

'It's never pleasant finding out something like this, Mr Johnson,' Ryan told him, glancing again at his watch.

'When I hired you, I suppose I was angry. Now I know for sure, I don't know what to think.'

The other man's voice cracked slightly.

She was being shafted by another bloke, Ryan thought. End of story.

'The photos will be proof enough when the case goes to court. I wouldn't worry about the Judge finding for you. It's there in black and white, after all,' Ryan said coldly.

'I didn't really want it to come to this' Johnson murmured.

Ryan exhaled wearily and reached for a pencil. He began drawing circles on his pad.

'I don't know what I should do, Mr Ryan.'

Ditch the bitch, Ryan thought, smiling thinly.

'Well, you've got the evidence, Mr Johnson. What you do with it is up to you.'

'Perhaps I was hoping that it was just my imagination.'

Get off the fucking line, for Christ's sake.

'Do you think I should confront her with it?' Johnson wanted to know.

Make her eat the photos for all I care, just get off the line.

'You suspected her of having an affair; you now know for sure that she was. You hired me to get you proof and I've done that. What happens now is your responsibility, Mr Johnson.'

There was a long silence at the other end of the phone. Ryan glanced at his watch again.

He thought he heard sniffling.

On his pad he wrote PRAT then went back to drawing circles.

'Thank you for your help,' said Johnson, his voice quivering.

'My pleasure. If you could send the cheque as soon as possible, I'd appreciate it.'

Johnson sniffed.

'Yes, I will,' he said quietly. 'I suppose this is all in a day's work for you, isn't it?'

'Every day's different,' Ryan said conversationally. 'As I said, if you could forward the cheque, I'd be very grateful.' He took another drag on his cigarette. He could hear Johnson crying softly at the other end of the phone.

'Nice doing business with you,' said Ryan and hung up.

Three

He patted the receiver and got to his feet, gathering up the black and white photos and pushing them into an envelope. He slipped it into a drawer in his desk and reached for the half dozen letters he'd picked up as he entered.

Ryan Investigations' offices were situated on the top floor of a five storey building in Old Compton Street. The premises consisted of the office itself, a kitchenette and a toilet. The walls of the office sported framed photos and posters, including a picture of Ryan himself just after he'd joined the police force nearly twenty years before. The fresh-faced eighteen-year-old who looked happily out on the office bore little resemblance to the thirty-seven-year-old man sitting on the leather sofa opposite the desk, opening the mail. The icy blue eyes were the same, but now they were surrounded by wrinkles and the expression Ryan usually sported was one of indifference - not the expectancy he'd showed as a trainee policeman.

He'd risen swiftly to the position of Detective and had hoped to reach the position of Detective-Inspector. But that was not to be.

Despite his arrest record, and his part in breaking a particularly large drugs ring, he'd been repeatedly passed over for promotion.

The excuse had always been that he was more useful on the streets, but he'd known the real reason. His temperament.

More than once his superiors had referred to him as a hot-head. It had come to a climax when he'd broken the jaw of a suspect who'd taken a shot at him during a chase through Whiteley's shopping centre in Bays- water. Despite Ryan's protestations that the man was carrying a gun and could have killed innocent passers-by, as well as him, the incident was the last straw.

He had been officially reprimanded and suspended for two weeks.

On his return he tendered his resignation.

Within a year he'd set up Ryan Investigations. Now, four years later, business was booming.

Divorce, surveillance, serving writs. The scope of Ryan's

work was enormous; it had grown to such proportions that he sometimes needed to use outside help for what he saw as the more mundane tasks associated with the job. He had friends at some of the biggest security firms in the capital; they were happy to supply him with men for the jobs that required a little muscle.

So successful had business been lately that Ryan was considering not only moving to larger premises but also getting himself a secretary. It was the administrational aspect of the job that he found tedious. He had a temp come in once a week to type up his letters. She told him how exciting she thought it was working for a private detective. Even if it was only one day a week.

Ryan smiled as he thought about her. He sifted through the mail and found some circulars, a cheque and a letter from a woman who suspected her husband of having an affair with another man. Ryan raised his eyebrows, re-folded the letter and placed it in a plastic tray on his desk.

Most of the work was divorce work. His job was to gather evidence for his clients, which would then be turned over to their lawyers. It wasn't spectacular work but it paid well. His usual charges were fifty pounds an hour plus expenses. It varied according to the job, naturally.

He still had friends at New Scotland Yard, useful contacts who could supply him with information if he needed it. Not once in the past four years had he regretted his decision to leave the force.

He got to his feet and glanced out of the window that looked out over Charing Cross Road.

The thoroughfare was busy, as usual; people moved back and forth beneath the blistering sun.

In the cloudless sky the searing orb blazed with even greater brilliance than on the day before. The heatwave showed no sign of relenting. Ryan opened a window and the heat flooded in, carried on an invisible tide of carbon monoxide fumes from the hundreds of belching exhausts below. It was cooler inside the office, even though the mercury in the thermometer on the wall was nudging seventy-six Fahrenheit.

He looked into the street for a moment longer, then wandered through into the kitchenette, where he filled the kettle and flicked the switch to set it boiling. He rinsed a mug beneath the tap and flipped open the cupboard above in search of the coffee jar.

He found an empty one and muttered under his breath, tossing it into the nearby rubbish bin.

He turned off the kettle and decided to walk round the corner into Charing Cross Road. There was a small cafe there where he often picked up a sandwich.

On the way out he picked his newspaper up from his desk.

As yet, he hadn't noticed the headline.

Four

If the heat outside was intense, inside the cafe was like an oven.

Ryan felt the warm air hit him like a wall. The small eatery smelled of frying bacon; it always did. Whether it was early morning, lunchtime or late at night the smell of frying bacon was ever-present. Sandwiches and pies were assembled behind the clean glass counter for inspection. Steam billowing from the large tea-um at one end of the counter only served to add to the sweltering heat.

Ryan removed his tie and unbuttoned the top two buttons of his shirt, feeling perspiration form at the back of his neck. He wiped it away with his handkerchief. A large man with a massive stomach was waiting to be served. He was sweating profusely despite the fact that he was only wearing shorts and a vest. A tattoo on his left shoulder in the shape of a snake disappeared inside his vest, the head emerging on his right shoulder. Droplets of sweat rolling down his back made it look as if the snake was shedding tears.

Ryan fanned himself with his rolled-up newspaper and studied the array of sandwiches and cakes. He glanced around at the other occupants of the cafe; apart from the large man and himself, there were only three other people.

Two youths dressed in leather jackets, apparently impervious to the horrendously high temperatures, were talking animatedly as they thumbed through a magazine. Ryan realized that there was a gig on at the Marquee next door that night. Obviously, he reasoned, these two were taking no chances about being late.

On one of the high stools beside the mirrored wall an old woman sat nursing a polystyrene mug of soup, staring down into it every now and then. She had a plastic bag with her; the sleeve of a sweater hung out of it. The woman looked at her reflection in the mirror tiles, averting her gaze quickly, as if displeased by the image. Ryan shook his head and returned his attention to the sandwiches.

The large man with the tattoo was ambling off towards a table, balancing a huge lump of pizza in one hand and a mug of tea in the other.

Ryan stepped forward to the counter.

'Morning, Frank,' he said, nodding affably to the little man who beamed back at him and pushed his black hair away from his face. It looked as if someone had sprayed his face with water, so much perspiration sheathed it.

'What can I get you, Nick?' asked the little man, still smiling. Frank Scalini wiped his pudgy hands on his apron and leaned closer. 'You on a case?' he asked conspiratorially.

Ryan nodded and winked.

'The case of the empty coffee jar' he said. 'Give me a cappuccino, will you, and a bit of that gateau.' He pointed to the cake.

'My wife made it fresh today' Scalini announced.

'How is she?'

'She has the baby in about three weeks,' he told him proudly, handing him the piece of cake and the coffee.

'I'll be in for my cigar when she does,' Ryan said, and paid.

He wandered over to the nearest table and sat down, flipping open his paper, pushing a forkful of cake into his mouth. As he read the back page he rummaged in his pocket and found his cigarettes. He took a couple more mouthfuls of cake then lit up.

There was a loud crackle from behind the counter as a wasp flew into the insectocutor. It disappeared in a flash of blue sparks to be joined a second later by a large fly.

Ryan sipped at his coffee and turned to the front page. The headline glared back at him.

BODY FOUND ON CLAPHAM COMMON:
THE FIFTH VICTIM?

There was a photo of bushes and uniformed men standing around. Ryan read the beginning of the article.

The body of eighteen-year-old John Molloy was found on Clapham Common yesterday. The youngster is believed to be the fifth victim, in as many months, of the same killer.

His body had been mutilated and was partially decomposed.

Like the previous four victims, Molloy had been living rough on the streets of London for some time . . .

Ryan sat back in his chair and sipped at his coffee, glancing at the remainder of the article.

Details of the precise nature of the mutilations had been withheld, as had the names of two previous victims aged fifteen.

In every case the youngsters had been sleeping rough.

Ryan wondered who was in charge of the investigation. Maybe the bastard whose job he should have had? He folded up the paper and, finishing his cake and coffee, glanced down at his watch.

He lit up another cigarette and decided he should make a move. He'd grab a taxi outside.

The insectocutor crackled as it claimed another victim and Ryan waved to Saclini as he hurried out onto the pavement.

The concrete was warm beneath his feet, the heat from the sun intense.

He saw a cab approaching and stuck out an arm, stepping back as the vehicle pulled in. Once more he looked at his watch.

He didn't want to be late.

Five

The air-conditioning inside the office was so efficient that Ryan felt cold after the scorching heat outside. He had replaced his tie during the taxi ride and also slipped on his jacket. Now he sat opposite the large oak desk, his eyes flickering first around the room then back and forth between the two people who faced him.

Both were, he guessed, in their early fifties. The man, Graham Witton, was tall and thin, his face pale and drawn to the point of being gaunt.

His companion was an elegant woman with pinched features and hair drawn back with daunting severity from her forehead. She fixed Ryan in an appraising gaze and regarded his rumpled shirt with distaste. He noticed her stare and looked at her legs, suppressing a smile when she crossed them self-consciously. Denise Shaw coloured slightly.

As General Manager of The Royalton Hotel, Graham Witton carried the necessary air of simpering civility and practised officiousness that men in his position usually mastered effortlessly. His clothes and his appearance were immaculate; Ryan had the feeling that if he walked out into the street and into the inferno of the city, he would not so much as perspire. Every inch of his body was stiffly efficient.

Ryan leant forward and picked up his tea cup, hearing it chink against the saucer.

Denise Shaw kept her eyes upon him, looking at the

cup as if fearing that Ryan might shatter the expensive china simply by his close proximity to it.

He took a sip and replaced the cup, reaching for his cigarettes.

As he lit up, Denise Shaw wrinkled her nose.

'How long do you think the robberies have been going on?' Ryan asked, blowing out a long stream of smoke in her direction.

'We've had guests reporting items missing for about a month now,' Witton told him. 'But when the money was stolen, we thought it was time to act.'

'How much was taken?'

'Nearly three hundred pounds.'

'Why didn't you call the police?' Ryan wanted to know. r

'The guest in question didn't want to. Besides, we do have the good name of the hotel to consider,' Witton told him.

'What else has gone missing?' Ryan wanted to know.

'Travellers' cheques, items of clothing; pieces of jewellery in one or two cases,' Denise Shaw told him.

'And you're sure it's a member of staff?'

'If we were sure we wouldn't have called you in, Mr Ryan,' Denise Shaw said contemptuously.

Ryan eyed her indifferently and turned his attention back to Witton.

'And none of the guests have asked you to call the police?' he asked. 'I find that a little strange.'

'We . . . how shall I put it . . . we dissuaded them. We replaced money if it was taken, or we gave them the value of other items that were stolen. As I said to you, we cannot have that kind of publicity in a hotel like this.' Witton smiled his superior smile and pressed the tips of his fingers together.

'I was thrown out of here once,' said Ryan. 'For wearing jeans.' He smiled.

'We do have a very strict policy on denim in the hotel' Witton informed him.

'It isn't allowed in any part of the hotel' Denise Shaw echoed.

Ryan nodded. 'So at least you know your thief isn't the one in the Levi's.' He chuckled.

'When can you start your investigation?' Witton asked.

Ryan got to his feet. 'Tomorrow, if I can get someone in.'

'What do you mean?' Denise Shaw wanted to know.

'I mean that I'm going to have to use someone on the premises, someone posing as a member of your staff so that they can get close to the thief.'

'Why can't you do the job yourself?' Denise Shaw asked indignantly.

'Because I've got more important things to do than wander around dressed like a bell-boy trying to find out who's lifting some rich bastard's wallet or ring. I'll have someone here tomorrow.' He turned and headed towards the office door. 'Oh, and don't worry. I'll make sure he doesn't wear jeans.'

Six

The uniformed doorman glanced briefly at Ryan as he stood on the pavement in front of the hotel, then the man hurried to open the door for another departing guest.

As he pulled his tie free and stuffed it into his pocket,

Ryan watched the old woman move as graciously as she could out into the sweltering heat of the street. Why she was wearing a fur coat in temperatures nudging eighty and in the middle of the day Ryan could only guess, but she swept past him in a wave of perfume and make-up, heading towards a Mercedes at the kerb.

The private detective watched her scramble in, both the car driver and the doorman fighting for the privilege of opening the door for her. Ryan shook his head and scurried across the road, the full force of the sun hitting him as he left the shade of the canopy.

Piccadilly was busy, choked with traffic as usual. The heat, combined with the noxious clouds of carbon monoxide spewing from countless exhausts, made him feel light-headed. The perspiration was soaking into his shirt. A couple passed him, both dressed in matching shorts and tops, the man badly sunburnt on his shoulders and arms. The woman was carrying a large map of Central London. Bloody tourists, Ryan thought, almost colliding with a flustered woman pushing a buggy with twins in it.

Ryan was about to apologise when the woman told him to look where he was going. He raised his eyebrows, glancing at her as she stalked off, pushing the buggy through the crowds of pedestrians, cutting a swathe like a latter-day Boadicea.

All around him he saw faces flushed by the heat.

He coughed and felt a pain in his chest. Muttering under his breath he continued walking, wondering why the feeling of light-headedness had not passed. Heading down Berkely Street, past the Holiday Inn, Ryan hesitated a moment then turned and walked towards the main entrance of the hotel. He cursed when he felt another twinge of pain. Perhaps he should sit down for a while, wait until he'd recovered his wits and got rid of the bloody thing. It wasn't the first time he'd experienced it in the last few weeks.

He strode through the lobby of the hotel, smiling at a particularly attractive receptionist. She returned the gesture, colouring slightly.

He walked on through into the bar and sat down at a table near the window, laying his jacket on the seat beside him.

It was pleasantly cool in the bar and also pleasingly quiet. Apart from Ryan himself, only two other people were present. They were engrossed in conversation.

He sat back in his seat and wiped a hand across his forehead, feeling the perspiration there. As he turned he caught sight of his reflection in the mirrored wall to his right and was surprised at how pale he looked. The pain still jabbed inside his chest; Ryan winced as he felt needle-like prickles within his ribcage. He took a few deep breaths, his actions interrupted by the arrival of the barman.

Ryan ordered an orange juice and reached into his jacket pocket for a cigarette, relieved that the pain seemed to be diminishing slightly. If only this bloody giddiness would leave him too.

When the drink arrived he gulped half of it down immediately and ordered another, sucking in deep breaths and closing his eyes. It had to be the heat, he reasoned. He'd only felt like this for the last couple of weeks, ever since the temperatures had started to soar.

Yes. It was the heat.

Ryan tried to push the thoughts of pain from his mind and concentrate on the job at the Royalton. Reaching into his inside pocket he pulled out a small black diary and flicked through it until he reached the back and some phone numbers. He ran his finger down a list of names and numbers. Each of the men had worked for him in the past on one job or more. There were a dozen names; they were men he trusted (God knew there were few enough of them). He began looking for a likely name to work at the hotel. They were ex-policemen, bailiffs and security men. Each had a full-time job but would work for Ryan on a temporary basis because he paid well. He found the one he sought and made a mental note to call the man when he got back to the office.

He was replacing the diary in his jacket when he was struck

by another coughing fit.

'Shit' he muttered, pressing his hand to his mouth.

The pain was there again, too.

And the dizziness.

He hauled himself to his feet and headed for the toilets, pushing the doors open and crossing to the white hand-basins. The lights reflected off the brilliant white tiles; Ryan felt dazzled. He leant against one of the sinks, head down, then spun the cold tap.

As he looked up he saw how pale his skin was; it looked waxen, corpse-like.

He cupped his hands together, scooped water into them and splashed his face. The cold water felt good on his hot skin.

Ryan coughed again as he straightened up, hawking loudly, tasting mucus in his mouth. He spat it out.

The globule that hit the sink was thick with blood.

He stared at the crimson lump, watching as it slid slowly down the white porcelain, leaving a red smear.

He turned on the other tap and washed it away, cupping cold water to his mouth and swallowing. He coughed again and propelled another gob of fluid into the sink.

There was no blood this time.

The dizziness was beginning to pass off too.

He exhaled deeply, using the roller-towel to dry his face.

Ryan stood before the mirror and ran both hands through his hair, glancing at the dark rings beneath his eyes.

He thought of the blood.

'Fuck it,' he murmured, still studying his reflection. He switched off the taps, took a couple of deep breaths, then turned and headed for the door.

He'd finish his drink, then get a cab back to the office. There were things he had to do.

Seven

'I would have killed the bastard.'

Brian Webster sat back on his seat and ran his hands slowly up and down his thighs, aware of the other eyes on him but unconcerned.

'Every fucking night he used to come home pissed,' he continued. 'He never had a job but he always seemed to find enough money for drink. For as long as I can remember he drank. I hardly saw him when I was a kid. My mum used to put me and my brother to bed but he'd wake us up when he got home. I'd always hear him. Shouting and swearing and throwing things. Then, when he got fed up of breaking plates or cups, he'd start on my mum. I wondered why she put up with it. She knew other people used to talk about her, about my old man, but it didn't seem to bother her. I used to feel sorry for her but then, as I got older, I started to get angry with her. I told her to leave him.

'I remember, on my twelfth birthday, she made a cake. I had about ten friends round to the house, but my old man came in pissed and he wrecked everything. Then he whacked my mum. She had a black eye for two weeks, he hit her so hard. I used to imagine what life would be like without him. I used to wish that he'd just fucking die. Anything, so that me and my mum and my brother would get some peace. Then, when I got to sixteen, he started picking on me, too. He said that I was a man and that I should know how to look after myself. When he hit my mum I wanted to hit him back. I can remember hating myself for being scared of him, for not helping my mum. But that annoyed me even more. I was fourteen, my brother was twelve. Mum could have left him. We'd have gone with her. We'd all have managed somehow. But she stayed with him. She never even fucking moaned about him. If I told her she should leave him, she used to say that it wasn't all his fault. I couldn't believe that. He'd come home every night and beat shit out of her and she was telling me it wasn't his fault. Nobody asked him to go down the fucking pub every night.

'He put her in hospital twice. He broke her jaw and her nose. And she still stayed with him. After a while I started to hate her too. I hated her for being so stupid, for not having the guts to leave him. He could have killed her and it wouldn't have bothered him. When he was pissed, he didn't know what he was doing. He didn't care who he hurt.

'I used to dread holidays most. Christmas, Easter, that sort of thing. We never had one Christmas without that bastard ruining it. Mum used to cook a big dinner and he'd fuck off down the pub, then he'd come home at closing time mouthing off, throwing his weight about. Smashing things.

'One Christmas, just a couple of years ago it was, we were sitting round waiting for him to come home so we could have our Christmas dinner. He rolled in, smashed out of his head and, because the dinner wasn't on the table, he turned the fucking thing over. Wrecked everything. Plates, glasses, food. Everything ended up on the floor. Then he started hitting my mum and she just took it, like she always did. Never hit him back. Perhaps she was scared that if she did he'd lay into her even worse.

'There was a carving knife lying on the kitchen floor and I picked it up. I wanted to stick it in him. I wanted to kill the bastard but he saw me with it. He must have realized what I was thinking and he turned on me. And my mum tried to stop him so he knocked her down and, while she was lying there, he kicked her. I ran. I locked myself in my bedroom but he got in and he beat the fuck out of me. I couldn't go to school for a week, until the bruises went down and some of the cuts healed. But my mum didn't do anything even then. She just carried on, as if it was all part of life. Still, I suppose it was by that time. She was used to it.

'I knew after that, though, that I wanted him dead. If I'd stayed I know I'd have killed him. I wouldn't have put up with what my mum put up with. That's why I had to leave home.

'I would have killed the bastard.'

Eight

Because of the heat inside the room the windows were open. The smell of diesel fumes was strong in the air. Carried on the dry wind, the stink of hot oil and smoke mingled with the more pungent fuel odour to create a noxious cloud that seemed to hang over St Pancras Goods depot like a man-made blanket. The already stifling heat made the stench even more repulsive.

From his position on his bed inside Ossulston Street hostel, Brian Webster could see out of the window and over the Goods Yard. Shunters trundled slowly up and down the network of rusty rails, fumes belching from them.

Aware of the others' probing eyes he wound his hair around one index finger repeatedly, not looking at any one face in particular.

The others were all roughly his age, nineteen going on forty. The ravages of living rough had taken a toll on their features. Gone were the fresh, mischievous, expectant faces of youth; these bore the bone-weary expressions of people who had never even dreamed dreams, never mind had them dashed. It was as if someone had systematically sucked the life from every one of them, draining away hope and replacing it with despair.

Their ages ranged from fifteen to twenty; boys and girls.

Brian Webster had often heard the expression 'Shit Happens'. He knew it was true. It had happened to him, to him and everyone else in the hostel.

Now lost in his own thoughts, he watched another train move lethargically about its business, aware only of the cloying heat.

'What's the point of all this, anyway?' asked Suzi Gray. 'I mean, every week we sit around here and talk about why we left home or what we're supposed to do, and the next week we're all sitting here again talking about the same things. I don't see why we bother.'

Suzi was a year older than Webster and had probably, at one time, been a very pretty young woman. She still

had a good figure, even if poor nutrition had served to make her a little skinny. It was in her hair and skin that the deficiencies showed. Her face was pockmarked, her long hair lank and dull. She sat cross-legged on a chair, barefoot.

'What is the point?' she repeated.

Emma Powell was hard pressed to find an answer.

She'd worked in hostels like this one, both long- and short-stay, for the past eight years. In fact she'd begun work in her first the day before her twenty-second birthday. The hostel in Ossulston Street was just one of many emergency short-stay hostels set up by the DSS in a desperate attempt to keep youngsters or anyone who had no accommodation off the streets. It was a desperate gambit by a desperate government to keep down statistics. No one knew for sure how many people were without homes in London and those in power were intent on it staying that way. The short-stay hostels kept people off the streets for up to three months at a time. It was time enough to allow figures to be juggled and it sounded good for ministers to crow about what was being done for the less fortunate.

Emma Powell knew from bitter experience that the solution wasn't so much an insoluble one as an inconvenient one. London was like a gigantic rug; the homeless were swept beneath it into hostels like this to hide them from sight.

She shifted uncomfortably in her seat, aware that they were waiting for an answer to Suzi's question.

'If you all talk to each other,' Emma began, 'if you all find out why you left home, you might begin to understand your problems a bit better.'

'Bollocks,' said Alan Casey, his Glaswegian accent hard.

'Our problem is that we don't have anywhere to live,' Suzi echoed.

'This is all bullshit' Casey continued. 'We sit around talking and where the fuck does it get us? All we know is that in three months' time we're going to be thrown out of here and we'll be back on the streets again.'

'Or in some other hostel' added Webster, still twining his hair around his finger.

'You won't be thrown out of here after three months, Alan' Emma Powell told him. 'It's regulations. I'm as sorry about it as you are, but I'm only doing my job.'

'So were the SS' Casey said, and laughed. 'Only obeying orders. Orders from above. From some cunt who's never had to worry about going without food or a bed. The fucking rules are made by people who don't live in the real world. How many fucking starving politicians do you ever see? How many of their kids will end up getting mugged or fucking raped or worse because they've got nowhere to live except in a cardboard box or a fucking doss-house like this? I'll tell you. None of them. Bastards.' He got to his feet and crossed to the window.

Casey was a big, powerfully built figure, his size and the heavy growth of whiskers he sported making him look older than his eighteen years.

'It's not Emma's fault' a broad Liverpudlian accent interjected. 'She can't do anything about it. It's no good blaming other people for your own faults.' Janet Ferguson picked agitatedly at the side of one black varnished fingernail and shifted her considerable bulk on her chair. 'It's not her fault you're here.'

'I know it's not her fucking fault' Casey said, spinning round angrily. 'I'm just making a point.'

'If you don't like it, go back home' Janet persisted.

'Get real, for fuck's sake,' snapped Casey. 'If I wanted to be at home do you think I'd have left in the first place? Why the fuck don't you go home, too?'

Janet lowered her gaze, her cheeks colouring beneath

the coating of her pure white make-up. It was in marked contrast to the bright orange of her hair, swept up in a high cockscomb, held in place by enough hair lacquer to put another hole in the ozone layer.

'Isn't it time we called it a day?' said Webster wearily. 'This isn't getting any of us anywhere, is it?'

Emma Powell was forced to agree. She nodded and got to her feet, looking around at their faces.

She saw only blank expressions, tired resignation.

'I've got something to say,' Maria Jenkins interjected.

She was a pretty girl of sixteen, her dish-water blonde hair pulled back in a ponytail.

One or two people looked at her. Casey was already walking towards the exit.

'I want to go to John's funeral. Do you know when it is, Emma?' asked Maria.

Emma Powell looked puzzled.

'I can find out,' she said.

'Why do you want to go?' Webster asked. 'Molloy was only here for about two weeks.'

'He was a nice guy. I liked him,' Maria said defensively. 'I think it's right that one of us should pay our respects.'

'I hardly spoke to him,' Webster said.

'You hardly speak to anyone,' Suzi commented, chuckling.

'There's another reason one of us ought to go,' Maria said. 'We shared this hostel with John until he was murdered. It could just as easily have been one of us.'

Nine

There wasn't much in the file. The cumulative experience of sixteen years added up to less than half a sheet of A4.

Emma Powell opened the plastic file and looked at the card marked JOHN MOLLOY.

It carried his date of birth, his home address, his height, weight and the other minor details which were all that remained now. She wondered if the police had studied a similar sheet after they'd found his mutilated body on Clapham Common.

The newspaper on her desk carried the story of the discovery of his body but Emma had glanced only briefly at it. He was dead. It was enough to know that. She knew that he'd been mutilated. She had no desire to know how.

Emma replaced the file and flicked through others in the cabinet jammed into one small corner of her tiny office. There was no air-conditioning in the small room; she had the one window open wide in an effort to counteract the intense heat. As the afternoon wore on the temperature approached eighty-five. There wasn't a breath of wind.

She looked through the remaining files. There were over two hundred of them, all arranged alphabetically. Each one contained details of those presently resident at the hostel and also those who had previously stayed for the regulation three months. Each file contained details not only of age and physical matters but also of backgrounds, home addresses (if there were any), families and friends. It seemed pointless keeping the files. Emma knew that no one who had passed through the hostel could return; but it made her feel as if she were running something other than a refuge. Everything there was to know about residents past and present had been neatly typed, the sum total of their lives contained in a few lines.

Emma closed the drawer and crossed back to her desk. She sat down, running a hand through her hair, feeling how wet it was where it touched her neck. She took a tissue and wiped away the perspiration.

The office door was open but the knock startled her. She looked up to see Maria Jenkins.

'Come in, Maria,' Emma said, motioning towards a chair but

the young girl decided to stand. She glanced out of the window across the Goods Yard.

'Did you find out about John's funeral?' Maria asked.

'I rang his home but there was no reply.'

'What about the police? They'd know, wouldn't they?'

'They might not give out that information to someone who wasn't in the family.'

Maria sighed and finally sat down.

'It said in the paper he was mutilated,' she muttered, noticing the folded copy of the Mirror on the desk. 'Like the others.'

Emma merely nodded.

'It's very sad,' she said finally.

'Don't you ever get sick of all this?' Maria asked, making an expansive gesture with her hand. 'You must realize there's nothing you can do in the long run to help. You can only keep people off the streets for three months. After that, they're helpless again. Don't you ever feel like giving up?'

'I've never thought about it. Even a little help is better than none at all, isn't it?'

Maria nodded slowly.

'I wonder if John's parents are sorry now he's dead?' she mused. 'I mean, if it was their fault he left home, I wonder if they blame themselves for his death?'

'That's difficult to say, Maria. It was his choice to leave. He came to London because he wanted to. Just like nearly everyone else here or at any of the other hostels.'

'Nobody cares, do they?' said Maria, getting to her feet. 'People say they're concerned about the homeless, but no one really cares unless it's happening to them.' She made for the door. 'No one really cares that John's dead because he wasn't important. He just lived rough. No one knew him. No one cared- No one cares about any of us.'

Emma opened her mouth to say something, but merely ran her tongue across her lips. There was nothing to say.

'No one would care if we all died. At least we'd be out of the way for good then.'

As much as she wanted to, Emma found it difficult to disagree.

Ten

'Where will you go?'

Suzi Gray sat on the edge of the bed, watching as Maria Jenkins removed what few belongings she had from the locker. She stuffed them into a small nylon holdall: a couple of pairs of socks, a pair of leggings, some knickers. She accidentally dropped a T-shirt onto the floor. Janet Ferguson retrieved it and handed it to her. She smiled and pushed it into the holdall with everything else.

'There are other hostels around, aren't there?' Maria said. 'I could try one of them.'

'I wouldn't if I were you,' Suzi advised her. 'Most of them are useless.' She swept a hand through her hair. 'Especially the mixed ones.' She lowered her head slightly, the memories painful.

It had been less than two years ago, but Suzi could remember it with the same appalling clarity as if it had been yesterday.

There had been three of them. All in their early twenties. Two of them drunk or stoned - she had never found out which. It didn't matter much, either. All that mattered was that they had attacked her. Pulled the covers from her bed as she slept. While she was still recovering her wits two of them had held her down while the third had raped her. They had taken it in turns, covering her mouth with a piece of sheet to stop her making a noise. Then, when they'd finished, they had left her there and run from the hostel.

She had dragged herself into one of the bathrooms and scrubbed their filth away, but no matter how many times she washed she felt she would always carry their mark, like a glaring tattoo only she could see. She'd left the same night and had wandered the streets until daylight, her anger almost as strong as her disgust.

Two weeks later, in a shop doorway in Oxford Street, a couple of youths had lunged at her late one night.

The first she had almost blinded when she jabbed at his eyes with her fingers. The second had fared even worse. Suzi had laid his cheek open to the bone with a

piece of broken glass she'd snatched up.

She had watched in triumph as they'd run.

Now she pulled her legs up beneath her and accepted a cigarette from Janet.

'What will you do for money?' the large girl asked.

Maria shrugged.

'Beg, I suppose' she said, smiling bitterly.

'You could go on the game.' Janet chuckled. 'There's a lot of money in that.' She took a drag on her cigarette. 'A girl I met at King's Cross was doing it. She said she was getting fifty quid a fuck.'

'Fifty quid and Christ knows what kind of diseases,' Suzi added.

'Fifty quid's fifty quid, though, isn't it?' Janet countered. 'You'd only have to do it five or six times a week and you could buy a bloody hostel.' She chuckled again.

Maria ran a hand through her hair and sat down on the bed.

'When do you leave?' Suzi asked.

'In a couple of days.' She ran a hand over her pillow as if smoothing out the creases. 'I'd been thinking of going back home.'

'Why did you leave in the first place?' Suzi wanted to know.

'I had a row with my mum and dad.'

'Join the club,' giggled Janet.

'What was the row about?' Suzi enquired, drawing on her cigarette.

'My mum had been having an affair. Dad found out about it. They were always rowing. I tried to stop them one night, but it didn't help. I just couldn't stand seeing them fighting all the time.'

'How long ago was that?' Janet asked.

'Two years.'

'So what makes you think things are going to be any different now?' said Suzi, flatly.

Maria could only shrug.

'Perhaps I was just hoping' she said softly.

'What's hope?' Suzi exclaimed, her eyes cold.

'So what are you going to do?' Janet repeated.

'Keep away from the other hostels. I mean it. Especially the DSS ones' said Suzi. 'No one knows what the insides of those places are like until they've seen them. I've seen them and I'm telling you, you're safer on the streets.'

Eleven

Ryan heard the shouts as he stepped out of the taxi.

He looked round as he dug in his pocket for change and saw two waiters from the restaurant opposite dragging a man to his feet.

The man was in his thirties, although it was difficult to be precise because of his unkempt appearance. He wore a long overcoat which was holed and filthy, stained in many places. His trousers bore a dark stain around the crotch. The two waiters were trying to lift him by hooking their arms beneath his, but the very act of touching him seemed distasteful. They pushed him away from the front of the restaurant.

Ryan looked on impassively then slipped the driver a tip, glancing one last time at the tableau across the street.

The sun was still high in the sky, beating down mercilessly on the city. It sent tempers as well as

temperatures soaring. In New York they called these searing, heat-shrouded times Dog Days.

Ryan selected his key and was about to open the main door when it swung back and two young men emerged. They nodded briefly at the private detective, then headed off down the street. Ryan returned the terse greeting with an equally swift nod then entered, climbing the stairs towards his office.

The young men worked in the graphic design studio on the first floor. Like Ryan, they shared the building with a small advertising agency and a tiny film production company which specialized in making TV adverts. The owner of the company was a man in his mid-twenties who'd been to Los Angeles a few times and insisted on calling Ryan 'dude' whenever he saw him. Something which never failed to irritate the private detective, especially as the young man was from Wembley Park. Not exactly West Coast California.

Ryan climbed the stairs to his office, feeling breathless by the time he had reached the third landing. He coughed gently, relieved when he felt no pain in his chest. The lift was, as usual, out of order.

When he finally reached the top floor he paused for a moment, sucking in deep lungful's of warm air, both angered and surprised by his inability to climb the flights without feeling this way. He exhaled wearily, then sucked in another breath which wheezed asthmatically in his lungs.

In his office heat and exhaust fumes poured in to greet him. He pulled his tie out of his pocket and tossed it across the room, looking over at the answering machine. The green message light was flashing. As he passed it, Ryan flicked it from 'Answer Set' to 'Incoming Message'. The tape rewound, voices speeded up in reverse squealing through the cloying stillness of the office.

He ran the cold water tap in the kitchenette and retrieved a glass from the cupboard. Blowing the dust from it, he held it under the flow of water. He drank two glasses as the machine rewound then began to replay the messages.

Ryan splashed his face with cold water, listening to the voices on the tape.

There was a message from the manager of the Royalton hotel, thanking him for his time.

Very courteous.

Could he call a Mr Goldman who ran a car hire firm in Paddington and suspected that three of his cars had been stolen.

More work.

One of his men was calling to let him know that the writ they'd been ordered to serve today had been.

The message ended.

Ryan rewound the tape and took down Goldman's address and phone number, then pulled open the top drawer of his desk and took out a letter which had arrived that morning with the other post.

It was from his bank, agreeing to let him have the mortgage on a larger office in Covent Garden.

Ryan smiled, read it again and dropped it back onto the desk.

He picked up the phone and wandered across the office with it, peering down towards the restaurant.

The drunk was now lying in the gutter. One of the waiters gesticulated angrily at him before turning and walking back into the restaurant. Ryan could see the man in the gutter moving slightly, lying helplessly on his back like a turned turtle. He finally scrambled to his feet and lurched off across the road, bumping into a young man in the process. The youth shoved him and the drunk ended up flat on his back again.

Passers-by moved swiftly, only casting cursory glances at the drunk.

Ryan held the phone in one hand, jammed the receiver between his ear and shoulder and jabbed out the digits.

Then he waited.

Twelve

She was surprised to hear his voice but it didn't show in her face. She sat expressionless through the short conversation, only smiling as she replaced the receiver and stayed motionless on the bed.

'Who was that?' a voice called from the adjacent bathroom.

Kim Finlay kept her eyes on the receiver for a moment longer, then got to her feet and wandered through into the en-suite.

Her husband was standing in front of the bathroom mirror, running an electric razor over his cheeks and chin.

Kim sat down on the edge of the bath and watched him.

'Who was it?' he asked again.

'It was Nick,' she told him.

Joseph Finlay switched off the razor and studied his wife's reflection in the glass. He splashed aftershave on his face, patting it against his skin.

'What did he want?' he asked a little sharply.

'He had some news to tell me,' she said.

'Was it that important?'

'He didn't say.'

'Then why did he phone?'

'He phoned to ask me if I'd meet him tomorrow for lunch. He wants to tell me face to face.' She clasped her hands around one knee.

Her husband said nothing.

'Is it such a big deal?' she wanted to know.

'Go if you want to,' Finlay told her, re-adjusting his tie. Although I suppose you will, whatever I say.' He walked through into the bedroom and opened one of the large wardrobes, searching through it for a jacket.

'I didn't think I had to ask your permission, Joe,' said Kim.

'You don't,' he snapped. 'I just can't see why you have to see him. You've been divorced for three years.'

'Exactly. And I've been married to you for over a year. It's you I love. Why does it bother you if I see Nick for lunch?'

'Perhaps if the roles were reversed you'd feel the same way' Finlay said acidly.

'I haven't seen him for over three months. It's not as if he's ringing or calling here all the time.'

'I should hope not. It is supposed to be over between you, after all.'

'What's that supposed to mean?' Kim said defensively.

Finlay exhaled and turned to face her.

'You might not think anything of Ryan any more, but who's to say whether or not he still loves you?'

'He didn't have enough time to love me when we were married,' she said, a hint of bitterness in her voice. She moved closer and put her arms around him. 'Even if he does still love me, I'm married to you now. That's all that matters.'

'And you can tell me that you don't feel anything for him?'

Kim sighed wearily.

'Joe, don't start that again. He's the father of my child. We were married for twelve years. I can't just wipe him out of my life and out of my mind. It wouldn't be fair to Kelly to do that. He cares for her.'

'Is that why he didn't even bother contesting custody? Because he cares so much?' There was an edge to Finlay's words that Kim was not slow to pick up.

'He knew there was no way he could look after her. He knew that the best way for her to be happy was by staying with me.'

She stepped away from Finlay, who regarded her coldly for a moment.

'You're defending him again' he said quietly.

Kim lowered her gaze momentarily.

'Kelly's happy here and you know it' she said.

'And she'd be even happier if Ryan didn't just turn up whenever he felt like it, wanting to take her out. She doesn't know from one month to the next if she's going to see him or even hear from him. When was the last time he phoned her, for Christ's sake?'

'Why do we always end up having an argument when Nick is mentioned?' she said, smiling thinly.

'Because he has the knack of bringing out the worst in people. You should know. That's one of the reasons you divorced him, isn't it?'

'He's still Kelly7s father, Joe, and all the arguing in the world isn't going to change that.'

She sat down on the edge of the bed and ran a hand through her hair. She felt hot and flustered.

'I'd better go' said Finlay, reaching for his jacket. He pulled it on and inspected his reflection in one of the full-length mirrors behind the door.

'Don't go off in a bad mood' Kim said.

Finlay took a step towards her, leant forward and kissed her gently on the forehead.

'Go and have lunch with him' he said. 'Find out what his news is.'

Kim smiled, taking a playful swipe at him as he left the bedroom. He strode across the large landing and down the staircase, which turned twice at right angles before reaching the polished wood floor of the hall.

'What time will you be back?' Kim called as he headed for the front door, briefcase in hand.

'The meeting isn't until three,' Finlay told her. 'I'll call you when I'm on my way home.' Then he was gone.

Kim stood by the banister listening to the sound of his Jag starting up in the driveway, then heard the tyres crunch the gravel of the drive as he pulled away. She turned and headed back into the bathroom, turned on the shower, testing the temperature with her fingers as she pulled off her clothes. When she was satisfied that it was cool enough she stepped in, allowing the refreshing jets to play over her body for some minutes before finally shutting off the conduit. She stepped out and wrapped herself in a bath towel. She caught sight of herself in the long mirror and she admired her own reflection. At thirty-three she still had an excellent figure. Nothing sagging yet, she thought, smiling. She padded through into the bedroom and pulled on fresh jeans and a denim shirt, the clean material feeling cool against her skin.

From across the room a wedding picture of herself and Finlay stared back. She crossed to it and touched the frame fondly, straightening it on the bedside table.

Then she slid open the bottom drawer of the cabinet and rummaged under the clothes.

She pulled out another photo. A small snap only two inches square, it was curling at the edges.

It showed herself, Ryan and their daughter. It had been taken about six years ago, when Kelly was just eight years old.

She looked at the photo for a moment, then carefully replaced it in the drawer and slid it shut.

Kim didn't want Finlay to know she had it.

It might cause arguments.

As she made her way downstairs she wondered what her ex-husband was so keen to tell her.

Thirteen

The bruises and cuts on his face gave him the appearance of a human jigsaw puzzle.

Great purple and blue welts and deep gashes, some of them stitched shut, covered every inch of skin. There were even some on his hands and arms.

Nick Ryan couldn't have looked much worse if a truck had reversed over his face.

His upper torso was exposed to reveal more contusions; tightly wound bandages held his broken ribs in place. There was a cast on one of his legs. The limb itself was suspended from a pulley in the ceiling of the hospital room.

Kim sat beside the bed, her eyes red-rimmed and hollow. Her first reaction had been one of horror. She wondered how anyone could survive such horrendous injuries. She was even more flabbergasted to learn that he had been conscious upon admittance. Now she sat gazing at him, reaching out to touch his hand, to run her own fingers over cut and bruised flesh. Over two fingers which had been dislocated.

His lips had been split, one of them gouged open when a tooth had shattered and ripped through it. His nose was broken and there was cotton wool jammed into one nostril. She could see the blood soaking into it. Ryan was breathing through his mouth. Low, guttural inhalations brought pain from his smashed ribs. One of them had come within millimetres of puncturing a lung. The doctors had said he'd been lucky.

She dreaded to think what they classed as unlucky.

The police had already been in to question him and Ryan had croaked answers to their questions through his split and swollen lips, wincing every time he coughed. He hadn't seen the faces of the men who attacked him as he returned home, he told them. He'd counted three. Including the one who'd been carrying the baseball bat. He couldn't identify them; it could have been anyone. There were many people who had reason to want him in this condition. Husbands discovered in the throes of affairs by his investigations. Men cheating on their business partners. Those he served writs on.

It was an occupational hazard, being hated by those he

exposed. Sometimes it was by those who hired him. The wives or husbands confronted by evidence he'd found to prove their spouses' infidelities often seemed to blame him for actually forcing them to face the truth.

It wasn't the first time someone had taken a swing at him. It was just that no one had done it so comprehensively until now.'

'A hairline fracture of the skull, a depressed fracture of the left sphenoid bone,' the doctor began, reading the inventory of injuries from the clipboard he held. 'Three broken ribs, though thankfully no internal damage. A hairline fracture to the left radial bone. Broken tibia and fibula on the right leg. Severe bruising and lacerations over the entire body.'

The doctor leant closer, using a pen-light to look into

Ryan's eyes, a task made difficult by the amount of swelling round them.

'You're going to have quite a collection of scars, Mr Ryan,' he said, glancing at two nasty cuts on the private detective's chest.

Ryan looked at him impassively, then at Kim. She swallowed hard.

'Is he going to be all right, doctor?' she asked.

'There was no internal damage. The breaks will heal in good time,' she was told. The doctor turned and headed for the door, leaving them alone.

They sat in silence for a moment. Then Kim spoke softly.

'You saw who attacked you, didn't you, Nick?'

Ryan drew in a painful breath.

'Yes,' he said, wincing.

'Then why didn't you tell the police?'

'Because I'll take care of it myself when I get out of here.' He tried to shift position.

'Take care of it?' Kim snapped.

'He might have put me in hospital but I'll make sure that fucker walks with a limp for the rest of his life. Him and the two cunts with him.'

'Who was it?'

1 was investigating a firm called Allied Security,' he said. 'One of the partners hired me; he thought his mate was siphoning off money. It turned out he was right. I exposed him, he got the hump and did this.' He motioned to his battered frame.

'The police would have arrested him.'

'And done what? They'd never have proved it. The bastard would have walked. Well, not now. I'll see to him when I get out of here.'

'You always have to 'have the last word, don't you, Nick?' Kim said wearily.

He didn't answer.

'You were lucky this time' she continued. 'They could have killed you. And if it wasn't them it might be someone else. You don't know what's going to happen to you from one day to the next. It might not be a baseball bat, next time; it might be a gun.'

'Occupational hazard' he said, trying to move into a more comfortable position.

'Then maybe you're in the wrong profession' she said angrily. 'Get out now, before it's too late.'

'I can't get out' he told her. 'I've got a business to run.'

'You've also got a family to consider. Unless you've forgotten about me and Kelly.'

'Why do you think I work so bloody hard? It's for you and Kelly.'

'She doesn't see you for days on end, Nick, because you're working. That's all you ever do. Since you set up this bloody business it's the only thing that matters to you.'

'You haven't missed out on anything; you've never gone without.'

'I've gone without you,' Kim said exasperatedly. 'You never know when to stop, do you? You won't stop until someone kills you. Well, I don't want to be around when that happens.' Her voice cracked slightly.

'So don't be,' Ryan said flatly.

As she woke from the dream Kim found that her eyes were moist.

She sat up slowly, trying to re-orientate herself with her surroundings, blinking myopically in the gloom.

Beside her Joseph Finlay slept soundly.

There were no doctors. No hospital.

No Ryan.

She lay down again, feeling her hair matted against the nape of her neck.

Kim closed her eyes but it was a long time before sleep came.

Fourteen

'Spare some change, please?' Maria Jenkins asked as the group of middle-aged people passed by on the subway steps.

One of them, a man in a dark blue blazer, dug in his pocket and threw a coin towards Maria as if he were tossing scraps to a dog. She retrieved the coin, glad to see it was a pound. Out of the corner of her eye she saw the man's companion grab him by the arm and pull him away. The words drifted back towards her on the warm air:

'Why did you do that, John? She's probably got more money than we have.'

There was a chorus of laughter as the people disappeared up the steps.

Maria looked at the money she'd collected in the past hour, counting it with her finger like a Dickensian miser. She found that the collective generosity of her public amounted to £2.36. She pocketed the money and set off up the stairs from Piccadilly Circus tube, heading for the Regent Street exit. She emerged opposite a branch of 'Dunkin' Donuts' and went straight in and bought herself a cup of tea and two donuts. As she sat eating them she watched the crowds pass by outside, bathed in the neon light. All across Piccadilly the night was lit by a rainbow of colours from the signs.

It was her first night away from Ossulston Street hostel. She tried not to think too much about the place, concentrating instead on where she might spend the night. The city offered plenty of doorways and back-alleys, but she would have to be careful which she chose.

The Strand seemed to be her best bet, she thought. Piccadilly tended to attract junkies and rent boys, while Oxford Street was the domain of drunks. In the society of the homeless, even the unwanted knew where they were welcome. Maria decided to head for the Strand.

She finished her tea and donuts and set off across Piccadilly, moving through the crowds that thronged the hub of the West End, slipping in and out of the hordes of tourists and sightseers enjoying themselves. She carried her small holdall, apologising occasionally when she bumped people with it.

As she passed the Trocadero, Maria looked across the street towards a restaurant and saw people eating. She felt a combination of envy and bitterness. Next to it there was a fast food restaurant; two young girls no older than herself were emerging, sharing a hamburger between them. Kindred spirits, perhaps?

In Leicester Square a man with dreadlocks and a long dirty overcoat rummaged through a dustbin, delighted when he found a drinks container. He took off the top, smelled the contents and, deciding they were drinkable, swigged thirstily from the container.

Watching him drink suddenly reminded Maria how hot the evening was.

The city smelled of cooking food and diesel fumes. Rubbish bins, filled to overflowing, added their own pungent stench to the jigsaw of odours heightened by the hot air.

Maria swept her long hair away from her neck, feeling the perspiration there. She walked on through the crowds and through the heat, her mind turning constantly to the thoughts she'd had before leaving the hostel.

Should she return home?

Surely even the pain of seeing her parents' marriage break up around her was preferable to a life spent begging and sleeping rough?

She crossed Charing Cross Road into St Martin's Lane and continued on her way.

On the other side of the road a queue waited to enter Stringfellows. The poseurs and the rich bastards were milling about on the pavement, awaiting the decision of the Neanderthals posing as doormen to allow them in. Maria saw two young men turned away. They shouted angrily at the doorman as he pushed them aside. It was a world of which she knew nothing and wanted no part. Just as well; it would never be within her experience. She felt a twinge of anger. There were girls standing there only a few years older than she was. They had never been forced to beg for money to buy a cup of tea. They probably did their own kind of begging once they were inside, but their kind was achieved with a low-cut dress or a short skirt.

There was a cafe up ahead; Maria fumbled in her pocket to

see how much change she had left. She found that she had enough for a can of drink and got herself a Coke.

On the steps of St Martin-in-the-Fields she sat down and looked out over Trafalgar Square. Nelson's Column thrust skyward, puncturing the thin wisps of cloud that wafted across the firmament, blown by the warm breeze.

Perhaps she should phone home before she actually made that monumental step, thought Maria.

What if they didn't want her back?

For all she knew the marriage could have disintegrated by now. There might be nothing left to go back to.

She took a swig from her coke can and put down her holdall on the steps, using it as a pillow to rest on. Two people already slept close by the doors of the church, one of them bundled up in a sleeping bag despite the heat of the night.

Perhaps she should stay here for the night.

Stay here and go home tomorrow?

But how to get home? If she was going home, she'd need the train fare. Maria realized she had no alternative.

The first two people who passed hardly paid her any attention. The third tossed her a fifty-pence piece.

'Spare some change, please?' she said, beginning to sound like a stuck record.

'How much do you need?'

The voice startled her. She turned to see a tall man dressed in jeans and a white shirt looking down at her. He was in his early forties but wore his hair in a pony-tail. The rest of it was pulled back so severely from his face that it made his skin shine. He had both hands dug in the pockets of his jeans.

'How much do you need?' he repeated.

Maria eyed him warily.

'Is it for something to eat?' he continued.

Her stomach rumbled as if in answer to the question.

The man with the pony-tail smiled.

'I was trying to get home,' she told him. 'I need the train fare. It's twenty pounds, though.'

He took one hand from his pocket and pulled out a wallet. From it he took a brand new twenty-pound note.

Maria's face lit up momentarily, but the light in her eyes faded rapidly.

'I'm not a prostitute, you know,' she said quickly. 'Just because you give me twenty pounds . . .'

He cut her short.

'Take the money,' he said indignantly. 'I was trying to help, that's all.'

'Why?'

'Because I've got a daughter about your age and I'd like to think that someone would help her if she was in your position.'

'Thank you,' said Maria quietly, holding out her hand for the money.

It was suddenly withdrawn.

'How do I know you'll use it for your train fare or for food?' he said sharply. 'You could be spinning me this story so you can get money for drugs.' He prepared to put the money away.

Maria got to her feet.

'I'm telling the truth, honestly,' she said. 'I need it to get home. Please believe me. I'll get something to eat, then I'll use it to get home.'

The man shook his head.

'I don't believe you,' he said slowly. 'But there's a way you can prove it.' His smile returned. 'Let me buy you something to eat. At least I'll know you've had food before you go.'

Maria smiled too.

'Deal?' he said, holding out the twenty again, like some kind of promise.

She nodded.

'Thank you' she said as he handed her the note.

'Come on,' he said. 'There's a place just round the corner where we can get something.'

Maria walked alongside him, the twenty-pound note clutched in her hand. She thought of home.

The man occasionally looked down at her. He had both hands in his pockets again.

One of them gently touched the hilt of a flick knife.

Fifteen

The first time Nick Ryan had seen Tiddy Dol's restaurant in Shepherd Market he'd been chasing a suspect.

He'd been an Inspector at the time, working on a case involving the murder of a prostitute in Red Lion Yard. A high-class call-girl someone had decided would look better with her hands removed and both eyes cut out.

It turned out to be a pimp for whom the girl had once worked.

Ryan had tracked him to Shepherd Market and finally cornered him inside the restaurant itself.

He'd brought Kim to the place on their first date.

Now he sat close to the main entrance, a vodka and lemonade cradled in his hand, watching for her. Around him other lunchtime diners were busy eating and talking. The place was pleasantly cool compared to the stifling heat outside. Giant rotor fans in the ceiling turned gently like the upturned propellers of helicopters, spreading a pleasing breeze throughout the dining area. Constructed of bare stone as it was, the building seemed a more than adequate guard against the perpetually scorching sunshine. Even in his jacket and tie Ryan felt comfortable.

He saw Kim approaching the front door and smiled.

She was wearing a black trouser suit over a white blouse. A pair of sunglasses hid her eyes but she removed them as she entered the restaurant, spotting him immediately.

He took a step towards her, leaning forward to kiss her. She met his kiss with her lips but the gesture was one of friendship.

'Do you want a drink?' he asked.

She asked for a gin and tonic and sat down beside him.

He thought how gorgeous she looked.

She thought he looked like death warmed up.

There were dark rings beneath his eyes and his face looked waxen, but when he looked at her there was a vitality there.

Once she had her drink Ryan asked if they could be shown to their table. It was one of the more secluded ones, inside what looked like a railway tunnel entrance. They sat on wooden chairs and studied the menus.

All around, the babble of many conversations seemed to merge into one unintelligible buzz. Many of the accents were foreign, after all. Tiddy Dol's attracted tourists because it served Traditional English Food.

'You look great,' Ryan said, peering at his ex-wife over the rim of his glass.

'I wish I could say the same for you, Nick,' Kim told him. 'Are you feeling okay?'

'I've been a bit tired lately. I haven't been sleeping too well, that's all.'

'Too much work?'

'There's no such thing as too much work. More work means . . .'

'More money, I know,' she interjected.

They regarded each other in silence for a moment.

'How's Kelly?' he asked finally.

'She's fine. You should come and see her, find out for yourself.'

'I will soon, but things are really busy at the moment.'

'They're always busy, Nick.'

'That's the way I like it, Kim.'

'You don't have to remind me.'

She looked at the menu and made up her mind quickly. Ryan did the same, ordering them both another drink when the waiter took the order.

'So what's the news you had to tell me?' she asked, smiling.

He told her how the business was expanding. About the new premises in Covent Garden.

If anything, she thought, the job had become even more important to him.

'I'm very happy for you, Nick,' she said, smiling. 'It's great news.' She raised her glass. 'Let's drink to it.'

They touched glasses and drank.

'Did Joe say anything about you coming here today?' Ryan wanted to know.

'Why should he?' Kim asked.

'Did he?'

'It's really none of your business, Nick,' she said quietly.

Their food arrived, providing a momentary distraction before Ryan returned to the attack.

'And how is the millionaire property developer? Still buying up all the slums in London and re-selling them at twice the price?' There was an edge to Ryan's voice that Kim didn't care for.

'Joe's fine, if that's what you're trying to ask' she snapped.

They locked stares for a moment.

Ryan coughed, put a hand to his mouth, felt pain in his chest. It passed quickly enough.

'Are you sure you're okay?' Kim asked.

'I'm fine, I told you.' He took a sip of his drink. 'Thanks for the concern, though.'

'Don't sound so surprised, Nick. Just because we're not married any more doesn't mean I don't give a shit about you now. We were married for twelve years, in case you've forgotten. The only trouble was, for most of that time you were married to the job.'

'Don't start, Kim,' Ryan said irritably. 'You knew how important it was to me, especially when I started up the agency.'

'Yes, and I never tried to stand in your way, did I? All I ever asked was that you should remember you had me and Kelly as well as your bloody agency. I didn't ask for much, Nick.'

'You left me over it.'

'It wasn't just the agency; it was the chances you used to take. I couldn't put up with that. With never knowing if a call to the hospital was going to be to identify your body.'

'So now you're married to Mr Dependable and you don't have to worry about things like that. Or where the next penny's coming from,' he said sardonically.

'I love Joe. He's kind and generous and he loves me and Kelly, too. But I don't love him the way I loved you, Nick.' She swallowed hard and lowered her head. 'You were unpredictable, exciting. I never knew how you would react to a situation. Maybe Joe is dependable, you might even call him boring, but I don't care. At least I know he'll be there when I need him. That was something I never knew when I was with you. And now, if you give me a choice between boring or dangerous, I'll take boring every time.'

Ryan shook his head and sighed.

'What's he done to you, Kim?' he said, an ironic smile on his face. 'Taken all the life out of you? What use is living without a few fucking risks?'

She looked at him and wanted to hate him for what he'd said but couldn't.

'I hope he doesn't do the same to Kelly,' Ryan added.

'If you took the time to see her more often you might find out,' Kim chided. 'See if she's changed, too.'

Ryan regarded her.

There was a fire in her eyes he knew well. It still burned as brightly.

'You haven't changed, Kim' he said. 'You've just settled for something different.'

She didn't answer; didn't even look up from her food. Afraid to look at him?

She took a sip of her drink.

Afraid he was right?

They ate the rest of the meal in virtual silence.

Sixteen

So many faces.

After too long they all began to look the same. Vincent Kiernan had to blink hard, to convince himself he wasn't in the middle of a science fiction film in which the world was populated by identical beings.

The concourse of King's Cross Station was a seething mass of people all moving apparently directionlessly.

Kiernan sipped at his drink and looked across at the departure board, at the numbers and places flicking across it. People hurrying to catch the trains also stared at the board, sometimes anxiously. He saw a man, sweat soaking through even the light jacket of his suit, dragging a large suitcase towards the trains. Behind him a woman with a trolley laden with cases ran headlong, using the trolley as a means to clear a path for herself.

Elsewhere a line of people filed slowly round the station, waiting to board a train to Leeds. Kiernan glanced at their faces as they passed. Taking another sip

of his tea, he could feel the perspiration soaking into his shirt. It also glistened on his thick forearms, matting the hairs there.

He walked away from the Casey Jones stand and moved slowly through the throng of people, looking at each person he passed, but more particularly at each young girl. His glances were furtive; he kept his eyes low, ensuring they didn't see his surreptitious looks. Blonde girls, dark-haired girls, brown-haired girls, redheads. He looked at them all.

She'd been blonde the last time he'd seen her.

Now she could have dyed her hair any colour.

It had been long and curly, cascading over her shoulders.

What if she'd cut it?

There were any number of things she could have done to alter her appearance, but could she have changed so dramatically in five months as to prevent him recognising her?

Kiernan moved past W.H. Smith, glancing inside briefly, seeing more faces. He paused for a moment, draining the last dregs of his tea, then tossed the polystyrene cup into a rubbish bin. From the back pocket of his jeans he pulled out a thin red plastic wallet and flipped it open.

It bore a passport-type photo of a smiling girl with blonde curly hair. She was seventeen. The name on the card was Josephine Kiernan.

He looked around at the crowd again.

Talk about a needle in a haystack, he thought, making his way towards the ticket office. One girl mistook his appraisal for inspection, but smiled at him nonetheless. Kiernan smiled back and moved on.

No sign of her near the ticket office. He walked in, looked round, then emerged back onto the concourse again.

The public address system burst into life and station announcements reverberated through the huge, domelike edifice of the station. They mingled with the rumble of arriving and departing trains and the constant babble of chatter.

Kiernan felt strangely detached from it all, a part of the horde but also able to concentrate on each likely face. He wondered what the mathematical probability was of finding his sister in a place like this; a place where over half a million people a day passed through.

He dismissed the thought as rapidly as it had come. Along that road lay despair.

No matter how long it took, he would find her. He had convinced himself of that.

Kiernan walked down towards the platforms, glancing at the boards beside each gate describing the trains' destinations. Leeds. Leicester. Scotland. So many places. So many people.

Over by the public phones two young girls stood talking. One of them leant against a wall. She was dressed in a short, tight mini skirt, teetering on high heels. A leather jacket was draped around her shoulders, despite the heat. She puffed on a cigarette and pushed her blonde hair away from her face as she chatted animatedly with her companion, a smaller girl with raven black hair wearing jeans and trainers.

Kiernan paused, looking more closely at the blonde.

He took a step forward, narrowing his eyes to see her features more clearly.

His heart began to thud against his ribs.

Could it be Jo?

After all this time, after all this searching? The days and nights of depression following fruitless searches.

Dare he even hope it was her?

He moved closer.

The public address system roared out another message. The words drummed in Kiernan's ears as he approached. If he could just hear her speak. If he heard her Irish accent he'd know for sure.

She had changed. Her face looked pale, her eyes red-rimmed.

He was within feet of them now and they were aware of him; they were turning to face him.

And as he drew closer he knew.

It was not Jo.

Kiernan stood motionless for a moment, staring at the blonde, his heart slowing its frantic pace. He felt that all too familiar crushing feeling of defeat descend.

'What the fuck are you staring at?' the blonde snapped.

He merely shook his head and walked past her.

Jesus, how much fucking longer?

He headed towards the subway, wiping sweat from his forehead with two fingers.

She was ahead of him.

Twenty or thirty feet away.

Jo and two other girls were hurrying down the steps to the subway.

He shouted her name once, but she didn't stop.

Kiernan set off after her.

Seventeen

He crashed into a couple struggling with their cases, almost knocking the man over in his haste.

As Kiernan reached the top of the steps leading down to the subway he heard the man's angry shouts behind him but he ignored them, intent only on catching up with the blonde he was convinced was his sister.

He jumped the last three stairs, almost stumbled then hurried on, weaving in and out of other travellers.

Ahead of him, about fifteen feet, he could see her head through the crowd. She was turning left towards the ticket machines. He'd have to catch up with her before she got her ticket, before she descended into the subterranean depths. If he lost her now he'd never find her again.

His heart thudded hard against his ribs, more in anticipation than with the exertion of his movements. He was so close.

A man turned the corner and Kiernan collided with him.

The man shot out a hand to steady himself against the wall. Kiernan overbalanced and slipped.

'Sorry, mate,' said the man, extending a hand to help him. 'Never saw you coming.'

Kiernan leapt to his feet and pushed past into the crowded area that housed the ticket machines.

He looked round frantically.

He'd lost her.

'Jesus,' he hissed, his eyes darting back and forth over the sea of faces.

Which way?

For interminable seconds he stood motionless, panic beginning to grip him.

He spotted her off to the right, heading for the escalators. The other two girls were with her; all three were beginning to walk down the moving stairway.

Kiernan knew what to do.

He couldn't waste time getting a ticket; by the time he did she'd be gone. Perhaps this time forever.

He pushed past people trying to get through the electronic barriers and vaulted the swinging gates.

A guard saw him and hurried over, shouting something, but Kiernan shook loose of his weak grip and ducked through a couple heading the same way.

The London Transport worker followed him for a few yards but gave up as he found his way blocked.

Kiernan glanced behind him once, saw that the guard had given up the chase and pressed on, heading down the escalator.

Once more he had lost sight of Jo.

Cursing, he began to walk slowly down the moving steps. Halfway down and he still hadn't found her. Another few seconds and he would have reached the bottom.

What then? Which direction would she go?

At the bottom his path was blocked by a woman with a suitcase which was taking up the whole of one step. Kiernan knew he had no choice but to wait until he reached the bottom; he couldn't climb over the case.

In front, he saw the trio of girls step off the escalator and head through an archway towards the Northern Line.

There was the loud rumble of a train approaching.

The escalator slid to the bottom of the shaft and he leapt over the suitcase and bolted through the arch.

The platform was crowded; again he had lost sight of her.

Sweat was pouring off him, soaking into his shirt, running down his face as he sucked in lungful's of the stale air.

The rumbling grew louder and the train burst from the tunnel like a huge metallic worm breaking free of its burrow. The headlights blazed like white eyes and the sound filled the subterranean chamber. People moved towards the edge of the platform.

Kiernan walked quickly along looking for his sister, knowing that the doors would open soon and passengers would pour off. The crowd on the platform would swell.

He had to find her.

There was a loud hiss as the doors slid open.

Kiernan was breathing heavily, his breath coming in gasps.

She was up ahead, no more than fifteen feet away.

He saw her take a step into the train and he ran forward, shoving people aside in his haste.

'Jo' he called, oblivious to the stares.

One of the girls with her saw the young Irishman lunge

forward.

She stepped away, afraid of his frenzied attempts to reach her, of his flushed, sweat-drenched features and wild eyes.

He grabbed the arm of the blonde girl and spun her round.

'Jo,' he gasped.

The girl shook loose from his sweaty grip, frightened by his actions, puzzled when he let her go so easily. She stepped onto the train with her companions, wondering who the man was who had gripped her arm and stared into her face. Probably drunk, she reasoned.

She moved over to the other side of the train as the doors slid shut.

Kiernan saw the girl disappear behind the grey metal doors.

The girl he had been convinced was his sister.

He bowed his head and sighed defeatedly.

The train began to pull away, finally disappearing into the tunnel at the other end of the platform. A slight slipstream of warm, reeking air followed it, stirring paper lying on the tracks. A plastic cup rolled off the platform.

Kiernan wiped his face with both hands, his breath still coming in gasps.

He had been so sure it was Jo.

So sure.

He turned and headed back towards the exit.

Eighteen

Both men wore masks. Black leather hoods with zips where the mouths should have been and slits in place of eyes.

Apart from that they were naked.

The girl tied to the bed between them was also naked but for a black blindfold over her eyes.

She thrashed her head from side to side as the first of them, a big man with a tattoo on his right shoulder, drove his erection hard into her.

The other man, pale-skinned but powerfully built and With a shock of red hair protruding from beneath his hood, pushed his penis towards her mouth, shoving the bulbous tip against her lips. He forced it into her mouth and he began to thrust back and forth, her saliva coating his penis. The two men matched rhythms as the girl writhed beneath their combined attention.

The music playing in the background seemed to grow louder, the thunder of drums and the relentless roar of guitars building to correspond to the frenzied movements of the men.

Red Hair pushed harder into the girl's mouth, making her gag on his organ. He withdrew slightly, his glans slippery, tendrils of saliva hanging from it.

Tattoo stopped thrusting and moved up the girl's body, grasping her breasts roughly, kneading them together before sliding his penis between them.

Red Hair forced his organ back into her mouth.

The music thudded on.

The girl continued to writhe.

'. . .Say your prayers, little one . . . '

Any sounds the trio were making were drowned by the music. Their lips moved but no sounds could be heard. Just the relentless accompaniment.

'. . . Don't forget, my son, to include everyone.'

The girl's breasts were red and sore from being manhandled so roughly by Tattoo, who was heaving his hips back and forth with renewed vigour, cupping the smooth flesh of her breasts into a tunnel with which he enveloped his organ.

She was held firmly by the ropes around her wrists and

ankles.

'Tuck you in, warm within, Keep you free from sin . . .'

The hemp had chafed flesh from her limbs. The skin around her left ankle in particular had been rubbed raw, as if someone had gone over it with a rasp.

Red Hair reached out and cupped his own testicles with one hand and the girl's face with the other, holding her steady as his strokes became more powerful.

Her nipples were bulging red; Tattoo's grip on her breasts was strong and unrelenting. He moved in time with his companion, whose face was contorted.

'. . . Till the Sandman he comes . . .'

Perspiration had formed on all three of them. It ran in rivulets down Tattoo's back and Red Hair's chest.

The girl retched as she gagged on the erection in her mouth.

'. . . Sleep with one eye open . . .'

Red Hair grabbed a handful of her hair and pulled her mouth even further onto his shaft, his face twisting into a grimace of pleasure.

'. . . Gripping your pillow tight. . .'

He nodded to Tattoo who was gasping loudly, pushing the tender flesh of the girl's breasts around his organ with powerful force.

'Exit light, Enter night. . .'

Red Hair closed his eyes tightly and released the first spurt of semen into the girl's mouth, pulling back slightly, holding the tip of his penis against her lips as more of the sticky white fluid jetted from his organ. It landed in thick gouts in her hair and on her cheek; some of it ran down her chin.

'. . . Take My hand

Tattoo thrust once more between her breasts, his body tensing as he too ejaculated.

The girl twisted beneath his weight, her mouth open to reveal the oily discharge of Red Hair on her tongue.

More semen spattered her face and neck and Tattoo kept on driving his penis back and forth until the last drops of fluid had coated the girl's face and body.

He moved off her and climbed off the mattress that had been laid on the floor.

Red Hair was smiling as he looked down at the girl. She was

still moving within the restraints of the ropes, her face and upper body now flecked with white ejaculate.

Blood had begun to seep from the cut on her left ankle as the rope bit ever more deeply.

With the blindfold still firmly in place across her eyes, she could only hear as Tattoo moved towards her again.

Her screams were inaudible as the music swelled.

'. . . We're off to Never-Never land

Nineteen

'Do you need to see any more?' asked Edward Caton, leaning forward in his seat, one hand poised over the 'Pause' button of the video.

Charles Thornton smiled and shook his head.

'No,' he said. 'I can see you two have surpassed yourselves again.'

'Better than the last one?' asked Don Neville, smiling.

'I'm a businessman, not a film critic,' Thornton told him. 'Just run me seventy-five copies off. That should be enough to start with.' He looked at the TV screen.

Caton had hit the 'Pause' button so that just the girl was in shot.

Thornton sipped at his drink. The heat inside the small second-storey room was quite intolerable. The fan on the wall was boosted by another on the desk but all they served to do was to circulate the dry air more quickly. Outside, the traffic in Beak Street filed the air with fumes.

Neville got to his feet and crossed to the window, pulling up the blinds, allowing sunshine to flood in. Motes of dust twisted in the searing rays.

'Are you sure seventy-five will be enough?' Neville asked. 'The last lot went well, didn't they?'

'Better than I thought they would,' Thornton admitted.

'Are you doubting the quality of our merchandise, Mr Thornton?' Caton said with exaggerated disdain. 'We're

craftsmen, you know. Every one of these films is a labour of love.' He and Neville laughed.

'I couldn't give a toss about the quality of your merchandise' Thornton told them. 'It sells, that's all that matters to me and my partner. Like I said, I'm not a connoisseur of this type of film.' He smiled again, a gold tooth glinting briefly. It matched the thick gold bracelet he wore, exposed because his sleeve was rolled up. A nasty scar ran from the wrist to the elbow, vividly white against his tan. It had taken more than thirty stitches to close the ragged edges of the wound when a carving knife had first laid the arm open. But that had been more than twenty years ago.

He'd received the wound protecting his boss. The same boss who, five years later, he'd personally shot. Thornton looked on those early years as a kind of apprenticeship. He'd left the army after six years in the Paras. Unable to find a job, his older brother had got him a place at a club in the West End as a bouncer. From there he joined a firm and worked his way up.

Now he had men to protect him.

It had been that way for the last fifteen years. Charles Thornton had ruled London's gangland almost without interference for all that time. There'd been the odd run-in every now and then with the Triads; the slit-eyed little bastards were always chiselling away at his businesses but they usually kept their distance. Thornton preferred co-operation. After all, he was a businessman, and there was business enough for himself and anyone else who wanted to make an honest or dishonest living in the Capital. Violence was always a last resort.

Unless someone was paying a good price for it, of course.

But Thornton's days of direct involvement had ended long ago. He looked upon himself as an entrepreneur, a

supplier of commodities he knew the public needed. Clip joints, casinos, magazine and video shops, cinemas or restaurants. If there was money to be made from it, Thornton was interested. If the public suddenly began to express an interest in crapping in the street then Thornton would be able to offer them a nice line in commodes.

At the right price, naturally.

He lived well and it showed in his features. He was tanned and looked healthy, he rarely drank alcohol and he followed a rigorous exercise programme every day. One of the reasons, he was convinced, that he looked younger than his forty-three years.

Caton was three years his junior, Neville four, and they too had the physiques of men much younger.

They had been making videos like the one Thornton had watched for the past year and selling them at a huge profit to men like Thornton. They dealt with every other gang boss in the City and out of it; Thornton knew it and it didn't bother him. As he kept saying, there was enough money to go round.

'I'll send the cheque when the shipment's delivered, right?' Thornton said, sipping at his Perrier.

'It'll take us a couple of days to run off the copies,' Neville told him.

'No problem.'

'We'll let you know when the next one's ready,' Caton said.

Thornton nodded.

'As soon as you two have got your bloody strength back, I should think,' he said, grinning. 'How do you work the camera while you're filming?'

'We put it on automatic,' Neville said, smiling. 'If we want close-ups we just stop the action. We can edit everything together afterwards.'

'We always shoot two different endings,' Caton said.

'We have a different one for the copies that go to Germany and Italy.'

Thornton looked intrigued.

'What's the difference? Do you bring on a Doberman or an Alsatian?' He laughed.

'The krauts and the wops are into heavier stuff. It's not just sex with them' Neville told him. 'At least not with the people we deal with.'

'We do something different with the girl or the bloke at the end,' Caton informed him.

'Like what?' Thornton wanted to know.

Neville smiled and pulled at his ponytail.

'We kill them' he said. 'Snuff movies are very big on the Continent.'

'Each to his own' said Thornton matter-of-factly. 'I'll stick with the usual stuff. My punters are more discerning.' He looked at the screen where the screaming girl was still frozen in the freeze-frame.

'Run it on to the end, will you,' he asked, watching as the images sped by.

The last shot was of the girl's blindfold being ripped away.

Thornton nodded, thinking that she was pretty. A bit on the thin side for him, but still pretty. He studied the contours of her face. Pretty kid. This video should go well at eighty quid a throw. He smiled. A nice little bit of business.

From the. frozen frame of the picture the semen- spattered face of Maria Jenkins screamed silently.

Twenty

The stench rising from the pile of rotting vegetables was almost intolerable. The rancid odour seemed to permeate the air throughout Berwick Street market.

Stall owners plied their trade surrounded by the invisible fog of putrescence, the smell aggravated by the unrelenting heat.

In a cloudless sky the sun hung mercilessly, covering the city in a fearsome blanket of radiance. As he walked slowly through the market, Vince Kiernan began to wonder how much hotter it was going to have to get before paving slabs began to crack like parched earth. He swigged from the can of coke in his hand, rolling the can across his forehead every so often, the droplets of condensation from the cool metal mingling with the beads of perspiration on his skin.

At one fruit and veg stall a customer was arguing animatedly with the owner about the quality of a watermelon, pushing an index finger through the green skin of the fruit. The vendor was shouting angrily.

A dog nosed through the piles of rubbish in search of food but seemed unable to find anything the heat had not putrefied. Flies and wasps swarmed over pieces of rotten fruit that had rolled into the gutters. Kiernan grunted as he trod in the remains of a rotten plum, slipping on the furred fruit. He wiped the worst of it from the sole of his trainer and walked on.

The market was busy, as it always was. Every day he

passed through and every day it was bustling. So frequent had been his passage through this area that several market traders now nodded cursory greetings to him as he passed.

It was part of his pattern.

From his earliest days in London Kiernan had set himself a search pattern he followed rigorously every day. He rarely deviated from it.

Upon arrival from Dublin he'd found a cheap hotel in Edith Road, Hammersmith. The Broadway wasn't exactly a five star residence but it served its purpose for the young Irishman. Of the twelve rooms it offered only two, apart from his own, were occupied; he could live there comfortably enough for about a hundred pounds a week. It had been his home for the last two weeks and, every day, he'd followed the same routine.

The quest to find his sister had been as relentless as the scorching sunshine.

He rose early every morning, ate breakfast, then walked to Hammersmith tube station where he caught a train which took him to King's Cross.

Kiernan would then spend thirty or forty minutes wandering around the station before venturing out into the neighbouring area. He would walk up the Caledonian road as far as Richmond Avenue. Here he would cut across until he reached Liverpool Road, then make his way back towards Pentonville Road and the station once more, where he would search again for twenty or thirty minutes.

A quick journey by tube to Euston and he patrolled that particular station's huge concourse for anything up to half an hour. He took another tube after that, this time to Tottenham Court Road; from there he'd walk through into Soho Square and then down Dean Street, across Flaxman Court and Wardour Street to Berwick Street. Brewer Street finally took him into Shaftesbury

Avenue, then down to Piccadilly Circus, up Coventry Street and through Leicester Square and down Charing Cross Road to Trafalgar Square.

After that he'd walk up the Strand as far as Burleigh Street and from there up into Covent Garden. Then he would retrace his steps, ending up back at The Broadway around eleven most nights.

There was a kind of monotonous routine to it all that Kiernan found unavoidable but also deeply depressing. He knew he was clutching at straws in his attempts to find one seventeen-year-old girl in a sprawling metropolis like London. But it was all he could think to do, and he had sworn not to give up until he found her, although he realized his task was all but impossible. Armed with just her bus pass and blind hope, he made his journey every day like a strange kind of pilgrimage.

He would stop and ask people if they recognised the photograph's smiling girl with the curly blonde hair, but none so far had been able to recall the face. They'd been unable or unwilling; Kiernan wasn't always sure which.

Every now and then he'd be seized by the icy conviction that he would never find her, but it was a thought he had to force to the back of his mind. His emotions were curiously muted. He had to believe that he could find her, yet his sense of logic told him that he could not. The size of his task, the impossibility of it simultaneously terrified him and drove him on.

He caught a glimpse of his own reflection in a shop window as he walked past but he looked away. He was beginning to look round-shouldered. Weighed down by the burden of the search? Ha fucking ha.

Perhaps he was a different man to the twenty-eight- year-old who'd left Dublin just over a fortnight ago. There was a light covering of whiskers on his cheeks and chin. Dark rings had begun to form beneath his piercing blue eyes. He'd lost a little weight, too.

He wondered how much weight Jo had lost.

He reached Piccadilly Circus and looked across at the statue of Eros perched above the heaving throng of people.

What have you seen? Have you seen my sister?

Kiernan glanced at his watch; it was almost 1.15 p.m. He ducked into a nearby Wimpey and ordered himself a hamburger and a milkshake. The young Irishman found a seat in the window opposite two young girls not much older than his sister. They were both dressed in shop uniforms of some kind, chatting and poring over a magazine.

Kiernan watched them for a moment, his face set in hard lines.

Then he glanced out of the window at the dozens of people passing.

So many people.

'Where are you, Jo?' he said quietly.

One of the girls opposite looked at him and nudged her friend. The two of them got up and left, chuckling to themselves.

So many people.

Kiernan bit into the hamburger.

Twenty-one

There was a delicate chink as the wine bottle brushed the lip of the crystal glass and the waiter steadied his hand as he poured.

Charles Thornton tasted the 1983 Bollinger and nodded to the waiter, who poured full glasses for both men. He then left the bottle in the ice-bucket and disappeared to deal with his other duties.

Morton's in Berkeley Square was relatively quiet for lunchtime. Only nine or ten of the tables upstairs were occupied, including the one that overlooked the square where Thornton now sipped his champagne. The windows were open but the breeze that blew in was warm. Thornton prodded his starter and began to eat.

'Why the champagne, Charles?' his companion asked. 'Are we celebrating?'

T like the best of everything,' said Thornton. 'Why not have the best champagne? At eighty quid a bottle it ought to be good.' He chuckled. 'Besides, I get bored with Perrier.'

Joseph Finlay nodded in agreement and sipped his own drink.

'How are the family?' Thornton asked.

'They're fine. And yours?'

'My mum hasn't been too well lately, so I packed her off to the Canaries for three weeks. Poor old sod.' He smiled benignly.

'What about that young lady you were seeing?' Finlay enquired, hiding his sly smile as he sipped his drink. 'What was her name? Amanda, wasn't it?'

'We weren't compatible,' said Thornton, raising an eyebrow. 'She wasn't too keen on some of my business interests, if you get my drift.' He shrugged. 'Plenty more fish in the sea, Joe.'

'So why did you want lunch today?' Finlay asked. 'What's so important?'

'Do I have to have a reason? I hadn't seen you for a while and I thought it would be nice to have a civilized get-together. Do I need a better reason?' He smiled.

'You never do anything without a reason, Charles.

I've been doing business with you for ten years now, I know you well enough to know that.'

Thornton shrugged.

'As a matter of fact, there is something,' he confessed. 'I've got plans for expansion.'

'You always have. And you want me to help you get planning permission, is that it?' Finlay asked.

'No,' Thornton said, shaking his head. 'I don't need it. I'm not looking to build, I'm looking at conversion. I know the place I want and I know what I want to do with it. I want to open another restaurant.'

'You own five already,' Finlay said.

'Six,' Thornton corrected him. 'Yes, I do, and they're all doing good business. But this next, one will top them all.'

'What had you got in mind?'

'A Japanese place,' Thornton told him. 'A club and a restaurant all in one. This Karaoke shit is really big, and so is Japanese food. Sushi, stuff like that. I must say I've never been too keen on the idea of eating raw bloody fish but there's no accounting for taste, is there?' He smiled. 1 figure the two together will go down a treat, especially right in the middle of the West End.'

'Where had you been thinking of?' Finlay wanted to know.

'You know it well, Joe. In fact, you own it.' He sipped his champagne. 'That place in Cavendish Square. Three-storey building on the west side of the square. That is yours, isn't it?'

Finlay ran his index finger around the rim of his glass.

'Yes, it's mine,' he said flatly.

Thornton smiled.

'Thought so,' he beamed. 'No problem then. Name your price.'

'It's not for sale, Charles.'

'What do you mean, it's not for sale?' he chuckled. 'I just said, name your price.'

'And I just said it's not for sale.'

The two men eyed each other for a moment, the smile fading from Thornton's lips.

'I need that building, Joe. It's ideally situated for what I want,' Thornton said.

'There are plenty of other places in the West End you could buy.'

'I want that one,' Thornton insisted. 'What's so important about it? If it's the money

'The money's got nothing to do with it. I bought that place six years ago for peanuts. I could sell it now for ten times what I paid for it. I don't want to sell it, it's as simple as that.'

'How much do you want for it? You're embarrassed to say because you think I'll be offended; that's the reason, isn't it?'

'I'm not selling, not to you or to anyone else. End of story.'

'What the fuck are you going to do with it?' Thornton snapped, raising his voice a little. Heads at a nearby table turned. He leant closer to Finlay and lowered his voice. 'You've been sitting on it for six years with no tenants, no rent. What use is it to you? I'll give you whatever price you want.'

'Find somewhere else, Charles,' Finlay said flatly.

Thornton exhaled deeply and sat back in his chair.

'Right,' he said, holding up both his hands as if in surrender. 'We're both businessmen. If you don't want to sell then you must have your reasons. But when you change your mind . . .'

Finlay cut him short.

'I won't,' he said defiantly.

'Famous last words,' Thornton said, his smile not quite as broad. The lights glinted off his gold tooth. 'We'll talk about it again in a few days. Perhaps, by then . . .'

Again Finlay interrupted him.

'We can talk about it every day for the next five years,' he said calmly. 'My answer will be the same. The building isn't for sale.'

Thornton regarded his companion coldly.

Beneath the table one fist was clenched tightly.

Twenty-two

'Fucking bastard.'

At the sound of fury from the back seat of the Mercedes Colin Moran glanced into the rear-view mirror at his boss.

Charles Thornton was gazing out of a side window at the other cars, his eyes seemingly fixed on something.

'Sorry, boss, I can't go anywhere until the lights change,' said Moran.

'What?' Thornton said, turning to look at the back of Moran's head.

His driver was a powerfully built man with a thick neck and a short haircut which made his head seem too small for his considerable body.

'I said I can't move the car until the lights change to green...'

'I'm not on about the bloody lights,' Thornton hissed, exhaling deeply. 'It's that cunt Finlay. I was trying to do some business with him at lunchtime but he's not having it.'

Moran slipped the car into Drive and pulled away.

'Is this that place in Cavendish Square you're after?'
he wanted to know.

'Yeah. I mean to say, I told him to name his price and he still won't sell the fucking thing. What more have I got to do?'

'It's important you have the building, right?' Moran said, as if he was telling his boss something he didn't know. 'But Finlay owns it and he don't want to sell, right?'

'Your grasp of the situation is breath-taking, Colin' Thornton chided. 'But unfortunately, it is of no help to me since Finlay won't fucking sell.'

'Blow him away' said Moran flatly.

'What the fuck am I? A gangster?' Thornton shouted, indignantly.

Moran glanced into the rear-view mirror, as if considering his answer.

'I'm a businessman' Thornton reminded him. 'Just because someone won't do a business deal with you, you don't go blowing their fucking heads off, do you?' He scratched his chin. 'Well, not unless it's absolutely necessary.' He sighed. 'Besides, I need him.'

'For what?' Moran wanted to know.

'He's important. He's got lots of contacts high up, architects, councillors. He's in with all of them. If it hadn't been for him a lot of my business over the last few years wouldn't have been done. He's pushed through planning permission, stopped trouble with builders, that sort of thing.' He shook his head. 'I don't want him blown away just because he won't sell me a fucking building, do I?'

'Then why don't you look for another building?'

'Because I want that one. It's in a prime position.'

'But you could buy one anywhere.'

'I know that. Fuck me, what's the good of trying to explain the niceties of economics to you?'

'I still think you should blow him away.'

'And I think you should concentrate on your driving.'

Thornton sat back in his seat, gazing abstractedly out of the window again. Why the hell was Finlay so insistent on holding onto the building? The two of them had been working together for years; Thornton couldn't understand the other man's reticence. Maybe in time he'd change his mind, but Thornton doubted it. He ran a hand through his hair. It would be simpler to find another building, but the one in Cavendish Square was what he wanted. And what Charles Thornton wanted he usually got.

Still, he had time. Finlay might reconsider. Thornton frowned. No, Finlay would reconsider. He smiled to himself. He'd make the property developer see sense. Business was sometimes a matter of psychology, he told himself. Finlay would be persuaded. Probably just holding out for a better price.

'Name your price'.

He must have his reasons for not wanting to sell.

He'd give him a couple of weeks, then speak to him again. They were both civilized men, both able to talk and reason.

Besides, thought Thornton, if the bastard didn't sell it to him eventually, he'd have his fucking legs broken.

Simple economics.

Twenty-three

At this hour of the morning the smell was tolerable. Only when the sun rose high in the sky did the stench become unbearable.

As Phillip Welsh gripped the black bin bag and heaved it onto his shoulder, some of the rubbish spilled out onto the pavement in the process. One of his colleagues trailing behind with a bag in each huge fist kicked the refuse into the gutter.

It was just after 6.15 a.m. and London was coming to life, stirring in the coolness of early morning, preparing for the onslaught that would surely come as the day wore on. Even now, with a faint nip in the air, Phillip could feel beads of perspiration forming on his back. He hurled the bag into the back of the truck and stood aside as his companion did likewise with his load. The big man wiped his forehead with the back of one filthy glove and rummaged in the overalls he wore, producing a packet of Marlboro. He lit one for himself and offered one to Phillip, who declined.

One of their other companions, a short, red-haired man with a profusion of freckles, joined them, tossing his own bag of rubbish in with the others.

'They always say you can tell more about people from their rubbish than you can by looking round their houses,' he said, nodding at the bag he'd just hurled into the dustcart.

There were half a dozen used condoms spilling from a rent in the bag.

'Do you reckon the whole bag's full of them?' said Phillip, smiling.

'If it is then someone had a good night last night,' the freckle-faced man said, accepting a cigarette.

'A bloody exhausting one, too,' his large companion offered.

The three men laughed.

'I tell you, this lot,' the freckle-faced man made an expansive gesture with his hand designed to encompass the immaculately-kept facades of houses in Belgrave Square. 'The rich. They're the worst of them all. The richer they are, the kinkier they are. I bet they've all been to fucking public school, all these geezers.'

Phillip looked on in amusement as the man continued his diatribe.

'Breeding grounds for snobbery and perversion, that's what public schools are,' he said authoritatively. 'The only two things you get from a public school education are a top job in management and an interest in perverse sexual practices.'

The other two chuckled.

'That's why fucking British management's so ineffective. As soon as they get in the boardroom, they're all slamming each other's dicks in the door.'

The three men's laughter echoed around the square.

The driver peered out of the cab and tapped the face of his watch.

'Sorry to disturb you,' he called. 'But we have got other bins to empty.'

The freckle-faced man performed an exaggerated Nazi salute and the driver ducked back into the cab.

'Miserable bastard,' the freckle-faced man said. The three of them wandered off to collect more rubbish as the truck rolled along slowly.

Phillip moved towards three bags bundled together at the top of a flight of stairs leading down to a basement flat. He reached for the first and recoiled from the stench emanating from it. He coughed and took a step back; the smell was almost palpable. Flies buzzed around the bags and crawled inside. Phillip saw something white wriggling against the black plastic and realized it was a maggot. The bloody bags must have been out in the heat for a couple of days at least, he thought, lifting the first of them, blowing hard.

Further up the street his colleagues were collecting bags, waiting until the wagon drew nearer before hurling them inside. Phillip decided he needed help with these three.

Besides, the smell was appalling.

He reached for the third.

The top of the black bag tore as he pulled it, the plastic ripping, the bag toppling over.

Flies swarmed from inside, a cloud of parasites buzzing madly around Phillip and the stinking contents of the bag. There were more maggots, too, flooding out across the pavement.

In amongst it all was a shape Phillip did not instantly recognize.

It was bent double, the skin mottled blue and grey where it wasn't covered in blood.

He smelled an odour so rank, so fetid that it was all he could do not to vomit.

Then he saw the head as it sagged forward, cracking hard against the pavement. One sightless eye gazed up at him. The other had gone; the socket was now filled with hundreds of writhing maggots.

The body of Maria Jenkins lay at his feet.

Twenty-four

Dear Vince,

How the hell are you, big brother? I bet you thought you wouldn't be hearing from me again, didn't you? Well, here I am. I'm writing this letter at about twelve in the morning. I've just got up. I get up late most days because there isn't much to do until the night-time then me and some of the other girls go out together. There are girls from all over the place living around here. I met a girl from Swords last week, but I can't remember what her name was. She was very nice. I don't know where she went. We all hang around together as much as we can. None of us like what we do and we hate the men we go with but it's the only way to earn money. There are no jobs. It's better than being at home, though. I will never come back now and I don't suppose dad would want me back. If he knew what I was doing and some of the things I've done here in London he'd go mad. Ha ha.

I can't give you an address to write back to because I move around quite a lot. I've been living in one place in Islington for about a week now, but we've got to move on again. Me and a friend of mine called Stevie are thinking of finding a squat.

I'll write again soon.

Love, Jo.

Vince Kiernan folded the letter and put it on the bed with the others. There were half a dozen, all written in the last year. The last one he'd received had been dated almost three months earlier. He'd heard nothing from his sister since that time. The postmarks on the letters showed that they'd been posted in many different parts of London: Paddington, Kensington, Islington.

A needle in a haystack.

All the letters had arrived not at his home in Dublin but at the health club which he and a partner ran on the outskirts of the city. His partner had agreed to take care of the business while Kiernan was in London. He phoned twice a week to make sure there weren't any problems, but he trusted his partner to keep things ticking over. Kiernan had more important things on his mind.

He hadn't bothered telling his parents or anyone else in the family that he was travelling to London in search of Jo. His parents wouldn't have cared and the rest of the family had always considered Jo something of a tearaway. Ever since she'd been arrested when she was fifteen for being in possession of a joint. Kiernan wished it was something so trivial now.

. . . We hate the men we go with . . .

He gritted his teeth as he re-read the letter. He felt a bead of perspiration trickle down his face but he didn't wipe it away. It hung from his chin for a second before dropping onto the mattress where it splashed one of the letters, smearing the ink like a tear. He dabbed at the wet spot with part of the sheet then got to his feet and crossed to the small basin. He spun the cold tap, bending low over the basin, wetting his face.

The water felt good against his hot skin. He didn't bother drying himself, merely allowed the water to drip down his face and chest.

In just a pair of jeans he sat cross-legged on the bed,

looking first at the letters then around him at the small room.

The walls were yellowed, the paint cracked around the coving. There was a green stain under the sink and the carpet and floorboards were rotten from constant drips. The bulky radiator that took up one wall was in need of a coat of paint. Its unwieldy frame was rusted in places, dented. It looked as though it would take just one firm tug to heave it clear of the wall.

Sunshine penetrated the windows with difficulty; the film of dirt on them was so thick as to make them appear opaque. Kiernan wondered how long it had been since they'd been washed. A pair of similarly grubby net curtains also hung there, yellowed slightly as if from constant exposure to cigarette smoke. He stubbed out his own cigarette in the ashtray, the smoke rising mournfully into the stale air.

On the battered wooden bedside table beside the phone there were a pile of magazines. Men Only, Club International, Mayfair and Escort. There were others, too, specifically contact magazines. It was the personal columns which interested Kiernan. In every one of the magazines there were hundreds, perhaps even thousands, of numbers prefixed by 0898. These, he knew, together with the 0836 numbers, were recorded messages. They promised such sanitized delights as 'Your hand on my crotch'. Kiernan flipped open the copy of Club

International, flicking quickly past the array of girls until he found the phone-lines.

The adverts screamed out:

WIVES CAUGHT TALKING DIRTY LET ME STROKE IT TRIPLE X TIGHT PULLED PANTIES Kiernan glanced at the models who fronted each panel and flicked on a few more pages.

There were ads for videos.

EXTREMELY STRONG HARD IMPORTED VIDEO FILMS. All guaranteed not cut or softened-down copies.

Kiernan shook his head. He skipped past a 'genuine offer of 28 video films from Cindy Thrust', ignored the invitation to 'CREAM OVER MY STOCKINGS' or to listen to a 'THREE IN A BED RUBBER ROMP' and found the page he sought.

CLASSIFIED

The numbers were all prefixed by 071, 081 or other recognisable city codes. Kiernan had already rung dozens of them, tiring of hearing answerphones promising 'elegant massages'. A few were answered by real live women, something of an oddity in the world of recorded sex. He'd already crossed out fifteen or sixteen and had reached an entry which boasted:

KNIGHTSBRIDGE. Fun-filled massage guaranteed 7 days. Call Ruth.

He took his marker pen from the bedside table and underlined the number, then lifted the phone onto the bed and dialled.

After a couple of rings he heard a woman's voice.

'I saw your advert,' said Kiernan. 'Can you give me some information, please?'

He ran a hand through his hair as the woman reeled off what was obviously a well-rehearsed speech.

She asked if he'd been before.

'No,' he told her.

She told him that Ruth could be found near to Knightsbridge Tube, that she was blonde, petite and measured 38" 26" 38". The price was twenty pounds for a basic massage but any other requirements could be discussed in private. He was welcome to call any day after one o'clock.

He put the phone down and crossed the number out, running his finger down the column.

There were numbers for Birmingham, Leeds, Manchester; there was even one for Milton Keynes.

All of those he ignored; it was only the London numbers he wanted. The others he crossed out.

Perspiration ran in salty rivulets down his face. He wiped it away, dialling with his free hand.

Emma's 'Lady' told him that his beautiful masseuse was very slim, five feet six and blonde. She reeled off some prices.

Kiernan hung up before she finished speaking. He scanned the numbers again.

Was the hope of finding his sister via one of these classified ads any more ridiculous than trying to hunt her down in Soho or King's Cross?

He didn't care. It was worth trying.

The next number he reached offered another stunning blonde. Surprise, surprise. She charged sixty- five pounds for half an hour, one hundred and fifty if she had to travel to his hotel. But he did get a choice of uniforms or fantasies.

Kiernan tried three more numbers before dropping the phone back onto the cradle. He sat in the sweltering heat of the bedroom for long moments, looking first at the collection of magazines and then at Jo's letters.

He reached for the next magazine, flipped it open at the classifieds and began dialling again.

Twenty-five

The glare of the late afternoon sunlight was dazzling. After the darkness of the cinema it seemed even more intense. Nick Ryan slipped a pair of sunglasses from his pocket and put them on.

As the remainder of the crowd poured out of the building Ryan looked around for his companion. He saw her a few feet away. Dressed in jeans and a T-shirt, her hair freshly washed and gleaming, she looked older than her thirteen years. He smiled, thinking how popular she was going to be with the boys in a few years' time. She glanced round, saw him and moved to him through the throng of people. They crossed the road together and then headed over the Bayswater Road towards Hyde Park. As they darted in front of oncoming traffic, she gripped his hand tightly. Ryan squeezed back, feeling the warmth in her touch. When they reached the other side his breath was sticking slightly in his lungs. He felt a twinge of pain but dismissed it.

'I would have thought you'd have wanted to have been out in the sun on a day like this,' he said, 'not stuck in a cinema.' He smiled at her.

'I wanted to see the film,' she said. 'Thanks for taking me, Dad.'

He reached out and put his arm around her shoulder as they walked, his hand brushing against her silky hair.

With his free hand he reached into his pocket and took out a packet of cigarettes, slipping one between his lips and lighting up.

'Do you have to smoke, Dad?' said Kelly, her tone a mixture of weariness and reproach.

He looked at her, raised his eyebrows, took the cigarette from his mouth and dropped it on the pavement, grinding if out beneath his foot.

She smiled.

'Happy now?' he asked.

Kelly nodded.

Christ, she looked like Kim, he thought. Some of her gestures and expressions made her look like a clone of his ex-wife. He realized how much he missed her.

They entered Hyde Park and set off across the expanse of green towards the Serpentine. All around them the grass was littered with people sunbathing, playing games, even picknicking. To Ryan it seemed as if there were children everywhere, from small babies to teenagers, shouting, laughing or crying. The warm breeze carried the sounds across the vast arena. Every now and then he heard a dog bark.

There was an ice-cream van parked close by and Kelly tugged his arm and began running towards it.

'Come on, Dad,' she called, looking back at Ryan. He set off after her, trying to ignore the pain growing in his chest. He gritted his teeth, angered that he was suffering now. He sucked in several deep breaths and it diminished slightly.

He caught up with Kelly in the queue for ice-creams.

They waited patiently until it was their turn, then Kelly ordered two 99's with nuts and juice, thrust one into Ryan's hand and wandered away while he paid.

The sun began to melt the ice-cream immediately and the private detective found it was dripping onto his hand. He licked it away and joined his daughter.

'If it stays this warm' Kelly began, 'Mum says we won't need to go away on holiday. We could just stay at home.'

'Where are you going?' Ryan enquired.

'Joe wants to take us to Barbados for two weeks.'

'You don't sound very enthusiastic, Kelly,' Ryan told her as they walked.

She shrugged.

Ryan rubbed her shoulders with one hand.

'You'll enjoy it,' he said none too convincingly.

'I told Mum I didn't want to go.'

'What did she say?'

'She told me not to be silly. She's always telling me not to be silly. I can't help it if I don't like him much.'

Ryan looked surprised.

'Why not? What's wrong with him? He doesn't treat you badly, does he?' His voice took on a slight edge.

'No, he's very nice to me. He's always giving me money or buying me things. I suppose I'm being ungrateful, but no matter what he does for me ...' She allowed the sentence to trail off.

'What?' Ryan prompted.

'Well, he's not my dad, is he? You are. I didn't ask Mum to marry him. I didn't ask her to leave you. No one says I have to like what's happening.' She turned and looked up at him. 'Why did you and Mum stop loving each other?' There was a hint of bitterness in her voice; Ryan found he could only hold her reproachful gaze for a second or two.

'We never stopped loving each other, Kelly. It wasn't that,' he said, tossing the half-eaten ice-cream into a nearby dustbin.

'It was your job, wasn't it?'

'Did your Mum tell you that?'

'I can still remember you and her arguing, Dad. That was why we had to leave, wasn't it? Because of your job.'

'You didn't have to leave. I didn't want you to leave. You or your mum. That was never what I wanted.' He wandered across to one of the numerous benches in the park and sat down. Kelly joined him.

'Then why did it happen?' his daughter wanted to know.

'It was my work,' he snapped, immediately feeling angry with himself. 'What I was doing, the things I was getting involved with, some of them were bad. Your mum was worried about me; it got her down. She couldn't stand it. It was best for both of you that you left.'

'How could it be if you still loved each other?' Kelly asked, with the kind of devastating logic that only a youngster can deliver.

'But your mum loves Joe now. She's happy and she and I still get on. We're still friends. We always will be.'

'And you still love her?'

Ryan exhaled.

'Yes,' he said flatly. 'I love both of you.' He snaked out an arm and pulled her close, kissing the top of her head. 'Especially you.'

'Then why don't you come and see me more often?' she asked quietly.

Again that awful, inescapable logic.

'Whenever I'm not busy I try'

'You're always busy, Dad,' she said coldly. 'You always will be.'

She got to her feet and walked on.

Ryan gritted his teeth. He hauled himself off the bench and

headed off after her.
 The truth hurts, doesn't it?
 'Fuck it' he rasped under his breath.

Twenty-six

The sunshine reflected harshly from the surface of the water. Kelly shielded her eyes as she tossed stones into the Serpentine, watching them splash and send rings sliding across the surface.

Ryan stood behind her, puffing on a cigarette and alternately glancing at his daughter and at a particularly gorgeous young woman who, clad in a skimpy yellow bikini, was stretched out on the grass close to the water enjoying the sunshine. The private detective could feel perspiration soaking into his shirt. Finally he joined Kelly by the waterside, squatting down beside her as she continued to throw the small pebbles into the waterway. He, too, watched the ripples spreading out.

'Kelly,' he began, 'do you blame me for what happened with your mum?'

Avoiding his eyes, she searched around for more pebbles and began tossing them in. They entered with a subdued plop.

'I don't know,' she said. 'You had to do your work, I suppose. I just wish . . .' She threw another pebble.

'What?' he said hurriedly.

'I sometimes wish we could be together again,' she told him, turning to face him.

Ryan found himself looking into her deep blue eyes. He felt as if he was floating.

'I'll come and see you more often,' he said quietly. 'I promise. We'll go out together more. When I'm not so

busy.' Immediately he wished he'd not uttered the last sentence.

She looked away from him and back to the water.

'Mum said you were ill' Kelly said after a long silence.

Ryan looked puzzled.

'You look tired,' she added.

'I haven't been sleeping too well lately, that's all,' he explained. 'That and too much work, but other than that I'm fine.' The twinge of pain in his chest did much to contradict his argument. He smiled thinly, hoping she hadn't noticed his eyes narrow as he felt the discomfort intensifying. 'Your mum worries too much.'

He picked up a stone himself and threw it into the water.

'Are you going to come and see my new office when I've moved?' he asked.

Kelly nodded.

'You didn't buy it from Joe, did you?' Kelly asked. 'He sells buildings.'

Ryan laughed.

'No, I didn't buy it from Joe,' he chuckled.

'Some of the girls at school know who he is. Some of their dads work for him.'

'What's school like?' he wanted to know. 'Have you settled in now?'

She blew out her cheeks.

'I don't like being away from home when it's term time, but most of the girls are nice. I didn't like sleeping in a dorm at the beginning, but you get used to it. The other girls' parents are rich, too, so I don't feel left out.' She looked at Ryan. 'Joe's very rich, isn't he, Dad?'

Ryan nodded.

'There's a lot of money in property, Kelly.'

'I suppose Mum must love him,' she said philosophically. 'But they have rows, too.'

'Every couple has rows.'

Ryan felt a flicker of delight at the thought that Kim and Finlay's marriage wasn't all sweetness and light, but he administered himself a swift mental rebuke for feeling pleasure at the thought.

'You still haven't told me why you don't like him,' he continued. 'You said he was nice to you. He's not nasty to Mum, is he?'

Because if he is I'll break the fucker's neck.

'No. I don't know what it is. Perhaps it's because he wanted to send me to boarding school in the first place. I thought he didn't like me when he did that. I thought he wanted me out of the way.'

'I'm sure that's not it, Kelly. He just wants you to have the best education you can get. Boarding school might be better for that.'

'It's all right for him, he doesn't have to go.'

'How does your mum feel about you going?'

'She says she misses me, but she agrees with Joe.'

She would.

Ryan looked at his daughter for a moment, then reached out with one hand and touched her cheek. He stroked it gently.

'Come on, princess,' he said finally. 'Let's go and get something to eat.'

She nodded and smiled.

'Pizza or hamburger?' he asked.

'Both' she chuckled, laughing loudly as he swept her up into his arms and held her high above his head before setting her down on the grass again. They set off together across the park.

As they walked, Ryan glanced at his watch. 4.36 p.m.

He made a mental note to call in at his office before he took Kelly back, just to check on any late mail or see if there were any messages.

He was expecting one.

Twenty-seven

It was after eight by the time Ryan arrived at Finlay's house in Hampstead.

He sat behind the wheel looking at the large house, then glanced across at Kelly who'd fallen asleep in the passenger seat. A combination of the heat and the long drive had made her nod off.

Ryan watched her for what seemed like an eternity. Her chest rose and fell slowly as she breathed, her eyelids flickering occasionally to signal that she was dreaming. About what, he wondered? About her day with him? About her new stepfather?

About the break-up of her parents' marriage?

That was all in the past, now. Only the memories remained, etched a little more deeply on a thirteen- year-old's mind, he thought, than on his own, but then memories were little more than spiritual wounds and the young's healed more quickly.

Ryan reached over reluctantly and touched her shoulder to wake her.

Her eyes snapped open and she sat up, taking a moment to recover from the disorientation. Then she looked at him and smiled.

'You're home,' he said quietly.

Her smile faded slightly.

'Tell your mum I'm sorry I didn't get you back earlier,' Ryan instructed her.

'Why don't you come in and tell her yourself?' Kelly enquired.

He glanced towards the house again and saw the Jag parked outside. Finlay's Jag.

'You tell her' he said, smiling.

She thanked him for the day out and he kissed her on the forehead then on the cheek, watching her as she clambered out of the car. She ran round to the driver's side and stuck her head through the window, kissing him again.

'I love you, Dad,' she said.

'I love you too,' he told her.

'When will you come again?'

Ryan swallowed hard.

'Soon,' he told her.

'You will come, won't you?' she asked anxiously.

'You try stopping me,' he said, smiling.

'When?'

'When I can.'

Her smile faded.

'When you're not working' she said flatly. Then she turned and scurried up the path towards the front door.

Ryan, watching her go, saw her press the doorbell.

As the front door was opened, he pulled away, not looking in his rear-view mirror.

He snapped on the radio, anxious to fill up the silence that seemed to have invaded the car.

A rock track was thundering out of the speakers:

'. . . You never know what you've got, 'til it's gone . . .' the singer intoned.

Ryan switched it off again.

Twenty-eight

She thought he'd been asleep; he'd been so quiet.

Kim glanced across at Joseph Finlay and the images from the television screen danced across the lenses of his glasses. As she looked more closely she saw that he was looking blankly at the screen, the book he'd been reading open on his chest.

He sat forward, putting the book on the coffee table beside him, removing his glasses and rubbing the bridge of his nose.

He reached for the glass of Glenfiddich and took a sip.

'Do you want a top-up?' he said, getting to his feet and walking across the room towards the drinks cabinet.

'No thanks, I'm fine,' she told him, lifting her own glass of Bacardi and Coke.

Finlay re-filled his own glass and stood there for a moment.

'Ryan was late bringing Kelly back,' he said finally.

Kim turned to face him.

'Only an hour or so,' she said. 'I knew she was safe with him.'

'That's not the point.'

'He didn't do it deliberately, Joe.'

Finlay sipped at his drink.

'I've been thinking. It might be best for Kelly if she didn't see so much of Ryan.' He crossed back to his seat and sat down.

Kim jabbed the mute button on the remote control, cutting off the noises coming from the TV.

'She only sees him half a dozen times a year now.'

'He's a disruptive influence on her, Kim.'

'For Christ's sake, Joe, he's her father. What kind of disruption can he cause?'

'I've said all this before, Kim, I don't want to keep repeating myself. You know my views on the subject.'

'And that's it, is it? End of story?' she snapped. 'I know that you don't want my daughter to see her father any more. Why?'

'She's your daughter now, is she?' said Finlay, acidly. 'Strange how every time we have this argument, she's your daughter. At any other time, she's ours.'

'You know what I mean.'

'I think you should remember who puts a roof over her head and clothes on her back. I think that makes her as much my daughter as yours.'

'Jesus Christ, Joe, this isn't a bloody competition. You can't buy her. Just because you support us doesn't mean you have any more claim to her than Nick.'

'And what does he contribute to her upbringing? A visit every few months if she's lucky. A phone call once in a blue moon. She needs more than that, Kim. You should know that.'

'I do know that. I also know that she likes to see him. She has a right to see him and he has a right to see her.'

'Perhaps we should ask Kelly what size thinks about this situation. She might be dissatisfied with it, too.'

'You're afraid of him, aren't you?' Kim said, challengingly.

'And you still love him, don't you?' he said flatly.

Kim didn't answer.

'Don't you?' he snapped.

'I loved him for twelve years' she said. 'I can't just wipe it out, Joe. I've told you, I love you. Do you think I'd still be here if I didn't? Do you think I'd have married you in the first place if I hadn't? Use your common sense. If it can get through that barrier of self-pity and hatred you seem to live behind.'

He took a hefty swig of whisky and banged the glass down.

'I don't want her seeing so much of Ryan,' he said, angrily. 'That's all I've got to say about it.'

'I'm sorry you feel like that, Joe, but it isn't that easy,' Kim informed him. 'There's nothing you can do to stop him seeing her.'

'We'll see,' said Finlay angrily.

The phone rang.

Both of them looked at it. At last Finlay crossed to it and snatched it up.

'Hello,' he barked.

Kim saw his expression change from one of anger to one of surprise.

'What do you want?' he said to the caller. 'Now?' He looked at his watch. 'It's almost ten-thirty. Can't it wait?'

It couldn't.

'I'll be there in an hour,' he said and put the phone down. He turned to look at Kim. 'I've got to go out.'

'What for?'

'Business. It's important,' he told her.

'You sound like Nick,' she said sarcastically.

Finlay glared at her and headed for the door to the hall.

'What time will you be back?' she wanted to know.

'One, perhaps later. Don't sit up.'

'I wasn't going to,' she told him.

Finlay hesitated and then strode out into the hall, closing the sitting-room door behind him. He took a light jacket from the stand in the hallway, picked his car keys up from the table by the front door and walked out.

Kelly saw him go.

Crouched on the landing, she saw him snatch up the car keys and leave.

Just as she had heard most of the argument. The words had drifted up to her as she lay in bed. When she heard voices raised in anger she had climbed out of bed and tip-toed onto the landing, straining her ears to hear what was being said. From her position she had heard nearly everything.

Now, as Finlay slammed the front door behind him, she scuttled back to her room.

Tears were running down her cheeks.

She swung herself into bed and lay there motionless, staring through the darkness at the ceiling.

Outside she heard the Jag pull away.

Twenty-nine

The thief at the Royalton had been caught. At least, Ryan's operative had gathered enough evidence against him to ensure a conviction.

The private detective sat at his desk with only the small table lamp turned on. He tapped his pen against his pad, the lamp casting thick shadows round him. The message had been on his answerphone when he'd returned to the office earlier. He'd thought about ringing the manager of the hotel but had decided to leave it until the following morning. Now he sat in the curious half-light gazing out of the window towards the dark sky and the dozens of bright lights illuminating it from buildings along Charing Cross Road and Oxford Street.

He'd ring the operative in the morning too and congratulate him on his work.

Work.

He glanced at his watch. 11.26 p.m.

He ought to be thinking about heading home by now. He'd driven straight to the office after dropping Kelly off, checked his messages and then wandered around the corner to Scalini's for a coffee and a sandwich. He'd returned to the office about nine and completed some paperwork, including some from Southwark Council concerning a series of eviction orders they'd asked him to serve.

He felt a twinge of pain in his chest and winced, gritting his teeth until it diminished.

It didn't.

'Shit,' he hissed and got to his feet, crossing to the window as if the movement would somehow lessen the pain.

It had the opposite effect. Suddenly he felt as if someone had filled his lungs with iron filings and were drawing a magnet back and forth across his torso. He coughed and put one hand to his chest.

Still the pain persisted.

He gritted his teeth and turned to the small drinks cabinet. He took a bottle of vodka from it, unscrewed the cap and drank straight from the neck, relieved and a little surprised when the pain diminished. He waited a moment and drank another few gulps. Perspiration had beaded on his forehead. He felt dizzy and shot out a hand to steady himself against the windowsill.

As the pain retreated slightly, he sucked in a deep breath, as deep as he could without starting the agony afresh. He stood there panting; drawing in shallow breaths then expelling deep ones to pump the pain away.

Ryan took another slug from the bottle and closed his eyes, practically falling into the seat by the window. He sat there, mouth open, a mixture of vodka and sputum bubbling on his lips as he exhaled. He felt light-headed. He told himself it was the effects of the drink on an almost empty stomach.

Who are you kidding?

He wiped his mouth with the back of his hand, wincing as he saw a dark stain there.

Blood.

It appeared like black ink in the murkily lit office but he could smell its coppery odour.

Ryan coughed again and tasted it. He pulled a handkerchief from his pocket and propelled the lump of sputum into the material, opening it a second later to see a bloodied ball of phlegm nestling in the cotton. The pain in his chest grew more intense. He rose to his feet, putting down the vodka bottle, stumbling through into the small toilet.

He barely made it.

A wave of nausea hit him and he dropped to his knees, head over the bowl, his stomach contracting, forcing its contents up his throat and into his mouth. An evil-smelling flux of half-digested food and blood poured out, spattering noisily into the lavatory. The smell made him retch again, but when the contractions finally died away, Ryan sat back on his haunches, his eyes closed, streamers of dark sputum hanging from his lips like rancid ribbons. His head was still spinning, the pain in his chest ever-present.

He crouched on the floor for what seemed like an eternity before he got to his feet. He flushed the crimson vomit away, slapping on the light.

In the harsh brilliance of the hundred-watt bulb he glared at himself in the mirror.

His skin was the colour of sour milk, and shiny, as if someone had stretched it over the bones of his face. Beneath his eyes there were dark rings; he could see a streamer of blood running from one corner of his mouth. He wiped it away with the flannel on the side of the sink, spun the cold tap and splashed his face with cooling water.

From the small cabinet on the wall, he took a bottle of aspirin and swallowed two. The bitter taste on his tongue almost made him retch again but he washed them down with two handfuls of water and stood supporting himself on the sink, staring into his own bloodshot eyes.

The pain in his chest persisted.

His reflection stared forlornly back at him. He coughed and spat blood into the sink.

'You're fucked,' he murmured to his reflection.

The blood disappeared down the plughole.

'Well and truly fucked.'

He waited a few moments then swallowed another couple of aspirins, shutting the cabinet door and leaving the lavatory.

He wandered back into the office, the pain lessening a little.

Another half an hour, he told himself. Just sit down. Take it easy.

He slumped in the chair beside the window, his eyes half-closed.

Half an hour.

Then he'd go home.

And call the doctor?

No way.

He was ill, he knew that. He didn't know what the

hell was wrong with him, but he didn't need a fucking doctor to tell him that all was not well.

He didn't want to know.

You're fucked. Well and truly fucked.

It was over an hour before he felt able to drive home. Well and truly fucked.

Thirty

Finlay found a parking space without difficulty and brought the Jag to a halt. Switching off the engine, he sat in the warm stillness looking up at the building in Cavendish Square.

He sat behind the wheel for some minutes just looking up at the place. The windows were blank, like dozens of blind eyes. Some had shutters, others had been boarded up. It looked derelict. Parts of the facade were crumbling, but other than that, the building was suitably impressive when viewed against its neighbours. Two large stone columns supported a canopy over the small flight of steps that led up to the large front door.

Finlay fumbled in his pocket and found a bunch of keys, selecting the one he knew fitted the massive front door. He swung himself out of the car, locked it and set off towards the main door, slowing his pace slightly as he reached the steps.

He glanced around to see if there was anyone passing then hurried up the steps and pushed the key into the lock, shoving against the door which swung back on rusted hinges.

He stepped inside and shut the door, waving a hand in front of him to dispel the clouds of dust he seemed to have disturbed.

To his right and left were closed doors; he was standing in what had once been a massive hallway. Lengths of bare wire hung from holes in the ceiling where lights had once been. Cables dangled like the innards of some monolithic creature.

Spiders had made webs in most corners of the hallway. As Finlay watched, a particularly large one crept along the wall, its bloated body resembling an eight-legged furry boil.

Ahead of him was a staircase, still covered by a threadbare carpet.

The whole place reeked of neglect. Damp, despite the scorching temperatures, was beginning to creep up the walls. Black spores had forced their way up beneath the wallpaper, making it blister and peel.

As Finlay began to climb the stairs, a couple of them groaned protestingly under his weight. He touched the banister and felt the thick dust there, brushing his hands together to remove it. It was difficult to see inside the darkened building but two or three of the windows on the first floor were unboarded and the half-light of night filtered through.

He reached the first landing and looked around. More closed doors faced him, and there were places on the walls where, at one time, pictures had hung. The patches were slightly lighter than the dark paper, much of which was peeling off. It hung like leprous flesh, dried and brittle. As he passed, Finlay pulled a piece from the wall, feeling it crumble between his fingers.

Unperturbed, he continued his climb until he reached the next landing.

To his left a door was ajar.

Finlay moved towards it, pushing it open gently.

The beam of light struck him in the face, making him recoil as if he'd been hit by a tangible object.

He put up a hand to shield his eyes from the glare, gradually regaining his wits as the light was lowered slightly.

'Good of you to come,' said a voice from the shadows.

Finlay heard a chuckle.

'You took your time though,' said Don Neville.

Thirty-one

'What the hell do you think you're doing?' snapped Finlay. 'Calling me at this time of night?'

'We needed to talk to you,' Neville told him, flicking the torch onto his face again before sitting down in an armchair.

Over by the boarded-up window Edward Caton was tapping gently on the metal cover of a halogen lamp.

The room looked as if it belonged in another house.

The floor was bare of carpet but also clean of dust. The walls, painted white, looked grey in the darkness. In the centre of the room was a bed and two armchairs. Dotted around them were arc lights and two halogen lamps. A bare bulb hung from a cord in the ceiling. A video camera had been set up on a tripod close to the bed. Neville turned it towards Finlay.

'And what's so bloody important that it couldn't wait until tomorrow?' Finlay wanted to know, keeping his distance from the two men.

'We hear a whisper that Charles Thornton wants this building' Caton said. 'Is that true?'

'Where did you hear that?'

'We have ears everywhere' chuckled Neville, pushing the camera on its tripod, allowing it to turn slowly.

'So' Caton continued. 'Is it true?'

'You do business with him, why don't you ask him?'

'We're asking you,' Neville hissed, angrily. 'Does he want the fucking building or not?'

'Yes' Finlay told them. 'But don't worry about it. I'll take care of Thornton.'

'He's a powerful man, Joey boy' Neville said, smiling. 'I hope you can.'

'What's the 'sp' on Thornton?' Caton wanted to know. 'Why is this place so fucking important to him?'

Finlay explained about the club and restaurant.

'He knows I own the building' he added. 'He thought it would be an easy purchase. He asked me to name my price.' He looked at the two men in the darkness. 'Perhaps I should have done.'

Neville shook his head slowly, mockingly.

'No, no, no' he chided. 'You know that wouldn't have been

good business. You're better off sticking with me.' He chuckled again, pulling his ponytail away from the back of his neck. 'You know it makes sense.'

Caton lifted an attaché case into view and laid it on the bed, flipping it open.

Finlay took a step closer.

The case was stuffed with money, great thick wads of fifty-pound notes piled on top of each other, bound by elastic bands.

'We brought you a present' Caton told him. 'Your cut.'

He pushed the case towards Finlay, who glanced at both men in the gloom and then shut the case.

'You don't want to count it?' Neville said.

'He trusts us' Caton told him, and both men laughed.

Finlay felt a single droplet of perspiration trickle down the side of his face.

'Twenty per cent?' he said.

Neville nodded.

'As agreed' he added.

'You'd better not get careless.'

'What the fuck are you talking about?' Caton said.

'Don't tell us how to run our business, Finlay' Neville rasped. 'We know what we're doing. Besides, if we stop, then your little bonus dries up.' He nodded towards the attaché case. 'I don't hear you complaining about that.'

'We're supplying a commodity' Caton added. 'And there's a big fucking market for it and that market's getting bigger all the time.'

'But if you want out, just say,' Neville told him. 'We can find somewhere else to make the films.'

'You should be grateful I let you use this place for nothing' Finlay snapped. 'Anyone else would charge . . .'

'The rent is in the fucking case' Neville interrupted angrily, pointing to the attach^ case. 'You let us make the films here because we give you a good cut of the profits. Let's not make any mistakes about that. And maybe you should remember, Finlay, if we're caught, you're an accessory. You know what goes on here. If we go down, we're taking you with us.'

Finlay picked up the attach^ case and took a couple of steps back.

'Leaving so soon?' Neville said, smiling. 'I thought you might be interested to hear how good business is, especially the sales to our European customers. Snuff movies are very big on the continent.'

'Snuff movies?' Finlay said, surprised. 'What are you talking about?'

'Don't play dumb, Finlay. You know what we mean' Caton insisted.

'You're killing people.' There was genuine shock in his voice. 'Is that what you're saying?'

'They're big business, these films, like I said,' Neville continued. 'And as long as there's a market there we'll carry on.'

Finlay swallowed hard, feeling perspiration on his face.

'I want no part of this,' he said, quietly, his voice wavering. 'It's filth. Murder, that's something else. Don't involve me in it.'

'Too late,' Neville told him. 'You are involved.' He nodded at the attach^ case again.

'I want it to stop. I want you out of this building,' Finlay said. 'This has got to stop.'

Caton hawked loudly and spat on the floor, a glob of mucus landing only inches from Finlay's foot.

'You want us out, you move us,' Neville said challengingly.

Finlay hesitated a moment longer, then spun round and headed towards the door.

'Nice talking to you, Joe,' Neville said, smiling. 'We'll be in touch.'

They both heard Finlay's footsteps receding down the stairs.

'He's too jumpy,' Caton said. 'If he loses his bottle, we're all fucked. I think he's going to drop us in it.'

'Don't worry about it. He's in too deep and he knows it. He won't give us any trouble.' He pulled the ponytail away from the back of his neck, wiping sweat off with the back of his hand. 'We'll make sure he doesn't give us any trouble. We'll have to take ourselves a little insurance.'

Thirty-two

The door of the Brewer Street Buttery was open but that one concession to the continuous scorching heat did little to alleviate the discomfort of the half dozen patrons inside.

In one corner a man in a shirt and tie sat fanning himself with a copy of the Financial Times, perspiration rolling off his face. At the table next to him three Japanese tourists babbled excitedly to each other as they passed round thick wads of photographs.

Vince Kiernan sat at the table closest to the door, alternately glancing outside and at his newspaper. He took sips of his coffee and looked again at the front page of the paper which was folded over at the headline: VICTIM NUMBER SIX DISCOVERED IN BELGRAVIA Beneath it was a photo of the pavement outside the house in Belgrave Square where the body of Maria Jenkins had been found. There were two detectives in the picture, both examining what was, apparently, evidence.

Kiernan had read the story three times, checking to see if the victim's name had been mentioned. It hadn't. All the paper would divulge was that the victim was female, about sixteen years old and that she'd been mutilated in the same way as the previous five victims. Like them she had been living rough for some time prior to her death, the paper said.

Like Jo?

Kiernan took a cigarette from his packet and lit one, blowing out a long stream of smoke into the warm air. He wondered how the latest girl had come to be living rough, what had driven her to seek an existence on the streets of London.

What drove any youngster to forsake home for that kind of life?

Every one of them probably had a different reason, Kiernan thought.

Like Jo?

He reached into the back pocket of his jeans and pulled out her bus pass, looking at the photo. Jesus, she looked so happy then. Not a care in the world. He wondered how she looked now. Still smiling? Still carefree?

He pushed the pass back into his pocket and reached for his coffee cup with his free hand.

A sudden wave of anger swept over him. It was a feeling he had grown used to since she'd left Dublin, more so since he'd discovered she'd come here to London's netherworld. But his anger had so many causes. He felt anger towards his parents for not stopping her, for not being more attentive to her. They had said she was too wilful.

What an archaic fucking word that was.

They didn't know how to handle her.

She had said she didn't want to spend the rest of her life in Dublin. There were no prospects for her there. The only things to look forward to were a dead-end job, marriage and a family by the time she was twenty. That was not for Jo. She'd spoken to him many times about leaving Ireland, and each time, he'd tried to talk her out of it. Tried to persuade her to at least wait until she was a little older. But, he'd thought often, it wasn't his job to be telling her. He was her elder brother and he loved her dearly but her own mother and father should have offered more guidance than they did.

His mother and father.

They'd effectively washed their hands of her when she'd left. As far as Kiernan was concerned, they'd abandoned her to her fate.

Whatever the hell that might be.

He glanced at the paper again.

Was it just a matter of time before he saw Jo's name printed beneath such a headline?

The thought made him shudder. He reached for his coffee cup and drained the last few dregs, getting to his feet. He paid and walked out into the street, into the heat.

He left the newspaper on the table. Forgotten.

Like Maria Jenkins?

Kiernan pulled a pair of shades from his pocket and slipped them on as protection against the bright sunlight. Then he set off, continuing his daily search.

He had the awful feeling time was running out.

Thirty-three

The car had stalled.

Ryan leant out of his window and peered ahead, past the other stationary vehicles in the road, towards the source of the hold-up. A choking cloud of exhaust fumes seemed to envelope him, the stinking air heated by the scorching sun. The private detective had the ventilators full on but they were merely sucking in more of the rancid warm air, turning the Sapphire into a mobile sweat-box.

He saw BSM signs on the stalled Metro and watched as the helpless driver struggled to escape the wrath of the motorists behind.

The Metro had blocked the junction of Holland Park Avenue and Royal Crescent and all the banging of hooters and angry shouts in the world weren't going to speed its departure.

Ryan drummed on the wheel with one hand, taking the butt of his cigarette from his mouth with the other and tossing it into the road.

He sucked in a deep breath, wincing at the pain.

Fuck. That hurt.

He suppressed a cough, knowing it would only increase the discomfort he'd felt all night. It had been building steadily since he rose at seven that morning. He'd not had much sleep the night before. Swallowing four paracetamols with some brandy had ensured at least three hours uninterrupted sleep, but the pain had woken him intermittently throughout the night. At last, sick of trying to doze off, he'd hauled himself out of bed at about four and drunk more brandy. He'd fallen asleep on the sofa and felt like shit when he'd woken up three hours later.

Ryan glanced at his reflection in the rear-view mirror. His hair looked uncombed, his face was pale and the rings beneath his eyes looked as if he'd been the canvas for some kid with black crayons. He felt like shit and he looked like it too.

He coughed, wincing at the pain as it intensified.

Up ahead, the learner was still struggling to move the car. It refused to budge. Someone hit their hooter. They were joined by another. Like some ridiculous fanfare, half a dozen horns were sounded. The learner glanced round sheepishly.

Ryan coughed harder, pulling a handkerchief from his pocket, spitting bloody phlegm into the material and balling it up. He wiped the corners of his mouth; the coppery taste was still there.

'Come on' he murmured, reaching to the glove compartment and pulling out a tape. He shoved it into the cassette and turned up the volume; the music competed with the symphony of protest coming from the other cars. '. . . Hey, little sister, scene's sure getting old . . .' He tapped his fingers in time as the tape rolled on.

The learner was now sitting almost motionless as the instructor clambered out and began pushing the vehicle aside. Immediately a big enough gap opened up, the closest car swung round and others followed.

'. . . Don't you think it's time we got to go . . .'

Ryan pressed down on his accelerator and eased away, casting a cursory glance at the stricken Metro which now had its bonnet up, steam rising mournfully into the warm air.

Ryan felt perspiration sticking to his shirt and shuffled uncomfortably in his seat as he drove. Each movement brought fresh pain and he was beginning to feel light-headed. He told himself it was the result of losing so much sleep the previous night. He'd get to bed early tonight, catch up.

The stream of traffic slowed again as traffic lights blinked onto red and, once more, he was left sitting in the unrelenting heat.

A particularly savage stab of pain made him gasp. He put one hand to his chest, trying to breathe in but finding it difficult.

'Shit,' he hissed under his breath.

Maybe a trip to the doctor's wouldn't be a bad idea.

No.

He'd just suggest two weeks' rest, or bollocks like

that. Tell Ryan not to work so hard, to take it easy for a while.

Fuck it. He couldn't afford to do that. Especially not when there was so much work around. He wouldn't turn anything down if it paid well enough. There were always others who would take his place. No. He couldn't be away from work. Besides, cooped up in his house alone twenty-four hours a day he'd go nuts.

Forget the doctor.

He drove on, wiping sweat from his forehead, feeling the pain worsening in his chest.

He gritted his teeth, feeling faint.

Come on, get a fucking grip.

He turned the volume up on the cassette, as if to shock himself back to normality, as if the thunderous music would somehow drive away his dizziness and pain.

He was driving up towards Notting Hill Gate now, trying to concentrate on driving, on the thought of the day's work ahead.

On anything except this fucking pain.

There was a zebra crossing ahead. No one in sight.

The young woman stepped onto it from behind two men and Ryan slammed on his brakes, barely stopping in time.

He glared at her through the windscreen, ignoring the shout from behind, from another driver who'd barely missed him.

The man banged his hooter.

Ryan leaned out of the window and looked at him. He was a middle-aged man with a bald head and a collar that looked too tight.

'What's your fucking problem?' hissed Ryan, eyes blazing.

The man looked past him, waiting for him to move on. He dutifully did.

The music pounded inside the car. Inside his head.

'... Let's move it, time to say so long ...'

The pain throbbed in his chest.

He passed Notting Hill Gate tube. Ahead, a bus was slowing down.

Ryan swung out to pass it.

As he did so the pain seemed to reach intolerable proportions; it was as if someone had suddenly pumped his skull full of air. He felt his hands slipping on the wheel, felt the car going out of control.

He was blacking out.

Jesus fucking Christ.

The world swam in front of his eyes, colours suddenly flaring with incredible brilliance, like fireworks exploding.

The car swerved across the road.

There was a Range Rover coming the other way. Heading straight for him.

He heard hooters, tyres screaming.

The cassette roared.

Ryan felt his hands slip from the wheel. His feet pressed down for the brake but the car didn't seem to respond.

Blackness slipped over him.

The car hit the kerb, bounced up it and hurtled on, smashing into the window of a restaurant.

Ryan had the presence of mind to cover his face but his arms were like rubber. All he felt was the terrible fire in his chest.

He heard shattering glass, screams, hooters, music.

His head snapped forward and slammed against the steering wheel.

He was unconscious before his forehead struck it.

Darkness.

Thirty-four

At first he thought someone had sewn his eyelids together. Try as he might, Ryan couldn't seem to open his eyes.

Fuck it.

Perhaps he was dead, he thought.

The undertaker had stitched his lids closed with nylon thread.

That was it. He was dead.

It didn't seem so bad after all. Just a bastard not being able to see anything and . . .

He felt pain in his chest.

In his head.

His arms.

His whole body was one mass of suffering, his mind able only to comprehend discomfort. Yet the pain wasn't as appalling as he'd known it in the past. His chest was sore, very sore. But he couldn't feel the gnawing pain he'd come to know only too well.

If only he could open his eyes.

He felt dizzy. Light-headed and disorientated. Yet he was lying down.

But lying down where?

He made another effort to open his eyes, feeling the lids part slightly, as if some kind of film were being peeled back. Light forced its way through and dazzled him. Artificial light. The light of fluorescent tubes. And now he noticed the strong smell, of antiseptic.

Ryan tried to move, tried to raise one hand to push his eyelids apart, rubbing at them, wincing as he felt the pain. But at least now he could see. Images swam before him momentarily as his vision cleared.

He was in bed. Grey blankets were pulled tightly across him, as if to restrain him. Only his arms were outside the covers.

There were drips running from both of them.

Ryan swallowed hard as he saw the narrow tubes running from plastic containers suspended above him to the needles embedded in his arms, held in place by surgical tape. He could feel them prodding him as he moved.

The drips didn't prevent him from moving his arms, though, and he pushed at the covers, easing them down slightly to expose his upper body.

His chest and stomach were swathed in bandages. He reached down to touch his pectoral area and felt padding there, and gauze beneath the bandage. Ryan tried to suck in a deep breath but found the effort almost impossible.

He glanced up and saw the clear solution in one of the drips trickle from the container down the tube towards his arm, where it was swallowed by the open vein.

What the fuck were they pumping into him?

The skin not covered by bandages looked blackened in places where it was bruised. Some of the discolorations were already beginning to yellow at the extremities. He had several more abrasions on his shoulders, one or two of which were already beginning to scab over. He tried to kick the covers off, anxious to see whether or not his legs had been damaged, but the effort was too much. He sank back onto the pillows, feeling as if he'd just run a mile.

Ryan tried to remember what had happened but his recollections were as fuzzy as his vision. It was as if his mind had been wrapped in cotton wool and thoughts were trapped inside. He blinked hard. He felt as if he could close his eyes and drift off to sleep again.

Despite the pain.

He pulled the covers back up to his neck and lay there, gazing around the room. Now sounds too began to filter through to him. He could hear footsteps outside the door, people passing back and forth. He heard a trolley being trundled past, one wheel squeaking loudly.

Somewhere in the distance he heard a siren.

The door of the room opened and a man with short dark hair strode in. He was tall, his features thin and he looked as if he could do with some sleep. His long white coat was flying open; beneath it he wore a shirt and trousers. His tie was loosened around his thick neck. He carried a clipboard in one hand.

The doctor looked apprehensively at Ryan for a moment, unsure whether or not the private detective's eyes were actually open. When he saw that they were, a slight smile touched his lips.

He moved across to the bed, reaching for Ryan's left wrist and jabbing two fingers against it to search for a pulse which he checked off against his wristwatch.

'How long have you been awake?' the doctor asked, still looking at his watch.

'A few minutes,' Ryan told him, his voice croaky. It felt as if someone had been scrubbing the back of his throat with sandpaper. When he tried to swallow, it took more effort than he would have liked. The doctor released his wrist and reached for the jug of water on the bedside cabinet. He poured Ryan a beaker full then supported his head while he took a few sips, wincing as he swallowed.

He nodded when he'd drunk enough and lay back.

'Where am I?' he wanted to know.

'St Mary's Hospital, Paddington,' the doctor told him, jotting something down on the clipboard. He crossed to the first of the drips and peered at the fluid level.

'What happened to me?'

'We were hoping you were going to be able to tell us that, Mr Ryan.'

'I can't remember much, just blacking out. I remember the car going out of control, then nothing.' He shrugged. There was a stab of pain in his chest.

The doctor regarded him impassively for a moment and then began pulling back the covers.

'I think I'd better have a look,' he said, motioning towards the private detective's heavily bandaged torso.

'What's the damage?' Ryan wanted to know.

'A couple of cracked ribs, cuts and bruises. You've got a bang on the head, too.'

'How long have I been unconscious?'

The doctor looked at him impassively.

'Two days.'

Ryan looked incredulous.

'Two days?' he repeated, as if that would somehow lessen the shock. 'But you said my injuries were minor. I didn't bang my head that badly, did I?'

'You were unconscious when you were brought in. You did come round, but after the operation you slipped under. You've been in a coma for the past forty-two hours, Mr Ryan.'

'Coma?' Ryan blurted. 'What the hell are you talking about?'

'You were brought here with minor injuries, as I've said,' the doctor informed him. 'We did routine X-Rays to see whether there was any internal damage.'

'And?' Ryan interrupted, a note of fear now in his voice.

'When we checked the X-Rays we found a shadow on both lungs' the doctor told him calmly. 'We opened you up and performed an operation. We did a biopsy on part of a growth we took from one lung.'

Ryan was looking directly at him now, his eyes blazing.

'Yeah?'

The doctor licked his lips swiftly.

'You have cancer.'

Thirty-five

'Cancer.'

Ryan repeated the word as if it was the first time he'd ever, heard it. His voice was even, his expression one of bemusement rather than concern. He looked down at his chest and took as deep a breath as the constricting bandages and the pain would allow.

Gerald Newman was beginning to wonder if Ryan had heard him correctly, so unresponsive were his reactions. The doctor had seen some people break down when they were given the news. Others fainted. Most just sat motionless as the realization dawned.

Ryan now lay silently, running one hand across his chin, perhaps grappling with the disclosure.

'In the lungs, you say?' Ryan finally added.

Newman nodded.

Ryan shook his head slowly.

Perhaps I should have gone to the doctor, he mused, a slight smile on his lips.

'You must have been in considerable pain for some time now,' Newman said.

Ryan didn't answer.

Fucking right.

'Didn't you tell anyone?' the doctor persisted. 'Your own doctor, perhaps?'

'No' Ryan said flatly. 'I never got round to it.' He shrugged.

Newman regarded him impassively.

'How far advanced is it?' Ryan wanted to know.

'Well, as I said, we found large growths in both lungs and there are signs that it is beginning to spread to the pancreas and the spleen.'

Ryan nodded.

'What did you do to me when you opened me up?' he enquired.

'There wasn't much we could do,' Newman confessed. 'Initially it was an exploratory operation. We were surprised at how far advanced the cancer was.'

'You didn't attempt to remove it, then?'

'That wouldn't have been possible, Mr Ryan.'

'Why not?'

'It was too deeply embedded, too far advanced. In both lungs there are up to four tumours. One of them in the right lung is the size of my fist.'

Ryan's eyes narrowed slightly, but otherwise he seemed more intrigued than perturbed. Newman wondered if the full gravity of his words had reached the patient. When hearing particularly bad news, he had found, the human mind sometimes shuts out what it cannot countenance.

'So what now?' Ryan demanded.

Newman shrugged. It was a question he had been dreading.

'What can you do?' the private detective continued.

'There's nothing we can do, Mr Ryan. The cancer is inoperable and, as I've already told you, it's beginning to spread.'

'What about chemotherapy?'

Newman shook his head.

'It's too late for that' he said bluntly.

Ryan smiled bitterly.

'In other words I'm fucked' he said. 'You can't operate, you can't treat the cancer. Right?'

'That's correct.'

'Why don't you just come out and say it?' Ryan asked challengingly. 'Why don't you tell me it's terminal?'

'I would have thought that was more or less apparent without my having to say it, Mr Ryan. I'm very sorry.'

'Don't be' Ryan hissed. 'How long have I got?'

'That's impossible to say' Newman explained.

'Take a fucking guess,' Ryan rasped angrily.

'If the cancer continues to grow at the rate it's growing now, and if the spread accelerates, then perhaps six months.'

Ryan fixed him in an unwavering stare.

'You're telling me I'll be dead in six months?' he said quietly.

'It may not take that long,' Newman admitted. 'On the other hand, we could operate on the tumours in the pancreas and the spleen. We could remove those, but they're not the real problem. They're secondary cancers. The primary tumours in the lungs are inoperable. The cancer could be arrested but not cured.'

'A stay of execution' Ryan quipped.

'There are drugs which will help relieve the pain and which will slow down the growth of the primary tumour. Unfortunately, they won't cure you either.'

'Which drugs?'

Newman shrugged.

'I have a right to know,' Ryan snapped. 'It's my fucking life.'

'Chlorambucil, triaziquone or cyclo-phosphamide,' the doctor told him. 'There are a number of others. Morphine to stop the pain, usually in liquid form, to be swallowed.'

'Thanks' Ryan said quietly.

Newman looked down at the private detective, feeling the same sense of helplessness he had known far too many times throughout his career.

'There's something else I have to know,' Ryan said finally. 'The symptoms. How will the disease progress?'

'Why do you need to know?'

'Because I'm the one who's going to be living through it,' Ryan reminded him. 'I'm the one who's got to face it. Now tell me what'll happen to me.'

'The cancer cells will continue to divide, to grow,' the doctor began. 'Breathing will become difficult, more painful. Finally impossible. The lungs will simply cease to function. Effectively you'll suffocate.'

Ryan nodded.

'I'll be able to walk about, though? Live life more or less normally?' he wanted to know.

'As the lungs become more diseased it'll become almost impossible to move around. You simply won't have the strength. You won't be able to take in enough oxygen to aerate your blood supply. In a weakened state you'll also become more susceptible to germs, to other infections and viruses.'

'I'm not going to lie here and wait for it to kill me, Doctor,' Ryan said defiantly.

'You might not have any choice, Mr Ryan.'

'I won't wait for it to kill me,' the private detective said through clenched teeth. 'No way.'

Newman nodded, then re-checked the drips before moving towards the door.

'I'll send a nurse in,' he said, one hand on the handle. 'In the meantime, if there's anything you need just press that button beside your bed.' He turned to leave.

'There is one thing,' Ryan told him.

'What is it?'

'I could murder a cigarette.'

Thirty-six

He drifted in and out of sleep, never able to snatch more than thirty minutes at a time. The combination of his pain and the incessant heat made complete rest impossible.

As Ryan rolled over yet again he glanced at his watch on the bedside table.

The luminous hands glowed green in the gloom; it was almost 1.00 a.m. The rest of the hospital was silent. To Ryan, it seemed as if the sound of his own laboured breathing filled the night.

Every now and then he could hear footsteps passing by outside the door of his room, receding away into the distance, swallowed up by the cloying solitude.

Beads of perspiration had formed on his forehead and he wiped them away with the back of one hand, pushing down his covers with the other.

Christ, it was hot.

He surveyed the bandaged torso. The bruised limbs.

Cancer.

Fucking cancer.

Ryan felt suddenly cold, as if someone had injected him with ice water, as if the liquid in the drips had turned to freezing moisture. He momentarily forgot the heat inside the room. A stab of pain in his chest shocked

him out of his musings. He sucked in a breath, wincing in the process.

Six months.

'Shit' he murmured.

People rarely contemplated their own deaths. Not even in quiet moments, he thought. Certainly he had never thought about his own until Newman had given him the news of its impending arrival. Certainly everyone at some time wondered what it would be like to die. When they were going to meet their end. But to be told, that was something different. To know of that awful finality was bad enough but to be told to expect it in a matter of months was intolerable.

To be helpless against it was even worse.

Ryan felt a curious mixture of rage and foreboding. He shifted uncomfortably in his bed, feeling the perspiration soaking into the sheets.

He had been told he would die in less than six months.

That, according to Newman, was a fact. And one which there was no escaping.

And they expected him to lie there helplessly waiting for the end?

Fuck that.

Ryan gritted his teeth.

He would fight it. Fight this fucking disease which was trying to kill him. Fight it like he'd fought everything else in his life. He wouldn't allow it to get the better of him. All his life he'd been competitive, in his job, in his relationships. Now he was being forced to face the most potent opponent ever. Death itself.

Well, he would fight.

He'd read of others who'd been diagnosed as having terminal illnesses, who'd been given a limited time. And they had fought and some had won. Some had kept death at bay.

If others could do it then so could he.

Try and take me, you cunt, and I'll fight you.

He gritted his teeth, as if faced by a tangible adversary.

He would not surrender. He would not lie here and give up his hold on something so precious.

No way.

His thoughts were interrupted as the door to the room opened and light flooded through, causing him to shield his eyes. A figure was silhouetted there for a second, and then the nurse slipped inside, closing the door behind her.

'Perhaps you should be carrying a fucking scythe' said Ryan.

The nurse looked puzzled.

'Did I wake you up?' she wanted to know.

He shook his head.

'I can't sleep, anyway,' he told her.

'Would you like a sleeping pill?' she enquired, checking the drips and scribbling something on the clipboard which hung at the bottom of his bed. She crossed to him again and felt for his pulse, checking it against the watch which hung from her uniform.

Ryan eyed her through the gloom, noticing that she was in her mid-twenties, pretty. She smelled of newly washed linen.

She moved to pull the covers up again but Ryan held out a hand to stop her.

'It's too hot,' he said protestingly, wincing as he felt a stab of pain.

'Are you in pain?' she asked.

'You could say that,' he answered acidly.

'Do you want me to get you something for it?'

'Yeah, major fucking surgery,' he told her caustically.

'I'll get you a couple of Brufen. They'll help you sleep, too.'

'I don't want to sleep' he snapped. His tone softened. 'I'll have plenty of time for that in six months.'

She regarded him through the gloom for a moment as his expression relaxed.

'Is this an occupational hazard?' he asked.

She looked puzzled.

'Having to deal with moaning bastards' he continued.

She smiled.

'Yes. All the time' she told him.

'Why do you do it? It's not the fucking money, that's for sure.'

'Someone has to' she told him. 'Besides, I enjoy it. I like looking after people. My mum was a nurse too, then a midwife right up until she died.'

'How old was she?'

'Forty-eight. She had a stroke.'

She was lucky.

'What's your name?' he wanted to know.

'Debra White.'

'Pleased to meet you, Debra White.' He nodded at her, as if the gesture made the introduction formal.

'One of the interns told me you were a private detective,' she said sheepishly. 'Is that true?'

Did he tell you I was dying, too?

'Yes, it's true. So what?'

'It must be a glamorous job.'

'Does it look glamorous now? I can think of more exciting ways of spending my time.'

'But in films . . .'

He cut her short.

'Forget what you've seen in films' Ryan said. 'The people who make films about private investigators usually haven't got a clue.'

'Do you carry a gun?'

'I own two but I don't carry one with me. The police tend to object if you go around shooting people. Even when those people are threatening to take your fucking head off because you've found out they're having an affair or something like that.'

'My boyfriend will be interested when I tell him I've met a private detective' the nurse said, smiling.

'Don't forget to tell him the truth,' Ryan said. Perhaps he'd be less interested in a dying private detective. 'What does he do?'

'He works here in the hospital. He's a porter.' She smiled again. 'Have you got any family?'

Ryan's face darkened.

'No,' he said sharply. 'No one.'

The nurse looked a little sad.

She glanced round towards the door.

'I'd better go, Sister will be after me,' she said. 'Are you sure there's nothing I can get you?'

Ryan shook his head.

She smiled again and left, closing the door behind her.

Ryan exhaled, the action causing renewed pain. He closed his eyes and waited for sleep, knowing it would not come. Not yet. He wiped perspiration from his face with his hand; the drip moved on its stand as the tube was pulled by his movement. Ryan felt the needle prick and cursed under his breath.

He could not take this, lying here like a helpless invalid.

Like a corpse?

He would not take it.

Thirty-seven

The lighter flared once then went out, briefly illuminating her face with the glow.

Stephanie Collins flicked at it again, the JPS bouncing up and down between her thin lips as she tried to get the lighter to raise a flame. Despite her efforts it produced only sparks. Muttering to herself, she rummaged in her small shoulder bag, searching for matches. There were none. She took the cigarette from her mouth and dropped it into the bottom of the bag along with the other debris. A couple of empty cigarette packets. Lipstick. Some condoms. A small pocket knife.

Despite the heat she shivered.

The gloom inside the multi-storey car park on Waverton Street was almost impenetrable and the thick concrete pillar she leant against was cold.

The stink of oil and petrol was strong in the cloying night air, even though the last car had long ago departed.

She shifted from one stilettoed foot to the other, occasionally running a skinny hand over her spandex- clad legs. The short black leather jacket draped around her shoulders did nothing to warm her. Dressed all in black, surrounded by darkness, she seemed to be a part of the umbra, a shadow distinguishable only by a shock of platinum blonde hair.

She picked briefly at a tiny spot on her chin, hoping it was still adequately hidden by her thick make-up. Yet to reach her twentieth birthday, Stephanie looked ten years older. Her pale features were weary and drawn, her eyes dull and lifeless, like those of a fish on a skillet. Those same dull eyes which darted furtively back and forth in the blackness.

She heard footsteps; the sound echoed through the cavernous car park.

Instinctively she pressed herself up against the pillar. Peering in the direction of the sound, she realized it could have been someone walking past the car park. Sound carried at such a late hour.

It was almost 2.10 a.m.

The footsteps receded and Stephanie ran a hand through her hair, shuddering involuntarily. She tried to slow her breathing and quieten it. Every sound seemed to be amplified, carried through the darkness with increased clarity.

As she shifted from one foot to the other the clicking of her heels on the concrete sounded deafening.

She tried standing still but found it almost impossible.

Through the gloom she squinted at her watch once again, tapping the face with one false nail when she saw that the second hand had stopped moving. She raised the time piece to her ear checking to see if it was still working. She heard the ticking.

And suddenly, from behind her, she heard a whirring sound.

The lift was rising from the basement level.

Stephanie pressed herself more tightly to the pillar, her eyes on the yellow floor lights above the lift doors.

The one marked 'G' flared.

The lift began to rise again.

She swallowed hard, watching as it reached the first level. This level.

Interminable seconds passed before the doors slid open.

The lift was empty.

Silence descended again, broken only by Stephanie's harsh breathing.

The lift doors remained open, revealing the empty car beyond.

She took a step forward, her eyes fixed on the lift.

The blood roared in her ears and she could feel her heart thudding hard against her ribs.

Conscious of the noise of her heels, she leant forward so that she was walking on her toes, almost silently.

The lift doors still yawned open.

She swallowed hard and took a step closer.

The hand closed over her shoulder.

Unable to help herself, Stephanie Collins screamed.

The sound reverberated off the concrete pillars and low ceiling of the car park, drumming in her own ears as she spun round.

Donald Neville released his grip on her shoulder and took a step back.

He was smiling thinly.

'Jesus Christ,' she panted. 'You scared the shit out of me.' She wiped one trembling hand across her face.

Neville pulled at his ponytail and looked her up and down.

'Why all the creeping about?' Stephanie asked.

'We had to be sure you were on your own,' Neville told her.

'I've been waiting here for ages' she protested. 'You said midnight.'

'We had other business to attend to,' Edward Caton told her. 'You're not too high on our list of priorities.'

'I've been standing here fucking freezing,' she said. 'You got a light?'

Neville reached into his pocket and pulled out a zippo, striking it.

She leant closer, sticking the JPS between her lips, pushing the end into the flame.

In the sickly yellow light he saw the dark marks on the crook of her arm and on her wrist. Some of them had scabbed over; others were purple welts where the skin had started to heal, only to be broken again.

'What are you on?' Neville asked contemptuously. 'Stevie? That is what they call you, isn't it?'

She took a couple of drags on the cigarette.

'What's it to you what I'm on? What do you care?'

'I don't,' Neville said flatly.

'Have you got the money?' she wanted to know.

Neville nodded.

'Have you got what we want?' he asked.

'It's here,' she told him, motioning to a small cardboard box at her feet with BEANZ MEANZ HEINZ stencilled on it.

'How long you had it?' Caton wanted to know.

'Five weeks,' she told him.

He snapped his fingers and she bent and picked up the box, holding it to her chest.

'Two thousand,' she said.

'One thousand,' Neville said, reaching into the pocket of his jeans. 'That was the price we agreed.' He fixed her in an unflinching stare. 'Give.' He curled his finger at her.

'Bastard,' she muttered, shoving the box at Caton. He peered inside and looked at his colleague, nodding.

Neville began pushing fifty-pound notes into Stevie Collins' hand.

She took their money.
They took her baby.

Thirty-eight

'What the hell are you doing?'

Doctor Gerald Newman froze as he pushed open the door to Ryan's room.

The private detective was sitting on the edge of the bed pulling the second drip from his arm.

There was a trickle of blood from the vein as he pulled it free but he wiped it away with a tissue before turning to look directly at the doctor.

'Mr Ryan' Newman continued, moving into the room hurriedly. 'What are you playing at?'

'I'm not playing, Doctor,' Ryan told him. 'I'm leaving.' He stood up, steadying himself against the edge of the bed.

'That's impossible. You're very ill, you're . . .'

'Yeah, I know, I'm dying.'

Ryan crossed to the wardrobe and pulled open the doors, searching for his clothes. He pulled on his shirt.

'You can't do this,' Newman said. 'You've undergone an operation. You're more susceptible to all kinds of infections now.'

'Oh, no! You mean I could catch a cold, or something serious like that?' Ryan continued buttoning his shirt.

'You know bloody well what I mean. I can't allow you to do this. I can't allow you to leave.'

'Try stopping me' Ryan said, stepping into his trousers.

Newman moved towards the bed and perched on the edge of it, watching as the private detective continued dressing.

'You need help, Mr Ryan,' he said, his tone softening.

'But, according to you, no one can help me. I'm going to die anyway, aren't I? Well, I'm fucked if I'm going to lie here in some hospital bed waiting for it. Counting off the days.' He shook his head. 'Not a chance.'

'What you're doing is madness, you realize that?' the doctor said in a last attempt to dissuade Ryan from his actions.

'I'd be even more crazy to stay here, knowing what I know,' the private detective told him. He winced slightly as he felt pain in his chest but he continued dressing. 'I'd go mad, stuck in here. I might as well be on fucking death row. I know it's going to happen in the next few months; it'd just be a matter of sitting around here waiting for it to happen. I won't go out like that.'

'But there's medication you need. Special care.'

'What's the fucking point? It's all going to be over in six months anyway, isn't it? If I need medication, then write me some prescriptions.' Ryan looked at him impassively. 'If you want to help me then let me out of here.'

'The hospital has responsibilities to its patients. I have responsibilities,' Newman protested.

'I'll sign a letter absolving you and the hospital of all blame for me leaving. Don't worry, Doc, no one's going to hit you with a lawsuit if I drop dead on the pavement outside.'

'There's no need for that,' Newman said quietly. 'I'm just sorry you won't let us help you.'

'Help me in what way? Get your nurses to bring me bedpans when I'm too breathless to walk to the shithouse? Shove drips into my arms when I can't take solid food? Send someone in with crateful's of pills every day? I can do without that kind of help. Besides, there are people in this hospital who need that kind of help more than me. People who are going to get better'

'Your concern for the other patients is touching, Mr Ryan' said Newman, a note of sarcasm in his voice.

'Concern, bollocks. I'm just being realistic. I couldn't give a fuck about anyone else in here, but most of them have got a chance of leaving in one piece. If I stayed here the only way I could hope to leave would be in a wooden box.'

Newman reached into his pocket and pulled out a prescription pad. He began writing. He scribbled down several different medications in his neat hand.

Ryan looked at him as he held out the pieces of paper.

'Some of those drugs will stop the cancer growing so quickly, others are pain-killers. There are a couple of prescriptions there for morphine, when the pain becomes too much.'

Ryan nodded and took them, folding them up and slipping them into his jacket.

He gritted his teeth at the pain burning inside him, but thankfully the tremor passed. He extended his right hand and Newman shook it warmly.

'If you can't cope' the doctor said, 'come back.'

'Why?' Ryan said, smiling.

He stepped past the doctor and headed for the door, closing it behind him as he left.

Newman shook his head and looked across at the discarded drips.

Saline was trickling from one of them. Droplets of it fell onto the floor like tears.

Thirty-nine

He caught a taxi straight to his office in Old Compton Street. From there, Ryan rang Hertz and rented a Nissan 200SX until his own car was repaired.

He checked the mail that had arrived in the past three days, and the messages on the answerphone, but none required urgent attention. More work had come in, he was pleased to note. That was what he wanted now. Plenty of work, plenty to occupy his mind. He didn't want any time to dwell on his predicament.

No time to think about death.

Ryan sat at his desk and sucked hard on the cigarette he'd just lit, glancing at the Health Warning on the packet. He almost laughed. Who was to say it had been the cigarettes that had caused his illness? There could be a dozen different reasons for it. He took another drag on the Superking, blowing out the smoke in a blue cloud.

STOPPING SMOKING REDUCES THE RISK OF SERIOUS DISEASES

He ran an index finger over the warning again.

Fuck it. He knew guys who smoked sixty Marlboro a day who were healthier than he was.

Fuck it.

He'd nipped out earlier and picked up two of the prescriptions Newman had written for him. One lot of pills were painkillers, the others were for retarding the growth of the cancer. He had hung on to the morphine scripts; no sense in using them until it was absolutely necessary.

Ryan glanced at the phone, rested his hand on it then withdrew it again.

Soon.

He got to his feet and crossed the office, glancing out of the window at the bustling thoroughfare of Charing Cross Road. The clouds of exhaust fumes from so many vehicles rose in a noxious wave. In the cloudless sky the sun blazed unmercifully. Ryan wiped perspiration from his face with the back of his hand, noticing that he was quivering slightly.

As he turned he felt a twinge of pain in his chest but he gritted his teeth, intent on ignoring it - as a bullock will ignore a troublesome fly.

To his left there was a teak cabinet about two feet square. Fumbling in his jacket pocket Ryan selected a key, knelt and unlocked the cabinet.

Inside it, lying on separate shelves, both lined with black velvet, were two guns.

On the top shelf lay a Smith and Wesson 9mm Model 39 Automatic.

Below it, a .357 Colt Python revolver.

There were half a dozen boxes of ammunition in there too.

Ryan took the .357 and hefted it, feeling the weight, seeing the light reflect off the gleaming metal. He traced the barrel with his index finger, feeling the engraved maker's name and serial number.

He swung it up and squinted down the barrel.

Ryan had owned the guns for the last six years but had never fired them in anger. He practised regularly at a shooting club in Druid Street, south of the river, but he'd never shot at anything other than a target with either weapon. He'd carried one or both of the weapons on a number of jobs but had only had recourse to pull them on half a dozen occasions, always in self-defence. The sight of the weapons alone had always done the trick.

Now he held the pistol close, studying every contour of it.

Six months of suffering?

Ryan swallowed hard.

Did he want that?

Six months was better than nothing. Wasn't it?

He pressed the barrel of the .357 up under his chin, the steel comfortingly cool against his hot flesh.

So easy to end it all now.

No more suffering.

No more pain.

He pulled the trigger.

The hammer slammed down on an empty chamber, the metallic click loud in the silent office.

'Fuck' hissed Ryan, lowering the gun. He pushed it back inside the cabinet and locked it. Then he crossed to his desk.

This time he didn't hesitate. He snatched up the receiver and dialled.

Forty

Kim wasn't very happy by the time she reached the door of Ryan's office.

The drive into Central London had taken longer than usual because of an accident and subsequent detour. Once in the centre she'd had trouble finding somewhere to park and now she had been forced to trek up five flights of stairs because the lift was out of order. Kim Finlay was more than a little irritated as she banged on the door, perspiration trickling down her back in the warmth of the evening.

'This had better be good, Nick,' she snapped as Ryan opened the door and stepped back to let her in. She breezed past him and stalked into the office, noticing how dark it was in there. Lit only by the desk lamp, the room was filled with deep, thick shadows.

He offered her a seat but she declined, preferring to pace back and forth.

'Do you realize the trouble your phone call caused me?' she asked. 'I had a row with Joe before I left.'

'Do you want a drink?' he asked, apparently unconcerned by the tribulations his call had precipitated.

She regaled him with the details of her tortuous journey to his office.

Ryan sat down behind his desk and poured vodka into his mug. He lit a cigarette and took a drag, coughing. He touched his chest briefly, feeling the all too familiar pain.

'Well,' she said angrily. 'I've come all this way, you could at least tell me why.'

'Just sit down, will you, Kim?' he said.

She pulled up a chair and plonked herself in it.

In the dim light she saw that his face looked even more pale, how the dark rings beneath his eyes seemed to combine with his heavy lids to form black holes where his eyes should have been. The hollows of his cheeks looked as if they'd been inked over. His hand was shaking slightly as he raised the mug to drink.

'If you have to call, can't you do it when Joe's not there?' she asked, her tone softening.

'I didn't know he was going to pick up the bloody phone' Ryan said. 'Anyway, he might not have to bother about my calls for much longer.'

She looked puzzled.

'There won't be any more calls,' he told her.

'Why? Are you going away?'

He grunted.

'You could say that.' He downed what was left in the mug and poured himself another refill.

'Nick, what's going on? Are you in some kind of trouble?'

'Big fucking trouble,' he said, a bitter smile on his lips.

'What's happening? Presumably you got me over here to tell me?'

'I can't think of an easy way to say this, Kim, so I won't even try. I'm dying.'

There, it was said. Quite easy, really.

'Terminal lung cancer. Well, to start with, anyway. My liver and spleen are fucked, too. Cancer. I've got six months, tops.'

She felt very cold, despite the warmth in the office. It was as if all the blood was draining quickly from her body...

He raised his mug.

'Cheers.'

Kim wanted to speak but found that no words would come. Her lips moved but she found it impossible to make any sound.

Ryan explained what had happened. The chest pains, the blood, the vomiting. He told her about the blackout and the car crash, the subsequent operation and the doctor's words. Throughout it all she sat in numbed silence.

Ryan lit another cigarette, noticing as she glanced at it.

'It's okay,' he said. 'I've cut down. The fucking things kill you.'

She got to her feet and walked around the desk.

Ryan saw the tears glistening on her cheeks.

'Could there be some mistake?' she asked, moving closer to him.

Ryan shook his head, standing up to embrace her as she threw her arms around him.

'Oh God, Nick,' she sobbed, hugging him tightly to her. 'What are you going to do?'

'There's not much I can do,' he said. 'That's the worst thing about it.'

'I'm so sorry,' she said, tears streaming down her face.

'It isn't your fault. It isn't anyone's fault. I can't even blame some other fucker for it.' He chuckled humourlessly.

'I'm sorry for you' she said.

'I don't want your pity, Kim,' he said through gritted teeth.

'It isn't pity,' she snapped, pulling back from him slightly. 'I don't want anything to happen to you. I never did. I love you.'

The words took him by surprise; he pulled her close again.

'I love you,' she whispered.

Ryan screwed his eyes tightly shut, so tight that white stars danced behind the lids. He felt a curious mixture of emotions.

She held on to him for a little longer, then reached out and touched his face. He took her hand and pulled it away.

'Kelly will have to be told,' Kim said.

Ryan wiped a tear from her cheek.

'Not yet,' he said.

'She has a right to know, Nick, before it's too late.'

'You mean before I'm down to five stone, and all my fucking hair's fallen out and I need a respirator to breathe? Is that what you mean?'

'I'll tell her.'

'No. She mustn't know, Kim. Promise me that' he said, a hard edge to his voice. 'Promise me you won't tell her.'

Fresh sobs racked her body as he pulled her tightly to him.

The darkness inside the room seemed to swallow them up.

Forty-one

The child lay in a cardboard box about three feet by two. It was wrapped in blankets to keep it warm, but even so its skin was tinged red about the cheeks and upper body.

'What if it fucking dies?' Edward Caton said, looking down at the child.

'Stop worrying,' said Don Neville. 'It's only port I've given it. My mum used to swear by it for the smaller kids when they cried. We're probably taking better care of it than the slag who sold it to us. If it survived five weeks with her it'll stand another couple of days with us.' He wandered slowly around the room in the building in Cavendish Square, checking the video camera and the lights. Double-checking that everything was in position.

'Are you going to offer this one to Thornton?' Caton asked.

'I'm not sure,' Neville said, wiping sweat from the

back of his neck. 'I reckon we'll do better abroad with a film with a baby in it. Mind you, I'm sure Charles Thornton's got plenty of punters who'd go for this kind of thing, too.' He smiled.

'And the other member of the cast?' Caton said, grinning. 'Maybe we should use a geezer this time.'

'Maybe, but the baby's a boy, isn't it?'

Caton shrugged.

'I don't know,' he chuckled. 'I didn't look.' He leant forward and pulled the blankets away from the child to get a better view. 'Fuck me, you're right.'

He laughed and covered the baby again.

'Finlay was right, you know,' Caton said, his tone changing.

'About what?' Neville wanted to know.

'Well, we've done six now. The law have found four of them.'

'And where the fuck has it got them? They're no closer now than they were when we first started and they never will get any closer. Those kids we took were just names or numbers, sometimes not even that. No one gives a fuck about them. They're expendable, Eddie boy. The shit that fills the gutter of society.' He smiled at his own philosophical musings. 'We've just been cleaning up that gutter a bit. Removing some of the unwanted debris from it, you might say.'

Caton grinned crookedly.

'No,' Neville continued, 'the law don't know where to start.'

'What about that little slag who sold us the baby?'

'What's she going to tell them? We should have used her in the next video. Give it another nine months and she'll be trying to sell someone else another kid of hers, if she hasn't O.D.'d by then.' He looked at his companion. 'You're not going soft on me, are you, Eddie? Not losing your bottle?'

Caton shook his head.

'Never' he said, flatly. 'I was just thinking about Finlay and what he'd said.' He ran a hand through his hair, wiping the perspiration off on his jeans. 'What the fuck do we do about that cunt? What's his fucking game?'

'The only game Finlay plays is with himself,' Neville said.

'But what if he blows the gaff on us?' Caton wanted to know.

'He can't. If he tips off the law there's no way we'd go down without implicating him. He knows that. He knows we've got him by the bollocks.'

'Have we? What proof have we got to tie him in to us? I don't know, Don, don't you think we might be better off abroad with this kind of thing?'

Neville thought for a moment and then smiled thinly. 'I can take care of all that,' he said quietly. 'Tying him into the business in a way he'd never have expected.'

Forty-two

The public bar of The Roebuck in Great Dover Street was empty but for three people. Two of them, men in their forties dressed in suits and looking decidedly uncomfortable in the heat, were standing at the bar.

One sipped mineral water; the other nursed a shandy in a large hand.

Nick Ryan stood in the doorway, looking at the two men. He glanced at his watch.

'Drink after the job's done' he said acidly. 'You might have time to waste but I haven't.'

The two men spun round, the taller of the two spilling some of his drink.

'Are you Ryan?' the taller man asked.

The private detective nodded.

'Malcolm Webber,' said the tall man, pressing a finger to his own chest. 'This is Peter Crane.' He nodded towards his shorter, stockier companion. 'We're from the Council. We've been waiting for you.'

'Then why the fuck weren't you waiting for me across the road at the flat of the bloke we're serving an eviction notice on? As far as I know he hasn't paid his rent. I didn't think you had to check out his local first. You're bailiffs, right? Not fucking Weights and Measures Inspectors.' Ryan walked out again and the two men followed, striding briskly across the road after him.

As he reached the flight of stone steps that led to the first floor, Ryan lit a cigarette, sucking hard on it.

'You got one to spare?' asked Crane hopefully.

'They had a fag machine in the pub, didn't they?' Ryan snapped. 'You should have bought some. Come on.'

He led the way and the other two men followed him up the steps, Crane raising two fingers at his back.

The trio reached the first landing and Ryan pulled a piece of paper from his pocket, checking the address. He noted the numbers of the other flats as they passed them. One. Three. Five.

The door to number seven opened and a woman stuck her head out, glancing warily at the three men. Behind her a small child shouted something Ryan

couldn't hear. The boy was about five and pushed past his mother to get a better view. She made a perfunctory grab for him but the child slipped out and scurried onto the landing, watching the men until they reached the door of flat number fifteen. The woman too was watching, leaning against the frame of the door, her arms crossed.

'What are you looking at?' asked Crane. 'There's nothing to see.'

The woman didn't answer.

Ryan banged hard on the door, noticing that some of the red paint had flaked off. There was no answer so he knocked again.

Still nothing.

'Mr Hughes,' he called.

Silence.

'Mr Hughes, can you hear me?' he said, sucking on his cigarette. 'Open up. My name is Ryan; I'm here with an eviction order from Southwark Council. I'm not moving until you open this door.'

They heard the sounds of movement from behind the door.

'Fuck off,' a voice shouted.

Ryan banged again.

'I told you to fuck off,' Hughes shouted again.

The private detective continued banging.

'Get away from the door,' Hughes told him.

'Open it,' Ryan called back.

'Shall we handle this?' Webber asked, stepping forward.

Ryan glared at him and the bailiff hesitated.

Further down the landing other doors had opened now, other inquisitive occupants of the block peering out. The small child moved closer to get a better view.

Ryan dropped his cigarette butt and ground it out.

'I've got a gun in here,' Hughes shouted. 'You get away and you won't get hurt.'

'Put the gun away, you old bastard,' Crane snapped. 'We'll have the police here in five minutes.'

'Shut it,' hissed Ryan.

'Either you open the door or I'll kick it in,' Ryan said, leaning against the frame.

'Didn't you hear me?' Hughes bellowed. 'I've got a gun. I'll fucking use it, too. The first cunt through that door gets both barrels.'

Ryan shook his head, stepped back and aimed a kick at the door.

The impact sent it hurtling back on its hinges, pieces of paint and wood flying into the air. As Ryan stepped into the narrow hallway he smelled the acrid stench of stale urine and sweat. But it was what he saw that caused him to slow his pace.

Donald Hughes was standing at the end of the hallway, a Viking 12 bore shotgun gripped firmly in his hands. The twin barrels yawned menacingly as Hughes raised the weapon.

Ryan looked from the barrels to the man's face. He looked pale and frightened.

Frightened men were unpredictable, Ryan thought. Especially when they were pointing a shotgun at you.

'Put the gun down,' Ryan said, advancing a couple of steps.

Hughes backed off.

'Stay back or I'll fire, I'm telling you. I'll fucking do it,' he rasped.

Ryan continued to advance.

'Put it down,' he said through clenched teeth, his eyes locked on the older man's.

'I'll get the police,' Crane called.

Ryan didn't hear. His full attention was fixed on the man in front of him.

'Get back,' shouted Hughes.

Ryan took a step closer.

Hughes swung the Viking up to his shoulder, peering down the barrel.

'Go on, then, if you're going to do it,' Ryan said quietly.

Fire.

'One more step,' Hughes gasped, his breath coming in shallow, rapid gasps.

Ryan took that one step.

'Come on, then, pull the fucking trigger,' he urged.

Do me a favour. Help me out.

'I'll kill you,' Hughes told him.

Be my fucking guest.

Ryan was still moving forward.

'I swear to Christ. . .'

'Then fucking shoot,' roared Ryan, seeing the uncertainty flash behind Hughes' eyes. The shotgun wavered in the air slightly. 'Pull the trigger,' he urged. 'Come on, you gutless fucker. Do it.'

Please.

There was a loud metallic click as Hughes thumbed back the hammers.

He was shaking now.

'I'll kill you,' he said none too convincingly.

Ryan raised a hand, reaching for the wavering barrels.

One touch on those triggers now and that was it.

Pull them.

'Last warning,' Hughes said, whimpering.

'Fuck you,' snarled Ryan and snaked out a hand.

His fingers closed around the Viking, and with one powerful twist of his wrist he wrenched the weapon from Hughes' grip.

The older man slumped back against the wall, his head lowered, sobbing quietly.

Ryan looked at him contemptuously.

'You gutless bastard' he snarled, hefting the shotgun.

'You're mad' Hughes told him.

Ryan held the gun for a moment then spun it round so he was holding the barrels more firmly.

'Why didn't you kill me?' he said. There was a note of anger in his voice.

The private detective lashed out with the butt end of the Viking, driving it hard into Hughes' face, satisfied when he heard the strident crack as it shattered the nasal bone. Blood burst from the smashed appendage, spilling down Hughes' shirt front. He went down in a heap clutching his face.

Crane stepped into the hallway and looked down at Hughes, his face now a bloody mask.

Ryan tossed the shotgun to the bailiff and pushed past him, digging in his pocket for his cigarettes.

'Job done' he said flatly.

Forty-three

'So it's thirty-two days and still no rain. No need to take your umbrellas out with you today, either, because there's no sign of any break in the weather. Temperatures are expected to remain in the high eighties and . . !

Vince Kiernan switched off the radio and slumped back on his bed, sweat already running in rivulets down his face. He had the windows in his room open but they brought little respite from the sweltering heat.

In the street outside dustmen were collecting reeking
bags of refuse; the stench of mouldering garbage rose on the warm air to fill his nostrils. He tried to ignore the smell and concentrate on the task in hand.

He ran his index finger down the list of numbers in the personal columns of the magazine, past those he'd already rung or those outside London, searching for new numbers, for the falsely enticing delights promised in the numerous adverts. He jammed the phone between his ear and shoulder and dialled a number that promised a 'stimulating massage by a superb blonde'.

It rang a couple of times and then a chirpy voice announced that she was Jenny's 'lady', but that his masseuse would be five eight, extremely curvaceous (something Kiernan thought to mean overweight) and full of fun.

He hung up before she got to the prices.

As he dialled another number offering 'sensual massage in opulent surroundings', he felt more than a little dispirited. True, his entire time in London searching for his sister had been little more than a catalogue of disappointments, but in the last couple of days the futility of it all had begun to creep up on him. Kiernan wondered if the day would ever come when he would wake up, pack his bags and return home to Dublin, finally defeated.

He shook his head. No, never. Best not to think about it.

The phone was answered and Kiernan listened as the woman told him prices and all the usual crap but there was something else on the line that caught his attention.

There were children's voices in the background. They were

playing happily, as far as he could tell.

He gripped the receiver tightly.

'Do you travel?' he asked.

'Where to?' the voice asked.

'Central London' he told her.

'That's forty pounds plus the taxi fare.'

He hung up.

Glancing at his watch he saw that it was approaching 10.30 a.m. He had time to make a few more calls before he began his daily rounds of London's streets. Some of the prostitutes had come to know his face by now; one or two even spoke to him as he passed on his endless trek.

He dialled another number.

He'd thought about varying the route, but it had become something of a habit with him. He could have walked it blindfolded. Perhaps he should ask the women who spoke to him if they'd seen Jo. Maybe if he showed them her picture it might just spark off something in their memories. Something that would lead him to her. He jammed a cigarette in his mouth and lit it, as much to cover the stench of the rubbish outside in the street as to satisfy the desire to smoke.

He tapped his lighter gently on the phone as he waited for it to be picked up, his eyes scanning the columns for more numbers.

So many to choose from.

The receiver was picked up at the other end.

'I've just seen your advert,' Kiernan said, his eyes flicking over the page, the words well rehearsed from constant repetition. 'Can you give me some details?'

The voice that answered him was Irish.

It took him only a second to realize it was his sister.

Forty-four

Kiernan froze.

Was it really Jo's voice?

He gripped the receiver so tightly it threatened to snap in two.

Dare he begin to think that it was her?

Was he mistaken? Was his desire to hear her voice so strong his imagination had now got the better of him?

The voice belonged to an Irish girl.

So what? London was full of Irish girls.

But there was something there that gradually persuaded him that the girl on the other end of the line was the sister for whom he had searched for what seemed an eternity.

The longer she went on, the more certain he was.

He wanted to tell her, to shout to her that it was him.

Jo, it's your brother. I've found you.

But all he could do was listen, dumbstruck. As if the sudden shock had robbed him of his power to speak.

What if you're wrong?

No. He couldn't be wrong. Not after waiting so long. Could God or fate or whoever was to blame for this be so cruel?

There'd been so much disappointment. What if he was wrong?

Just tell her. Speak to her.

Vince Kiernan slammed the phone down and sat back staring at it as if it were some venomous reptile.

For what felt like an age he sat motionless in the heat of the room staring at the phone, wanting to pick the receiver up, wondering why he didn't feel the all-embracing elation he'd expected to feel. He felt only anxiety and fear. Fear that, after coming so close, he could be wrong.

He dialled again and waited.

Waited.

'Come on,' he whispered, his heart thudding hard against his ribs.

Waited.

'Hello,' he said as the phone was picked up, in as London an accent as he could manage. 'I'd like some information please; I've just seen your advert.'

Let her talk. Listen to her voice. Be sure.

She repeated the information she'd given him moments earlier.

Kiernan shifted the phone from one ear to the other.

Jesus Christ, he was sure this time. It was Jo.

By a monumental effort of will he managed to remain silent as Jo repeated her well-rehearsed words.

'Would you like to make an appointment?' she asked.

Kiernan shook himself.

'Yes, I would,' he said, trying to sound calm but realizing he was failing miserably. 'As soon as possible.'

'Thursday's the earliest I'm afraid,' she told him. 'I'm going to be away for a couple of days.'

Two fucking days.

Kiernan gritted his teeth.

'Thursday's fine,' he said. 'Do you have an address for me? It only says Finsbury area in the ad.'

She gave him an address.

'How's four o'clock for you?' she wanted to know.

'Great.'

'See you then. It's cash only, by the way,' she added.

She hung up.

Kiernan held the receiver for a long moment before dropping it back onto the cradle. Sweat sheathed his body.

'Fuck,' he whispered, his eyes screwed tightly shut. His breath was coming in gasps, as if he'd just run a mile.

And now?

One part of his mind told him he should go straight over to Finsbury now, find the address and take her away from there. Another part of his mind posed a question he had been trying to avoid until now.

What if she didn't want to leave?

But in her letters to him she had complained how she hated the men she went with.

Hated the men, not the lifestyle.

It was all the same, wasn't it? She would want to leave, wouldn't she?

To be returned to a family who didn't want her? Who had openly disowned her? To be removed from one place of no hope or future to another.

Returning one lost daughter to the bosom of her not so interested family, not a bad attempt, Mr Kiernan. Would you like to come back next week and try for the star prize? Trying to find out how you can make her stop doing it again? The choice is yours.

'Fuck' he murmured again.

Thursday. Two fucking days away.

He'd find out the truth then. He'd see the sister he'd imagined lost, possibly even dead.

Why then, he asked himself, did he still feel that crushing weight of weary anxiety and the other feeling he could not quite identify?

Was it fear?

Of what? Of what she'd become? Of how she would react to him?

It would be another two days before he found out.

Kiernan grabbed the magazine and, with a grunt of anger, hurled it across the room.

Forty-five

Seated in a window booth of Burger King in Coventry Street, Neville could see the hordes of people stream back and forth between Leicester Square and Piccadilly Circus. Many were pouring into the Trocadero across the street, pushing past a man with a billboard which proclaimed:

GOD IS COMING

As he turned Neville saw that the reverse side of the board carried the legend:

ARE YOU PREPARED TO MEET GOD?

Neville smiled to himself and glanced down at his cold cup of coffee.

He looked at his watch. 12.36 p.m.

He pulled the ponytail from his neck, feeling the sweat there, then got to his feet and crossed to the counter, where two French tourists were trying to work out the difference between a pound coin and a ten-pence piece. They babbled to each other and then to the member of staff serving them, but he seemed unable to help. They finally pushed change towards him and he selected the right amount. The tourists nodded and retreated to a nearby table clutching their hamburgers and chips.

The smell of frying food was overpowering in the fast-food place. The hiss of hundreds of frozen French fries being dumped into hot fat competed with the steady crackle of the insectocutor.

'Coffee, please' Neville said, digging in his pocket for change.

The assistant scuttled off to return a moment later.

As Neville paid, the assistant said, 'Enjoy your meal,' with practised ease. Neville glanced at him and smiled. He wandered back to his table and sat down, occasionally looking out into the street, scanning the hordes of faces that passed. Where the hell were they all going? None of them seemed to be moving with any purpose, some were pausing to take photos, others were gazing around aimlessly, some tourists were consulting maps.

They were late.

He'd give them until 12.45, then ring Caton who was back at their office in Brewer Street processing orders for the last two videos. The sooner they began shooting the newest effort the better. Stevie Collins' baby was running a temperature. Neville didn't know how much longer it would last. He didn't want the fucking kid to die before it had served its purpose. Besides, it would be a thousand quid down the drain if it did.

He took another sip of his coffee.

The hand that tapped his shoulder was large and powerful and he spun round in his seat.

Paul Thompson smiled down at him.

'How you doing, Don?' the younger man said, seating himself opposite Neville. He was in his early thirties, dressed in a faded black T-shirt with the arms cut off to reveal large biceps. The T-shirt, which hung loosely outside his jeans, bore the slogan:

PURE FUCKIN'ROCK

'Where's Mac?' Neville wanted to know.

'Over there,' Thompson told him, nodding towards the counter.

Neville looked round and saw a squat, thick-set man dressed in a shirt and jeans heading back towards the table carrying a bag full of food.

'You know Mac' Thompson said, grinning. 'He likes his grub.'

Colin Macardle sat down next to Thompson. Pulling a hamburger from the paper bag, he took a bite and smiled at Neville.

'You're late,' he said.

'Fuck it,' Macardle said, pieces of half-chewed hamburger dropping from his mouth. He grinned even more broadly.

'Where's Eddie?' asked Thompson.

'He's got other business to attend to,' Neville said.

'So what business have you got for us?' Macardle asked, his heavy Glaswegian accent muffled by the handful of chips he was shoving into his mouth.

'One night's work,' said Neville.

'How much?' Thompson wanted to know.

'Two grand.'

'Each?' asked Macardle, stuffing more chips into his mouth.

'Fuck off,' Neville snorted. 'A grand each is a fucking fortune compared to what you usually get for your little jobs. What's the going rate now? Fifty quid to break someone's leg? A ton if he has to spend a week in hospital? This is a different league,

Mac.'

'What have we got to do?' Thompson asked.

Macardle held up a hand.

'We haven't agreed yet,' he snapped.

'You got more urgent business to attend to then, have you?' Neville asked.

There was an uneasy silence between the three men. It was finally broken by Neville.

'Have you got shooters?' he asked.

'What the fuck is this, Don?' Thompson said.

'We need a job doing. I'm offering you a grand apiece to do it. What's the big deal?' He looked at the two men seated opposite. 'You either want it or you don't.'

'We'll do it' Macardle said, shoving hamburger into his mouth. He chuckled. 'For a grand you must want someone hurt pretty bad. Do you want us to shoot the cunt?' He laughed.

Neville didn't speak.

'Money up front' said Macardle.

'Half before, half when the job's done' Neville told him.

'Would we fuck you over?' Macardle asked, sounding hurt.

'I'm not going to give you the chance, Mac' Neville told him.

All three men laughed.

'When do you want the job done?' Thompson enquired.

'I'll give you all the details. Come to our office in Brewer Street. We'll sort out the money then, too.'

'Done,' said Macardle, smiling.

Neville nodded, reaching across to take a chip. He sat back in his seat, smiling.

Forty-six

There was building work in progress on the office block opposite. Joseph Finlay stood in shirt sleeves in his own office, watching as workmen moved hastily back and forth over the scaffolding with the assurance of monkeys on climbing frames. The men were sheathed in sweat from their exertions; Finlay was thankful for the air-conditioning that kept his own place cool. He watched as two workmen tipped barrowloads of rubble into a large chute, seeing it hurtle into a skip fifty or sixty feet below. Dust from the shattered concrete rose in the cloying air, motes of brick dust floating about like rusty cinders.

Apart from his own building, most of the other properties in Furnival Street, off High Holbom, were undergoing renovation or modernization of some description.

Finlay paced back and forth in front of the large window, lost in his own thoughts.

A polite cough from behind him reminded him where he was. He turned and looked at his secretary, who was sitting with her pad on her knee looking expectantly at him. She was drawing small circles on the comer of the pad with her pen while she waited. Finlay regarded her indifferently for a moment and she lowered her gaze.

She was a pretty girl in her early twenties who'd worked for Finlay since leaving school five years earlier, working her way up to her current position of personal assistant. She crossed and uncrossed her legs as she waited patiently for him to continue.

'Where did I get to?' he asked distractedly.

She read back what she had transcribed so far, stumbling once over her own shorthand.

Finlay considered the words for a moment then continued dictating.

'In view of the present situation,' he said, slowly and deliberately.

His secretary scribbled away in an effort to keep pace with him.

'. . . I would suggest that you seek legal advice before embarking on any such scheme . . .'

He moved back to the window.

So Nick Ryan was ill, was he?

The news had not caused him the grief it had evidently caused Kim. Upon her return from her ex-husband's office the previous evening she had been distraught when she'd told Finlay that Ryan was very ill. She hadn't been specific as to the ailment and Finlay hadn't asked. Probably something to do with drink, he'd surmised. Ryan drank like a bloody fish.

'. . . There are many pitfalls that can be avoided by undertaking . . .' He was struggling for the words he wanted. 'By following the . . .' Again he was struggling, annoyed with himself for not being able to think straight.

Christ, it was all Kim had spoken about since she'd returned from Ryan's office. His illness. How bad he looked. Finlay had done his best to show some interest initially but his mock concern had rapidly disappeared to be replaced by a smouldering resentment. She wasn't married to the bloody man any more.

'. . . The . . . er . . .'

'Guidelines?' his secretary offered.

'I know what I'm trying to say, Helen,' he snapped, rounding on her angrily. 'Or perhaps you'd rather write the letter for me. Perhaps you feel you're more capable. Is that it?'

'I'm sorry, Mr Finlay,' she said, her cheeks colouring.

'Just write what I tell you to write,' he snapped, turning back towards the window.

Something else bothered Finlay about this business with Ryan's illness, whatever the hell it was. Kim had said that Ryan might need her help, that he had no one else to turn to. Finlay didn't want her going back and forth to the private detective. He already suspected she thought more of her ex-husband than she admitted. If she began to pity him, that pity might turn into something more.

By following the guidelines described in my earlier letter, dated 23rd of this month, I feel that you will see the sense of considering this venture more carefully.' He coughed. 'New paragraph.'

Finlay had been relieved that Kelly didn't know of her father's illness. It was bad enough having Kim wandering around the house worrying about the bloody man without burdening Kelly with the knowledge, too.

What if he had called her today? What if she was with him now? Ryan could easily have called the house.

Helen Whiteside sat waiting for her boss to continue. She was tempted to tap her pen against her pad in an effort to shock him from his thoughts, but then she thought better of it. She crossed her legs, pulling down the hem of her skirt so it covered more of her thigh.

Finlay was pacing up and down now, his gaze fixed out of the window.

Helen Whiteside exhaled but not so deeply as to be heard.

What if Kim was with Ryan now?

'We'll finish this later,' Finlay snapped, inclined his head towards the office door. His secretary got to her feet.

'Do you want me to type up what you've dictated so far?' she asked.

'Forget it,' he rasped. 'We'll finish later, I just said that.'

She nodded and turned to go.

He sat down behind his desk and drummed on it with his fingers.

Kim had said that she was going out with Kelly, he remembered.

Perhaps they were both with Ryan.

He clenched his fists.

For interminable seconds he stared at the small console on his desk, his mind racing.

She might be at home. If she was, he could ask her if she'd spoken to Ryan that day.

He shot out a hand and flicked one of the switches in front of him.

'Helen, get my wife on the phone,' he snapped. 'Now.'

And then he thought, Why am I wasting my time worrying about Kim ? What am I going to do about Neville?

Forty-seven

'Is something wrong, Mum?'

The words shocked Kim Finlay from her distracted gazing out of the car window. She looked across at her daughter and smiled.

'Sorry, I was miles away, wasn't I?' she said, gripping the wheel of the Peugeot.

'You've been miles away for most of the day,' Kelly reminded her as they waited for the stream of traffic to move. 'You haven't said much.'

'You should be grateful,' Kim joked, trying to sound happier than she actually was. 'You're usually complaining I talk too much.'

The traffic in Knightsbridge was heavy; the car could only creep along. Kim glanced around at the other drivers similarly trapped. Most had the windows of their vehicles rolled down, preferring the choking exhaust fumes to the cloying heat. There wasn't a breath of air but what there was felt as if it was being pumped straight from a furnace. Kim ran a hand through her hair and felt perspiration on her forehead.

Kelly toyed with the laces of her trainers, peering around her at the other cars and at the shoppers thronging the pavements.

'Were you thinking about Dad?' she said finally.

Kim looked round with concern.

'Who? Joe?' she asked.

'Joe's not my dad. Not my real dad' Kelly reminded her.

'I wish you wouldn't talk like that, Kelly,' Kim said wearily.

'But it's true, he isn't.'

'He does his best for you. He tries.'

'I know that, but he still isn't my real dad, is he?'

Kim edged the car forward, trying to prevent a black Ferrari which was pulling out from a side turning nosing in front of her. The driver glared at her, as if he thought his vehicle entitled him to some kind of consideration. Kim smiled to herself when she saw that none of the cars following would let him out either.

'I heard the two of you arguing again the other day' said Kelly. 'Was that about Dad, too?'

'You shouldn't have been listening' Kim joked, but it didn't lighten the tension between them.

'Joe doesn't like Dad, does he?'

Kim didn't answer.

Should she mention Ryan's illness?

No, he had specially asked her not to.

Kim swallowed hard. And what was she supposed to do when he finally died? Make up some story? Kelly would have to know then. She wanted so badly to tell Kelly, if only to share the knowledge with someone else. It was a terrible burden, being forced to endure the certainty that her ex-husband was dying. Yet she could not bring herself to pass on the burden to her daughter, too. Why should they both suffer?

'When can I see Dad again?' Kelly wanted to know.

'That's up to him' Kim told her. 'You know what he's like. He's very busy.'

'He always was. He always will be, I suppose.'

Not always, thought Kim.

Tell her now. She has a right to know.

She felt so bloody helpless caught in the middle. She was torn between her loyalty to her ex-husband and her concern for her daughter. She understood why he didn't want the girl to know of his illness, but he didn't appreciate how painful it was having to lie to her. He had no idea how much she hated lying to their daughter. There was no other way of looking at it. Kim would be forced to live a lie until Ryan was dead. She wondered if hiding the truth that way was really protecting Kelly, or merely making things worse when the time came to tell her about his death.

Questions. Decisions.

The car ahead braked quickly and Kim banged her hooter, gesticulating angrily at the driver, who sat there apparently unperturbed.

Kelly chuckled.

'What are you laughing at?' Kim asked, smiling.

'You,' Kelly told her. 'You don't usually get worked up when you're driving.' The idea of her mother becoming a demon driver seemed to have amused her.

Kim reached across and grabbed her waist, tickling her.

She looked at her daughter and felt as if she wanted to sweep her into her arms.

And tell her the truth?

The streams of traffic rolled slowly on.

It was past six in the evening by the time Kim finally swung the Peugeot into the driveway of the house. The journey from Central London had been a tortuous one and she could feel the beginnings of a headache gnawing at the base of her skull.

She and Kelly unloaded the shopping and carried it inside, Kim muttering to herself when she realized she'd left her car keys in the ignition. She wandered out to the car, taking deep breaths as she reached the driveway. In the stillness of the early evening she could hear the drone of a rotary mower as someone cut their lawn. A dog was barking; she heard children shouting. The noise carried on the humid air. She took the keys from the ignition and locked the car, then turned and headed back towards the house.

She didn't notice the battered blue Cavalier parked across the street.

Inside, the driver smiled and nudged his companion, who also looked across towards Kim and the house.

Colin Macardle nodded.

Forty-eight

The afternoon had dragged on interminably; Joseph Finlay had found it impossible to concentrate on anything. His already frayed temper had been ravaged further by his secretary's inability to reach his wife on the phone on three separate occasions earlier in the day. There had been no answer from the house.

Finlay vaguely recollected Kim mentioning her and Kelly going out shopping; she could have taken Kelly to see her sick father.

Bastard.

If Kelly knew of the illness it would only bring her
closer to Ryan.

Finlay sat tapping his pen against the blotter on his desk, one eye on the clock perched on the mantelpiece. There were photos of Kim and Kelly there, too, smiling out at him contentedly. He clenched his fists and rose, walking across to the window. The scaffolding was devoid of workers now. They'd left more than an hour ago. Finlay could see little sense in delaying at his office much longer himself. He pulled on his jacket and reached for his briefcase, anxious to be home, even more anxious to find out where Kim had been all day. He told himself that he would remain calm when he asked her, that he would believe what she told him. He promised himself he would not ask her whether or not she had seen Ryan that afternoon, but he knew the temptation would be strong.

He was about to leave when the phone rang.

Finlay muttered something under his breath, then crossed to his desk and snitched up the receiver, watching the winking red light go out as he did.

'What is it, Helen?'

'There's a call for you, Mr Finlay. The gentleman says it's very important,' his secretary announced.

'Tell him to call back tomorrow,' Finlay snapped.

There was a moment's silence, then the secretary spoke again.

'He says he has to speak to you, Mr Finlay.'

'Who is it, for Christ's sake?' he snapped irritably.

'His name is Neville. He said he's a business associate of

yours.'

Finlay felt the breath catch in his throat. He swallowed with some difficulty.

'Put him on,' he said quietly and sat down behind his desk.

There was a crackle of static as the call was transferred.

'Hello,' Finlay said.

'Joe, how are you doing?' Neville asked conversationally.

'Cut the crap, Neville, what the hell do you want?'

'It's about our little discussion of the other night,' Neville told him. 'You know, you expressed some dissatisfaction about the videos.'

'Get to the point.'

'Well, I discussed it with my partner and we're both agreed on one thing.'

'Which is?'

'That you can take a fucking jump. We're not moving, Finlay.'

'I warned you . . .'

Neville cut him short.

'Don't threaten me, you cunt. Fuck your warnings. What are you going to do? Go to the police?' He chuckled.

'I told you what I'd do,' Finlay reminded him. 'I'll throw you out of the building. I'll call Charles Thornton now and tell him he can buy it. You're finished, Neville.'

'No, Finlay, not me. You think you can just walk away from this? You start throwing your fucking weight around and expect us to take it? Well, fuck you. I've had enough of your shit. We're going on, and we'll do it rent-free. How does no fucking percentage at all sound to you?'

'You're out of that building, Neville.'

'Try moving me. What are you going to do? Ask your friend Mr Thornton to get us out? Don't forget, he makes even more money out of our little home movies than you do. Do you think he's going to give that up?'

'He wants that building for his restaurant and he wants it badly. He'll make ten times the money from a restaurant than he would from flogging your videotapes, so don't try and threaten me, Neville. I'll give you until tomorrow to get out. Then I'm having you thrown out.'

'Try it,' Neville said challengingly. 'You're not in a position to threaten or to bargain, Finlay.'

'We'll see' he said and slammed the phone down.

Forty-nine

7.36 p.m.

Kim looked at the clock on the kitchen wall, wondering how much longer Joe was going to be. He was usually home by seven, although if he had meetings she was lucky to see him before nine on some evenings. Strange, though; he usually phoned if he was going to be late.

Across the table from her Kelly was picking disinterestedly at her food.

'If you don't want it then leave it' said Kim, raising her eyebrows.

Kelly smiled.

'I think I ate too much in McDonalds this afternoon' she confessed.

'How many hamburgers did you have? Five or six?' Kim said, smiling.

'Mum, I only had one. A Big Mac and large fries' Kelly reminded her.

'Yes. And a milkshake and two apple pies and some chocolate cake when we stopped for a coffee this afternoon. No wonder you can't eat your dinner. When you get older you won't want to look at chocolate cake,

let alone eat it. You'll be too worried about your figure!'

'When I get older, Mum' Kelly chuckled. 'What, as old as you?'

Kim raised a hand in mock anger, relieved to see her daughter laughing again. It was a marked contrast to the solemnity of their afternoon out, some of which, she realized, was due to her own preoccupation with Ryan's illness.

'You can't eat that,' said Kim, nodding towards the plate of half-eaten lasagne, 'but I bet you'll eat ice-cream if it's offered.'

Kelly grinned and nodded.

As Kim swung herself off the bench and headed across the large kitchen towards the fridge, Kelly also got to her feet and switched on the portable TV on the work-top opposite. She flicked through the channels until she found the one she wanted. There was a soap opera on. There always seemed to be a soap opera on somewhere, thought Kim, glancing round at the set.

'You know Joe doesn't like the TV on while we're eating,' said Kim, returning with a bowl of ice-cream and pushing it in front of her daughter.

'Joe's not here, though, is he?' said Kelly, disdainfully.

No, he's not.

Kim glanced up at the wall clock again.

It was strange he hadn't phoned.

She was in the process of dropping a scoop of ice-cream into her own bowl when she heard the doorbell ring.

'Turn that down, Kelly' she said, scurrying across the kitchen towards the hall, wondering who it could be. Finlay, perhaps? He might have forgotten his keys.

She pulled the kitchen door shut behind her and wandered across to the front door, peering through the spy-hole before she opened it.

She could see no one standing there. Whoever was outside must be standing to one side of the door. Either that or it was kids mucking about.

She slid the chain off and opened the door.

The figure seemed to appear from nowhere. It loomed before her like a spectre.

Despite the heat of the night, the man was wearing a jacket. But it was not that which caused Kim to freeze. It was his appearance.

His face was distorted grotesquely.

The flesh looked dark grey, his nose was squashed and pulled towards his left cheek; his eyes, deep set, glistened like a dead fish's.

The shocking mask was simple but horribly effective.

'Step back inside the house,' a heavy Glaswegian voice told her. 'Move.'

She wanted to shout out, bellow a warning to Kelly, but the man reached inside his jacket and she understood why he wore the heavy garment.

The shotgun had been sawn off so that the entire fearsome weapon was less than twelve inches long, including the filed-down stock.

The barrels looked massive as Colin Macardle pointed them at her face. When he spoke, his voice was low.

'You scream and I'll blow your fucking head off.'

Fifty

He heard voices as he entered the hallway of the house but it took Joseph Finlay a moment or two to realize they were coming from the kitchen, and another second to ascertain that their source was the television. He frowned. It wasn't like Kim to watch TV in there. Also, Kelly's bedroom was directly above. The noise might wake her if she was sleeping.

Finlay glanced at his watch and saw that it was almost nine o'clock. The drive from London had been tortuous. A lorry had overturned and blocked one part of the Fulham Road, causing delays of up to an hour and a half. Like Finlay, other motorists had attempted to take alternate routes, with the result that all the arterial roads within a ten mile radius of the accident were also blocked. He felt the beginnings of a headache as he headed across the hall to the kitchen.

He pushed open the kitchen door and walked in.

The room was empty.

He crossed to the set and turned it off, then spun round and headed for the dining-room.

Empty.

He crossed to the sitting-room and peered in. They were probably both sitting in there, watching the larger TV; they might well have forgotten they'd left the portable on. They . . .

The sitting-room was empty, too.

Finlay muttered something under his breath. Kim

wouldn't have popped out for something at this late hour. All the local shops shut at six. Even the small supermarkets closed at eight. Besides, he'd noticed her car in the drive as he'd parked. Just to be thorough, he pushed open the door of the room opposite the sitting-room. It was about twelve feet square and contained a desk and chair, some filing cabinets, a fax machine and a phone. On the occasions he had to bring work home with him, Finlay used it as an office. He knew as he peered into the darkened room that there was no reason for Kim to be in there, but he wanted to check anyway.

He closed the door and began to climb the staircase, feeling uneasy.

The doors that faced him as he reached the landing were all

closed. The house was silent. Boards creaked protestingly under his weight as he crossed to the door of Kelly's bedroom and opened it.

There was no sign of the girl.

Posters of pop stars stared blankly back at him from her walls.

Finlay swallowed hard, aware now that there was something very wrong.

As he reached the door to his bedroom he saw a dirty mark on the carpet, as if messy feet had trodden there.

His heart thudding hard, he pushed the door open.

Kim was lying on her back on the bed, her legs and arms firmly tied with what looked like the cord from a bathrobe. There was a flannel stuffed into her mouth, secured there by a towel that had been tied tightly around her face. Her face was tear-stained, her eyes red-rimmed and bulging. There was a nasty bruise above her right eye.

Finlay rushed across to her and pulled the gag from her mouth, helping her to release the cord round her ankles and wrists.

'Kelly,' she gasped, frantically. 'They took Kelly.'

'Who?' he said, grabbing her. 'Who took her?'

She tried to shake loose of his grip, tried to grab the phone on the bedside table, but Finlay gripped her arm.

'Get off me,' she hissed. 'We've got to call the police.'

Still he held her, gazing into her red-rimmed eyes.

'Who took her?' he snapped. 'Tell me what happened.'

'There isn't time,' Kim blurted. 'They might have killed her already. Let me use the phone.' She made another grab for it.

'Kim, calm down. You have to tell me what happened.'

'My daughter's been kidnapped. How much more do you need to know? Every second you waste they could kill her. Get out of my way.'

She pushed past him and snatched at the phone, but even as her hand closed over the receiver it suddenly rang.

Kim jumped back and it was Finlay who snatched up the phone.

'Hello,' he said.

Silence.

'Who's there?' he repeated.

'You've got a nice house,' the voice said. He recognized it immediately as Neville's. 'So we're told.'

Finlay could only grip the receiver helplessly, his knuckles whitening.

Kim looked on helplessly.

'You've got a nice daughter, too' Neville continued. 'Pretty kid.' He chuckled. 'She'll be popular with the boys when she's a bit older. Or maybe she won't have to wait too much longer.'

'What do you want?' Finlay said, his voice a harsh croak.

'I want to do some business.'

'Just let me have my daughter back then we'll talk.'

'What am I? Fucking stupid? Now you listen to me, Finlay. We've got the kid and we're keeping the kid until you agree to what we want. If I were you, I wouldn't call in the police. I wouldn't even think about it. For a couple of reasons. First, if I even get a sniff that the Law know we've got your daughter you'll be collecting her in paper bags. Secondly, I think they might be interested to know of our little business partnership, don't you? It wouldn't look too good if the Law or anyone else found out about your involvement with us, would it? Whatever would your wife say?' Neville chuckled.

Kim moved closer, trying to hear what was being said. Finlay held up a hand to keep her back.

'What do you want me to do?' he said meekly.

'Nothing. We'll be in touch to talk about that business I mentioned.'

'How do I know you aren't bluffing? Kelly might be dead already.' He swallowed hard.

'Yeah, she might. You'll just have to trust me, won't you?' Neville told him.

'I want to speak to her. Now.'

'Don't make demands, Finlay. You're not in a position to do that.'

'Then there's no deal. Let me speak to her or I won't believe she's alive.'

'I don't know whether to admire your nerve or pity your stupidity,' Neville told him. There was a long silence then he spoke again. 'The kid's alive. Listen.'

Finlay heard voices, harsh voices.

Then:

'Help me, Mum.'

Kim heard the words too and tears began to flow freely down her face.

'Help me, please.'

Then the high pitched sound of Kelly's entreaties was replaced by Neville's harsh voice again.

'Satisfied?' he grunted.

'If you hurt her…' .Finlay began but the sentence trailed off.

'You'll fucking what?' Neville snarled challengingly. 'Just do what you're told. Be at your office in the morning. I'll be in touch again but, like I said, Finlay. One sniff of a copper and the kid comes back in fucking pieces.'

Fifty-one

'We can't call the police, don't you understand?' Finlay snapped, turning away from Kim and pouring himself a brandy. 'If we do they'll kill her.'

'How do we know they won't kill her anyway?' Kim wanted to know.

Finlay ran a hand through his hair.

'We've got no choice,' he shouted.

Kim sat motionless on the sofa, her legs drawn up beneath her. She was clutching a handkerchief which was sodden from her tears. Now she shifted it nervously from one hand to the other, gazing blankly ahead of her.

'What if she's already dead?' she said quietly.

'I heard her voice,' Finlay reminded her. 'So did you. She's not dead. We've got to believe that they won't kill her.'

'And if we raise our hopes and they do?'

Her words hung in the air.

Finlay took a large swallow from the brandy balloon, feeling the liquid burn its way to his stomach.

Jesus, he felt so helpless.

Helpless and angry. His rage was directed both at himself for ever getting mixed up with a man like Neville but mainly at Neville himself.

What was the bastard playing at?

Kidnapping? It didn't seem like his game.

'The man who came here,' Finlay said. 'What did he look like?'

Kim shrugged.

'He was wearing a stocking mask,' she said. 'I didn't get a good look at the one in the car, either. What does it matter?'

'Was he tall, short, dark, fair?'

'I told you, Joe, I don't know.'

'You must have got a glance at him?'

'He was wearing a stocking over his head,' she said, exasperated. 'How many more times?'

Finlay downed what was left in his glass and poured himself another.

'Getting drunk isn't going to help Kelly, is it?' Kim said acidly.

'I'm not getting drunk,' he snapped. 'Besides, what do you

expect me to do? I was told to wait, to let them call me tomorrow. That's just what I'm going to do.'

'They'll kill her, Joe, I know it,' Kim said, wiping her eyes.

'Not if we co-operate with them.'

'But we don't even know what they want.'

'That's why I have to speak to them tomorrow. To find out what they want.'

'It'll be money,' she said flatly. 'You're rich. Why else would they have taken her?'

Finlay paused for a moment but did not look at her. Perhaps he was afraid she would see something in his eyes.

Guilt?

He wondered if this was how the parents of the children killed in Neville and Caton's videos had felt when their youngsters first left home. Did they feel this sense of desolation? Of helplessness? Of anger? He suspected they did. And the fear. But Finlay knew only too well that he had more reason to be afraid. Whatever the outcome, whether Kelly was returned safely to them or killed (and that was one thing he dared not consider) then he risked exposure. His connections with Neville and Caton would be revealed. Then what? Financial ruin? Prison? He exhaled deeply and crossed to the sofa where he sat down beside Kim, sliding his arms around her.

She pulled him close to her, crying softly as she rested her head on his shoulder.

'What can we do?' she said, tears soaking into his shirt.

Finlay held her tight.

'Wait,' he said. 'All we can do is wait.'

Fifty-two

The parcel was about seven inches long and four inches wide, enclosed in brown paper and Sellotape. Finlay's name was written on it in black marker pen. Just his name and office address.

'It arrived a couple of minutes ago, Mr Finlay,' his secretary told him, handing over the small package.

He snatched it from her and glanced up at her.

'How did it arrive?' he wanted to know. 'Post? Courier?'

'A man came into the reception and left it. I went and fetched it.'

'You didn't get a look at him?'

She looked puzzled.

'No, he'd already gone' she told him.

Finlay nodded.

'You can go' he said and began fumbling on his desk for the letter opener, using the sharp edge to cut through the Sellotape wound thickly around the parcel. Despite the air-conditioning in the office, he felt beads of perspiration form on his forehead as he struggled with the parcel, finally pulling the wrapping free, tossing it to one side in the rubbish bin.

He sat staring blankly at the video cassette for a moment, turning it over in his hands.

It was unmarked. No labels. Nothing.

Then he saw a small corner of paper sticking out from inside one of the spools. He pulled it out and found that it was, in fact, a sheet of paper about six inches square, folded so many times hardly a centimetre of it was uncreased. He unfolded it and spread it out on his desk, scanning the words written there, also in marker pen:

ONE MILLION POUNDS
OTHERWISE THE KID IS DEAD
WAIT FOR US TO CONTACT YOU
REMEMBER NO POLICE

Finlay swallowed hard and re-read the note, then turned his attention to the video cassette, turning it in his hands as if unsure what to do with it. He had a VCR rigged up in one corner of the office, connected to a small, fourteen-inch TV.

He got to his feet, walked across the office and turned both machines on, sliding the video into place. He picked up the remote control and wandered back to his desk. Perching on one corner of it, he jabbed the 'Play' button.

There was hissing on the soundtrack and a blank screen. He stabbed the 'Fast Forward' until he had some semblance of picture, then pressed 'Play' again. The picture began to unfold before his eyes.

A bare floor, but clean. Bare walls, too. In the room there was only one piece of furniture. On the bed, held down by several leather straps, a piece of masking tape across her mouth, lay Kelly. She was naked.

'Oh God,' whispered Finlay as he watched two men approach her, one from either side. 'Oh, my God. No.'

The men were also naked, sporting large erections. One was masturbating.

To his horror Finlay saw that the other man was holding a baby.

'Oh, Jesus,' he murmured, transfixed by the screen.

The baby couldn't be more than six weeks old, he guessed.

But his eyes were riveted to the body of Kelly as she strained helplessly against the straps, her head thrashing from side to side as the man who was masturbating - both he and his companion wore black leather hoods - pushed his penis close to her face.

Finlay wanted to turn the tape off, to wrench it from the machine and hurl it away. Smash it into a thousand pieces. But he sat mesmerized, a mouse watching a snake.

He saw the other man put the baby on the bed beside Kelly. Then he, too, began rubbing his penis.

As the two men ejaculated, almost simultaneously, Finlay finally crushed the 'Stop' button, hurling the remote control across the office. He spun round, feeling the vomit clawing its way up from his stomach. By a monumental effort of will he managed to retain it. He stood against the desk, his back to the blank screen, his breath coming in gasps. He closed his eyes but the images he'd just witnessed on the screen seemed to flash before him. He put a hand to his heavy stomach and rubbed gently, wishing that the feelings would subside but unable to force the images from his brain. He shook his head, staggered back to the other side of his desk and sat down heavily. The ransom note stared up at him.

NO POLICE

His head was spinning. His stomach churned.

He sat gaping at the blank screen of the television set for what seemed like an eternity, unable or unwilling to move. Then, finally, he got to his feet and walked slowly across the room to retrieve the remote.

Once safely back behind his desk he pressed the 'Play' button again, watching with the same mesmerized horror. But this time he could not bear to watch the action at normal speed. He kept the 'Fast Forward' button depressed, his hand gripping the control so tightly he threatened to snap it in two.

What he saw before him, flying past at four times the normal speed, was beyond anything he could have imagined in his most depraved and warped nightmares.

Kelly untied.

Kelly and the baby.

Kelly held by one of the men while the other . . .

He lowered his gaze momentarily.

Kelly.

Kelly.

He switched it off, jabbed 'Re-wind' and sat back in his

seat, sweat sheathing his entire body. Finally, he dropped the remote, and looked at the note again.

NO POLICE

He put both hands to his face and felt the moisture there. His head still spun. His stomach still somersaulted.

ONE MILLION POUNDS

He allowed his head to flop back on his shoulders, his eyes turned heavenward. For long moments he stayed immobile then he leant forward, looking first at the TV screen then at the phone.

'Kelly' he whispered.

NO POLICE

He fumbled in one of his desk drawers and pulled out his Filofax, flipping through it until he found a number.

Picking up the receiver he glanced at the blank screen, his mind filled with the images he'd seen.

As he dialled he noticed his hand was shaking.

Part Two

'Never trust anyone as far as you can spit and even then, be careful.'
Anon

*'People always turn away, from the eyes of a stranger.
Afraid to know, what lies behind the stare.'*
Queensryche

Fifty-three

'Well, well, well. I never thought I'd see the day said Ryan, opening the door. He smiled thinly and stepped aside, ushering Joseph Finlay inside, noticing the sweat on his face and arms. The heat of the day had contributed to his condition but walking up five flights of stairs certainly hadn't helped, either.

Finlay wandered into the office, looking round at the desk, the filing cabinets, the leather chairs and sofa and the books that lined one wall. There was a VCR hooked up to a television in one corner of the room.

'Do you want a drink?' Ryan asked, crossing to the small kitchenette. 'Tea, coffee? Something stronger?'

'I'll have a brandy if you've got one,' Finlay said, sitting down opposite Ryan's desk.

The private detective raised an eyebrow, nodded and disappeared into the other room, emerging a moment later with a glass. He blew the dust off it, set it down on the desk in front of Finlay and poured him a large measure of Courvoisier. Then he sat down behind the desk and gazed across at the property developer.

Finlay saw two bottles of pills on his desk. As he watched, Ryan took two, swallowing them with a mouthful of water. He ran his index finger around the rim of his glass, glancing at Finlay.

'Kim told me you were ill,' Finlay said, sipping his brandy.

Ryan nodded.

That was fair enough. Terminal cancer was about as ill as you could get.

'She didn't say what it was. Nothing serious, I hope,' Finlay continued.

'Let's cut the shit, Finlay,' Ryan said flatly. 'You didn't come here to check up on my health. What do you want? You didn't say on the phone. Only that you needed to see me.' He raised his eyebrows, quizzically. 'Needed?'

'In a professional capacity,' Finlay told him.

'Don't tell me; you think Kim's having an affair and you want me to tail her, right?' Ryan said, smiling.

'This is serious, Ryan,' snapped Finlay, reaching for his jacket.

He pulled the ransom note from his inside pocket and the video from another.

Ryan watched, bemused, as the other man pushed the two items across the desk. He opened out the note and scanned it, his brow furrowing.

'What the fuck is this?' he muttered.

'It's Kelly. She was taken from the house last night.' His voice cracked.

'What do you mean, "taken"?' Ryan said through clenched teeth.

'Kidnapped. Do I have to spell it out?'

'What about Kim?'

'She's okay. They didn't hurt her.'

'Jesus Christ,' snarled Ryan. 'What the fuck have you done about this? Do the police know?'

'The kidnappers said that if any police were involved, they'd kill Kelly.'

'When did you speak to them?'

'Last night.'

'Where was she snatched from?'

'The house. God knows where they've taken her.' Finlay said.

Maybe the house in Cavendish Square?

It was a thought he dared not voice.

Ryan pressed both hands together in front of his face in an attitude of prayer.

'They sent this' said Finlay, prodding the video tape. 'It arrived at my office this afternoon.'

Ryan picked the tape up and looked at Finlay questioningly.

'Look at it' he urged. 'I can't. Not again.'

Ryan got to his feet and crossed to the VCR, switching both it and the television on. He pressed the 'Play' button and watched as the images sped by.

Finlay lowered his head, unable to look at the screen.

Ryan watched transfixed, his expression indifferent at first, but the knot of muscles at the side of his jaw were pulsing angrily. As the video continued, he dropped to his knees before the screen, as if worshipping at an electronic shrine. His eyes never left the images, the outlines of the figures reflected in the glazed mirrors of his eyes. He felt tears forming. Anger building. Anger unlike anything he'd ever known before.

He finally hit the 'Stop' button and sat back on his haunches, his breath coming in short gasps.

'Does Kim know about this?' he asked quietly, his head bowed.

'No' Finlay informed him. 'Only about the ransom note. I didn't want her to see that' he gestured towards the tape. 'It would destroy her.'

Ryan took the tape from the machine, gripping it in his fist so tightly he threatened to shatter it.

'Dirty fucking scum' he hissed, his body quivering. He closed his eyes tightly, as if to wipe away the images he'd just seen, but they stayed as clear as if they'd been burned onto his retina. He slammed the tape down onto his desk so hard his glass of water spilled.

Finlay looked at him.

'Will you help me?' he said.

'What do you mean?'

'I want you to find Kelly. Find her, Ryan. Help her.'

'This ransom' he prodded the note. 'They didn't say when they wanted the money?'

Finlay shook his head.

'They said they'd be in touch. It says that in the note.'

'I know what it says in the fucking note,' snarled Ryan. 'I can read.' He began pacing the office floor slowly.

Finlay sipped his brandy.

'Do you think they'll kill her?' he asked quietly.

'Without a doubt, if you don't pay up when they tell you. Can you get hold of that sort of money if it comes to the crunch?' Ryan wanted to know.

'It won't be easy, but I think so. Hopefully you'll have found them by then.'

'If I find them.'

'What the hell do you mean? She's your daughter, Ryan. Do you want them to kill her?' Finlay snapped.

Ryan spun round, glaring at Finlay.

'Yeah, you're right, she's my daughter.' There was a heavy silence between the two men, finally broken when Ryan spoke again. 'Leave the tape with me. Let me think about it'

'What is there to think about?' Finlay snapped. 'Your daughter is in danger. The longer you spend thinking, the more danger you put her in.'

'Get out' Ryan said, opening the office door. 'I'll call you.'

Finlay hesitated a moment then got to his feet and headed for the door, pausing there. They locked stares for long seconds, then he walked out. Ryan pushed the door shut behind him. He turned and headed back towards his desk, snatching up the video in the process.

He jammed the tape into the machine and stepped back.

Why the hell would anyone want to kidnap his daughter? He exhaled deeply, feeling a twinge of pain in his chest.

He looked down at the ransom note.

Then back at the VCR.

Reluctantly, he pressed the 'Play' button.

Fifty-four

He couldn't remember the last time he'd cried.

Even when he'd been told that he had just six months to live, he hadn't felt the tears of self-pity and fear he had expected. Only a feeling of empty desolation.

But now, as he sat in his darkened office, eyes fixed to the TV screen, Nick Ryan felt tears running down his cheeks.

He took a hefty swig of the vodka he'd poured himself, swallowing a couple of pain-killers, too, when the discomfort began to mount. He drew in several deep breaths and he felt pain. The pain seemed inconsequential, unworthy of consideration compared to what he was watching on the screen.

The pain his daughter was being forced to endure before his very eyes. That pain and humiliation repeated every time he rewound the tape and watched it again, now through a haze of tears.

Every time he looked as closely as he could at the room, searching for any clue as to its whereabouts, anything that might enable him to recognize it or its occupants, but both of the bastards wore black masks. One had tattoos. A dagger on his right shoulder. A snake on his left.

The other had red hair, some of it visible beneath the mask.

As Ryan watched them, his gaze was drawn hypnotically to the baby lying beside his daughter. He would look at the baby and then at his daughter's face contorted in fear and pain. Ryan clenched his fists, squeezing one so tightly around his glass it seemed it might break.

He watched as one of the men ejaculated onto his daughter's face.

Fucking bastard.

The man with the tattoos lifted the baby and moved it closer to Kelly's face, rubbing its tiny body over her face, sliding it through the semen.

Ryan squeezed the glass more tightly.

Tears flooded down his face.

He saw Kelly writhing helplessly on the bed.

Let her go.

Saw the other red-headed man wipe his penis across her

stomach.

His hand crunched the glass with ease.

It smashed in his grip, lumps of the crystal slicing into the palm of his hand, gouging into the flesh. Blood burst from the ragged cuts, spurting onto the desk. Ryan hardly felt it. He hurled the broken glass away. Looking down at his injured hand, he noticed a large shard protruding from the base of his thumb. He pulled it free and tossed it aside contemptuously, his eyes turning back to the screen.

Back to the two men. To the baby.

To his daughter.

He got to his feet and switched off the VCR, then snatched up the phone, his injured hand hanging at his side. He jammed the receiver between his ear and his shoulder and jabbed out digits.

It rang only twice before being picked up.

He recognized the voice immediately.

'Finlay,' he said sharply, blood dripping steadily from his gashed palm. 'I'll find Kelly.'

'Good,' said Finlay.

'And now I want to speak to Kim,' Ryan said flatly.

There was a moment's silence at the other end.

'Did you hear me?' Ryan said, more forcefully.

Another moment and she was there.

'Nick, please find her,' Kim blurted, her voice cracking.

'I'll find her,' he said, 'And the fuckers who took her. I swear it.'

'Just be careful. Please,' she urged. 'There's no telling what they might do. Not just to Kelly, to you as well. Please be careful.'

'They won't hurt her, Kim,' he said with a certain amount of assurance.

There was a long silence, finally broken by Ryan.

'I love you, Kim,' he said softly.

'I know,' she said.

Then she was gone.

Ryan crossed to the cabinet in the corner and unlocked it. Ignoring the pain from his cut hand he took both the guns from the container and carried them back to his desk, laying them side by side. The 9mm Automatic and the .357.

Ryan knew the men he was going up against were dangerous.

He was banking on it.

But he had nothing to fear from them. What could they do to him? Shoot him?

He hoped so.

Better a death like that than a long lingering death by cancer.

Jesus, he was almost looking forward to catching up with them. And when he did he'd make the fuckers pay. He would make them feel pain unlike anything they could have imagined. But he had to save his daughter first. And, to do that, he had to find her.

Fifty-five

It was the seventh shop that morning; they had begun to take on a weary familiarity after number four. By the time Ryan walked into Lovecave on Beak Street, he felt he was suffering from deja vu.

All the shops seemed to be decorated in the same putrid pastel colours: blue, pink or yellow. All of them seemed to carry the same kind of magazine and video. He was even convinced he'd seen the same customers in two or three of them.

Soho was filled with shops like these, turds floating in the sea of filth this part of London had become. But what the hell, everyone had to earn a living somehow. And there was certainly a good living to be made out of pornography. Most of the strip clubs had shops attached to them; Ryan had already been into one. But with the time not quite approaching eleven in the morning, most of the clip-joint book shops weren't even open yet. Their staff and their customers lived a kind of nocturnal existence, only emerging during the hours of darkness to ply their trade within the confines of darkened rooms. Men frequenting the establishments also seemed more at home in the absence of daylight.

Ryan had left his office at about 9.15 am. and begun his trek walking round the area close by his own place. Up Greek Street to Soho Square, across to Dean Street and then down as far as St Anne's Court, before moving over to Wardour Street.

Throughout his journey he'd ventured into selected bookshops and video sellers, browsing through their stacks of printed material but always claiming he couldn't find what he sought. A quick word with the assistant and he'd be shown through into a back room where 'harder' material was available. In one shop in Wardour Street, when he'd mentioned his interest in videos featuring children, he'd been practically thrown out. The Manager hurled a magazine at him as he left. Ryan had noticed that it bore a photo of a pregnant woman, her breasts oozing milk, being fondled by two men. A strange kind of weapon with which to express outrage, Ryan had thought, cries of 'sick fucker' ringing in his ears.

Two other shops, Adult Delight in Dean Street and Paradise

Showroom in Greek Street, had been more helpful.

Ryan had shown them the video, surprised when they had offered imported gear which was as strong. He'd asked to see it. He'd been told that it was a shop, not a fucking preview theatre, but they said that the youngsters involved were no more than five years old, sometimes younger. Imported from Holland, it was reckoned to be the strongest stuff available. Ryan had said he'd think about it and made his exit.

Now, as he walked into Lovecave, he looked around, pushing the plastic streamers that passed for a door out of his way.

The place was large, the walls lined with shelves.

Every one was piled high with magazines, most of which were in cellophane. There were several spinners in the middle of the shop which held a selection of paperbacks, also wrapped in cellophane, and more shelves accommodated some larger format, thicker books or manuals. They, too, were sealed. Not much fun for the casual browser in here, thought Ryan, glancing around.

The one member of staff he could see on duty was seated at the far end of the shop by a till on a raised platform that resembled a pulpit. The man was in his mid-thirties, his hair long and curly. He wore a T-shirt with the sleeves cut out to reveal powerful arms. He paid Ryan only fleeting attention, more concerned, it appeared, with reading his newspaper and dipping biscuits into his steaming mug of tea.

It was warm inside the shop, the only air-conditioning being in the form of a noisy fan droning loudly by the door. Ryan glanced at the two other customers in the shop, middle-aged men peering avidly at magazines which were not sealed up. Neither of them looked at him as he sidled up alongside, casting appraising eyes over the magazines on display.

The floor was bare lino, badly in need of a clean. The whole place smelled of body odour but Ryan couldn't be sure if it was the building or the customers. Ryan moved towards the assistant, who looked up only briefly from his paper, dipping another biscuit into his tea, cursing when it broke and flopped into the steaming fluid. He set about fishing it out with a spoon.

To the rear of the shop a red neon arrow pointed downwards. The tip of the arrow touched a sign announcing:

VIDEOS DOWNSTAIRS

Ryan pushed his way through another beaded curtain and almost tripped on the dimly lit stairway. He recovered his balance and descended the flight into the basement.

The lighting here was more subdued, not so much for the comfort of patrons, he thought, as to hide the profusion of filthy marks covering the threadbare carpet. There was the familiar musky smell of damp and body odour.

A radio was blaring from one corner of the room. It sounded like Madonna. Ryan looked quickly around at the endless rows of boxes on display. There were many imported films.

MEGA TITS caught Ryan's eye. It was on the shelf next to BLACK SHAVERS and LIEBESSPIELE (Love Games). Ryan was grateful for the translation. He passed by LUSTFUL POSITIONS and NEW PUSSY and headed slowly towards the assistant who was checking what looked like an invoice, leaning over a glass counter which badly needed cleaning.

The private detective studied the man; he was in his early thirties, dressed in jeans and T-shirt. His hair was long, his face burdened by a heavy forehead which made it look as if he wore a perpetual frown. He looked up as he saw Ryan standing there.

'Can I help you, mate?' he said, smiling.

'I'm looking for something,' Ryan told him. 'You don't seem to have it.'

The assistant looked surprised.

'Like what?' he wanted to know.

'You got any stuff with kids in?' Ryan asked.

The assistant eyed him suspiciously, running appraising eyes over the private detective.

'What sort of stuff?'

'I just said, with kids in. Young kids. Twelve, maybe younger.'

'Have you had stuff from us before?'

'No, but I wondered if you had anything like this.'

Ryan took the video cassette from his carrier bag and passed it across the counter.

The other man looked first at the tape, then at Ryan.

'If you're with the old Bill...'

Ryan cut him short.

'Do I look like a fucking copper?' he said challengingly.

'Just because you haven't got a tit on your head doesn't mean you ain't filth' the assistant told him.

'Have a look at it,' Ryan told him, pushing the cassette towards him again. 'I want some stuff like this.'

There was a TV and video recorder on the end of the counter, the lights on the electronic clock flashing repeatedly. The assistant took the tape and inserted it, pressing the appropriate buttons.

Ryan gritted his teeth as the all too familiar pictures came into view. He lowered his gaze.

'Fuck me,' murmured the assistant. 'This is good stuff. Where did you get hold of it?'

'A mate gave it to me,' he lied.

'Good picture quality, too. Do you know where he got it?'

'I wondered if he might have got it here,' Ryan ventured.

The assistant shook his head, his eyes never leaving the screen.

'We get pretty wild stuff, but not usually like this. I've got stuff out the back with kids as young as four or five. Was it that kind of thing you were after?' He stroked his chin thoughtfully. 'The girl in this must be about ten or eleven.'

Ryan clenched his fists by his sides.

'Not very often you see babies, though. Your mate must have paid a fortune for it. Something like this would usually set you back a ton, at least. We get a fair amount from Germany and Holland, but this isn't

imported.' He nodded towards the screen.

'How can you tell?' Ryan asked.

"The picture quality's too good. It's very sharp. Most of the imported stuff is shot on 8mm and then transferred to video; that's why the pictures lose their quality. Especially by the time they've run a couple of hundred copies off. This one looks like it was shot direct onto video.'

'Have you ever seen stuff like this before?' Ryan asked. 'That wasn't imported?'

'Only a couple of times. There's a geezer in Finsbury who does a lot of kids fuck movies. We call them Jellybaby movies.' He chuckled. 'He's about the only bloke I know who specializes just in using kids.'

'Do you reckon he'd deal direct with me?' Ryan asked, his heart thumping against his ribs.

'I don't see why not. He might check you out first, make sure you're kosher, make sure you're not with the fucking vice-squad or something, but it's worth a try. Do you want his address?'

'Thanks,' Ryan said, nodding.

The assistant scribbled something down on a piece of paper and handed it to the private detective. He took it and read it aloud.

'Raymond Howells. 35A Margery Street, Finsbury.'

'It's off King's Cross Road, almost opposite Mount Pleasant Post Office,' the assistant added helpfully.

Ryan nodded.

'Can I have my film back?' he said, motioning towards the video.

The assistant ejected the tape and handed it to him.

Ryan took it, turned and headed for the stairs, the piece of paper tucked into his pocket.

As he reached the top of the stairs he glanced back at the assistant, who was watching him. He waited until Ryan was out of sight before reaching for the phone.

Fifty-six

The pavement felt warm beneath the soles of his trainers. Vince Kiernan ran a hand across his forehead, wiping the sweat away. He noticed his hand was shaking slightly. Why, when he was so close to the end of his quest, did he feel so deflated? With any luck, in a few moments he would see his sister for the first time in five months. He should feel elated. All he did feel was a gnawing worry.

What if she wasn't here?

What if she wouldn't go with him?

Kiernan tried to force the doubts from his mind.

He checked his watch.

3.56 p.m.

The appointment was at four. So he was early; what did it matter?

It had taken him a while to find the place. The train journey from Hammersmith itself had seemed to take an eternity. Then he found himself walking through areas which had, over the past few weeks, become all too familiar to him. Yet he still had trouble finding the house. The girl on the phone two days earlier ... Jo? ... had given him this address; even now, looking up at the red-bricked building, Kiernan felt the sense of desolation building even more strongly. What if she'd given him a false address?

Why should she? She didn't know who he was or what he wanted. The girl who'd answered the phone had assumed he was just another punter.

Stop worrying about it and get on with it.

A little further down the street there were a few kids kicking a football around and yelling loudly, kicking it back and forth across the road, ignoring the cars which periodically passed. If any drivers pressed their hooters they were met by a stream of abuse. One car slowed down, the driver gesticulating angrily at the children as the ball bounced off his bonnet. They moved away from the car shouting, one of them spitting on the back of the car as it pulled away.

Kiernan looked up at the house and saw that two of the dirty windows were boarded up. Elsewhere curtains were drawn, to obscure the view, or the glass was simply so filthy it appeared opaque. The young Irishman peered at the ground floor windows, trying to catch signs of movement within, but there appeared to be none. Once more, the idea that he'd been given a false address surfaced in his mind and refused to budge.

A set of rusted iron railings guarded a narrow flight of stone steps that led down to a basement flat.

Kiernan pushed the gate open, hearing it creak protestingly, and descended, peering at the number by the door. He checked it against the address he'd been given two days earlier.

His hand quivering slightly, Vince Kiernan pressed the buzzer of 35A Margery Street.

Fifty-seven

Three times he pressed the buzzer.

Each time no one answered.

He swallowed hard, his worst fears growing.

What if she wasn't here?

What if there was no one here?

He cupped one hand over his eyes and pressed his face to the window, trying to see inside.

The dirty glass and the gloom beyond made it impossible. He pressed the buzzer of 35A again, coughing as the stench of rotting food assailed his nostrils. Two dustbins were crammed into the small space between the bottom of the stone steps and the front door; one of them overflowed with rubbish rotting in the heat. Kiernan wrinkled his nose. From down the street he could hear the kids still kicking their ball about, the noise interrupted every now and then by the banging of a hooter. He gave up on the buzzer and banged hard on the door.

Still no answer.

Kiernan kicked at it angrily, sweat soaking into his shirt as the sun beat down.

'Shit,' he hissed, his initial anger giving way as the door opened a fraction, swinging back on hinges that hadn't tasted oil for years.

A damp, fusty smell wafted out to join the rancid odour of decaying food but Kiernan ignored it, nosing inside the open door a foot or two, peering through the gloom. He blinked hard as he stepped inside, his eyes slowly becoming accustomed to the dingy hallway.

There were three doors leading off it. The floor was covered by a threadbare carpet; the walls were bare, but for some cracked and peeling yellow paint. The three doors were in a similar state of disrepair.

It was cooler inside. Kiernan was grateful for that, at least. He wiped his face with his handkerchief and approached the first door.

It swung open as he pushed it and he looked through into a small bedroom. He stepped inside, again struck by the smell of damp; dark mould crept up two walls. He half expected to see mushrooms growing on the skirting boards, themselves cracked. The bed had been made up. The sheets were dirty; the only light in the room was provided by a bare bulb which hung from the centre of the ceiling. He was surprised, when he flicked the switch, to find that it worked.

Besides the bed there was only a dressing table and a small wardrobe in the room. The mirror had been removed from the dressing table and the doors of the wardrobe hung open. The ashtray on the corner of the dressing table was full of dog ends. There was lipstick on one or two. The remains of a spliff had been stubbed out. The place didn't seem quite as derelict as it had first appeared. It had been inhabited recently, he guessed. Probably squatters, the Irishman told himself.

Kiernan moved back into the hallway, the conviction growing in him that he had been cheated. Jo wasn't here. Neither Jo nor anyone else.

He pushed the next door more forcefully and it swung back, cracking against the wall behind.

This second room was even smaller, cramped and diminished by the absence of light. It was a fifteen by fifteen box, the walls dull and grey in the gloom. Kiernan flicked at the light switch, but this time there was no brightness. The bulb had been removed.

He leant against the wall, feeling the perspiration soaking into his shirt. The young Irishman closed his eyes and exhaled wearily, gripped by a combination of crushing disappointment and anger.

Where the fuck was Jo?

He had the right address. This was the one she'd given him.

What the fucking hell was going on?

He was still wondering when the front door buzzer sounded.

Fifty-eight

When the buzzer was pressed a second time, Kiernan shook himself and scurried back into the first room he'd entered.

He slipped inside and pressed up against the wall behind the door, waiting.

The buzzer was pressed again. Whoever was outside this time kept their finger on the button. The strident sound lanced through Kiernan's ears and he gritted his teeth, waiting for the noise to die away. It did so abruptly as the buzzer was released. He heard the front door creak as it was opened and then tentative footsteps on the hall floor.

Moving closer.

Perhaps he'd been wrong; perhaps the place wasn't uninhabited.

Maybe it was Jo.

His heart began to race faster.

The footsteps came closer. Although he knew he was hidden from view behind the door, he pressed himself ever more tightly to the wall, as if to melt into the damp brickwork.

The footsteps hesitated at the threshold.

He could hear soft breathing in the heavy, cloying silence.

It was all Kiernan could do to slow his own breathing to make it even.

The door was pushed a fraction and the figure moved inside.

He frowned as he saw her.

Saw the skinny frame, the long, bleached hair.

Surely this couldn't be ...

'Jo' he said, taking a step forward.

The girl spun round, her eyes wide with surprise. She stepped back as she saw him, her mouth dropping open. She almost fell over a piece of rucked-up carpet, teetering on her stilettos.

'Who the fuck are you?' asked Stevie Collins, her eyes wide but filled with suspicion.

Kiernan frowned.

'I could ask you the same thing,' he said. 'What are you doing here?'

'I'm looking for someone.'

'Who?'

He took a step closer and she moved further from him apprehensively. He was a powerfully built man, his hair and eyes wild, his face unshaven.

'Who are you looking for?' he repeated.

'Are you a copper?' There was a note of contempt in her voice.

'I might be,' he told her. 'What difference would it make to you if I was?'

She raised one arm to brush hair from her face and Kiernan saw the dark marks and bruising in the crook of her right elbow. The track marks.

'Fucking junkie' he said dismissively.

They locked stares for a moment.

'So' she continued, 'are you a copper or not?'

Kiernan shook his head.

'You looking for Ray?' she asked. 'I haven't seen you here before.'

'Who's Ray?'

'The guy who lives here. Or lived here.'

'Who else lived here?' he asked, fumbling in his pocket for something.

'Tell me who you are first' she demanded.

'My name's Kiernan. Vince Kiernan.'

'You're Irish.'

'You're quick' he added sarcastically.

'Fuck off.'

'Maybe I will. But not with you. Now tell me what you're doing here. This place looks derelict. It's empty.'

'It wasn't until a couple of days ago.'

'What happened?'

'The police raided a house near here. They do that every now and then, just to prove they're making an effort.' There was scorn in her voice. 'Ray thought it was safer to move his operation.'

'Move it to where?'

'How the hell do I know? If I knew where he was I wouldn't have come here looking for him, would I?'

'Who is this Ray you keep talking about? What's his full name?'

'Ray Howells. He's a friend of mine.'

Kiernan shook his head and smiled thinly.

'What is he? Your supplier or your pimp?' he said acidly.

'Why should I tell you?'

Kiernan stepped towards her quickly, seizing her left arm in a vice-like grip, pulling her close towards him.

She could see the anger in his eyes, could hear it in his voice.

'Because if you don't tell me I'm going to break your fucking arms' he rasped, gripping her other arm too, pulling them out straight to reveal more puncture marks in the other limb. The veins looked black beneath her pale skin, hiding there like limp worms.

'Get off me,' she squealed.

'You tell me who Ray Howells is. Now.'

'I did tell you, you Irish prick. He's a friend of mine.' She struggled to pull loose from his grip but Kiernan kept hold of her. He suddenly pushed her away, advancing on her as she fell to the floor in a corner.

'Stay away from me,' she shouted.

'Was she a friend of yours too?' Kiernan snapped, pushing Jo's bus pass towards Stevie, allowing her to see the picture of his sister. 'Have you ever seen this girl?'

Stevie glanced at the picture, then up at Kiernan.

'Look at it,' he snapped.

She did.

'I've seen her,' she said more quietly. 'She used to live here.'

'Do you know her name?'

'I can't remember, I. . .'

He cut her short.

'Try,' he urged angrily.

'Look, I said I know her, right? I just can't remember at the moment. She lived here with Ray and a couple of other girls. I stayed here, too, for a while. I knew her quite well.'

'If you're fucking me around, I'll break your neck,' he hissed.

'I'm telling you the truth, you bastard,' she snapped. 'Her name was Jo.' She stabbed an index finger at the picture; the fingernail was bitten down to the quick. 'Jo.

That's right, isn't it?'

Kiernan swallowed hard.

'Isn't it?' Stevie demanded.

He nodded slowly and stepped back.

'Why is she so fucking important to you, anyway?' Stevie hauled herself to her feet.

Kiernan looked at the photo in the bus pass. The smiling seventeen-year-old. When he spoke again his voice was a hoarse whisper.

'She's my sister.'

The long silence was finally broken by Kiernan.

'How long since you saw her last?' he asked.

Stevie shrugged.

'Like I said, up until a day or two ago she was living here with Ray and a couple of other girls.' She took the bus pass from him and looked more carefully at the photo. 'Yeah, I know Jo. We used to have a lot of the same punters.'

'Was she working for Howells?'

'Both of us were. Us and Christ knows how many more. Not just girls, either. He had guys in his family, too.' She sighed. 'I wish I knew where he was. He's got some stuff for me and I paid him up front.'

'Could Jo be with him?'

'It's possible.'

'Where might he have gone?'

'There's a dozen places around London he could be. He'll turn up eventually, when the heat's off. Like I said, the police pull a little stunt every now and then just so people don't start moaning that they never do anything. Every thing'll be back to normal in a day or two. Your sister might turn up then.'

'How well did you know her?'

'We were good mates. I liked her.'

'Did she touch the same shit as you? Drugs, I mean?' he said irritably.

'Everybody uses it' she told him flatly. 'If it's not heroin it's coke or crack. It's the only way to get through life.'

'And Howells gets it for you?' Kiernan said.

'He can get anything. I've even seen him get hold of ice. He can get stuff no one else can get. Idiot pills, morphine, Dr Godfrey's, Space base. Even China White.'

'What a man,' said Kiernan caustically.

There was another long silence; this time it was broken by Stevie.

'We made a film together, me and Jo. Just the two of us and

four or five blokes,' she told him. 'Ray arranged it all.'

'Film?' said Kiernan, looking a little vague.

'Ray said he knew some blokes who wanted girls for some video work. Just suck-and-fuck movies. You know the kind of thing. We did about four of them. They paid us a few quid.'

'How long ago was that?'

'Five weeks, maybe a bit more.'

'Jo was into porno films?' he said, not really wanting to hear the answer.

'She needed the money, like I did. It's better than tossing some old bastard off behind King's Cross for a fiver. One of the blokes was quite horny.' She giggled.

'Shit,' murmured Kiernan, leaning back against the wall.

As he did, he saw the door swing open.

He turned, wondering what was happening, his eyes drawn to the figure in the doorway.

Stevie saw the newcomer too but, like Kiernan, she was looking not at the intruder's face, but at the gun he held.

The barrel was levelled at them.

Fifty-nine

For a second Stevie considered screaming, but she contented herself with moving a step backwards, her eyes never leaving the barrel.

Kiernan remained motionless, his gaze alternating between the gaping barrel of the .357 and the eyes of the man who held it.

Nick Ryan coughed and winced at the pain in his chest. But he kept the gun steady, one thumb on the hammer, ready to pull it back.

'Who are you?' asked Stevie, her voice low.

'An interested passer-by,' said Ryan, his face impassive. 'It seems we have something in common.' He glanced at Kiernan. 'Raymond Howells. I'm looking for him, too.'

'How do you know I want him?' Kiernan asked, his eyes flicking nervously towards the pistol.

'I know quite a lot of things,' Ryan said. 'I've been standing out in that hallway for the last five minutes listening to your conversation.'

'How did you get in?' Stevie asked.

'Same way as you two. Through the front door.' He motioned with the .357, a sharp gesture, at Kiernan. 'Move back.'

Kiernan did as he was told.

'What the fuck is going on here?' he asked.

'That's what I was hoping to find out,' Ryan announced. 'Drugs, porn movies, prostitution. This one's got everything, hasn't it? Oh, not forgetting runaway sisters.'

Kiernan regarded him warily, the perspiration beading on his forehead.

'What do you know about my sister?' he asked irritably.

'Only what I overheard,' Ryan told him, smiling thinly. 'Perhaps you'd like to tell me a little bit more.'

'Why should I?'

'I'm holding a fucking gun on you, for one thing. How much more incentive do you need?' Ryan snapped.

'I've been looking for her for the last five months.' He shrugged. 'At least, she's been missing for the last five months. She ran away from home.'

'Where's home?' Ryan wanted to know.

'Ireland.'

'You surprise me,' the private detective said acidly. 'I would have put money on Yorkshire.'

'What kind of fucking comedian are you?' snapped Kiernan.

'The kind with a gun who'll blow your head off if you don't shut it.' He looked at Stevie. 'What's your story?'

'You were listening at the door; didn't you hear it?' she said defiantly.

Ryan smiled.

'I've heard of tarts with hearts,' he said. 'What are you? A tart with a trap. Just tell me who you are and what you're doing here.'

'My name's Stevie Collins,' she said. 'I'm looking for Ray Howells, he . . .'

Ryan cut her short.

'He sold you some drugs and now he's fucked off with the money or rather he promised you some drugs and he's fucked off with the money. Right?'

'Ten out of ten,' she said sardonically.

'Vince Kiernan and Stevie Collins' Ryan said, looking at each of them in turn.

'You know our names' snapped Kiernan. 'Who the fuck are you?'

'Ryan. I'm a private detective.'

'And I'm the fucking Pope,' Kiernan snorted.

Ryan pulled some ID from his pocket, a business card, and threw it towards Kiernan.

'Then read that, Your Holiness' he said, watching the young Irishman snatch up the card and scan it.

He shrugged and glanced once more at the gun then at the private detective.

'Happy now?' said Ryan.

'You never said why you wanted to see Ray' Stevie reminded him.

'Business' Ryan lied. 'He's got a product I'm interested in. As a matter of fact, you might be able to help.' He glanced at Kiernan. 'Both of you.'

Ryan stepped back towards the door, the gun still aimed at the other two.

'Move it' he said. 'You're coming with me.'

'Why should we?' Kiernan demanded.

Ryan thumbed back the hammer of the .357 and aimed it at the Irishman's kneecap.

'Because it's better than learning to walk with a fucking stick' he rasped. 'Come on.'

'Where are we going?' Stevie asked, walking out cautiously.

'You wouldn't want me to tell you and spoil the surprise, would you?' Ryan said, pushing Kiernan out of the room too.

The Irishman turned and clenched his fists.

Ryan raised the pistol to within inches of his head.

'I wouldn't' he said quietly.

Kiernan stalked out behind Stevie, both of them heading down the hall and towards the stone steps that

led up to street level.

'Kiernan' said Ryan as they reached the top of the stairs. 'Take these.' He tossed him the keys of the Ford Sapphire which was parked beside the kerb. 'You drive. You can drive, can't you?'

Kiernan held the keys up and nodded.

'What if I refuse?' he said.

'I'll kill you' Ryan said. Then, looking at Stevie:

'That goes for you too. Either of you fuck me around and I'll blow your heads off. Now get in the car. I'll give you directions.'

'I want to know where we're going,' Stevie protested.

'Shut up and get in,' Ryan snapped. 'There's something I want you to see. Both of you.'

Sixty

'Jesus Christ.'

Vince Kiernan's muffled exclamation of revulsion seemed to hang in the heavy air of Ryan's office.

The private detective sat at his desk, a drink cradled in one hand, a cigarette in the other. He had his head lowered, his back turned to the video screen on the other side of the room.

Kiernan and Stevie sat on the worn leather sofa under the window watching the images. Stevie seemed relatively unmoved by it all. Kiernan looked on with his face twisted into a grimace.

Was this what Jo had been involved in?

Ryan downed another large measure of vodka and refilled his glass. He couldn't bring himself to watch the antics on the screen, couldn't force himself to look at what was being done to his daughter. As if the very thought were causing him pain he winced and touched his chest. With the vodka to wash them down he took two of the tablets and sat back in his seat, eyes closed but aware of everything that was happening on the tape.

The .357 was back in its holster now and had been since they'd entered the office about twenty minutes earlier. Both Kiernan and Stevie had seemed uneasy, even after the weapon had been put away, but Ryan preferred it like that. He wanted them off their guard, unsure what his next move would be. He needed them as allies; the fear factor might prove to be his ultimate weapon.

The tape came to an end. He reached for the remote control to switch the machine off.

'Where the fuck did you get that?' Kiernan said, his face pale.

Ryan ignored the question.

'Is that the kind of film you were making?' he asked Stevie.

She sat almost motionless, still staring at the blank screen. She shook her head almost imperceptibly.

'There were only blokes and girls' she said quietly.

'Was it always the same girls?' Ryan asked.

'No. Ray would use new girls for every film if they asked him to get them.'

'Who are "they"?' he wanted to know.

'The people he worked with. We never saw them. We only ever acted in the films.'

'You and my sister?' Kiernan interjected.

She nodded.

'It wasn't that bad,' she said, her gaze still fixed on the screen. 'We got well paid.'

'And I bet Howells took most of that, didn't he?' Ryan snapped.

She nodded again.

'He looked after us; he gave us somewhere to live. He took care of us. It was only fair' she said softly.

'And he got you the drugs you needed, too?' Ryan said.

'Was my sister on drugs?' Kiernan wanted to know.

'I told you, everybody was. Everybody is. You have to get through somehow. Jo and I were stoned when we made those films. If you've got five blokes all trying to stick their cocks in your mouth one after the other then it's better to be stoned.'

'How well did you know the girls who made the other films?' Ryan asked her. 'You and Jo weren't in every one, were you?'

She shook her head slowly and, for the first time, Ryan saw that her eyes were moist. As he watched a tear trickled slowly down her cheek.

'Ray said we were his girls,' she said, smiling thinly. 'He said we looked good on screen.'

Kiernan clenched his fists.

'He told us we were beautiful,' she continued, tears still trickling down her face.

'Where did he get the other girls, Stevie?' Ryan wanted to know.

'The streets,' she told him. 'Anywhere.'

Kiernan looked across at the private detective, who was watching Stevie intently.

'Do you recognize the girl in that film?' he said, his voice cracking slightly.

'She's very young. I've never seen a girl as young as that in one of the films before. She can't be more than about twelve or thirteen.' She wiped a tear away.

Very young.

'I don't recognize her,' said Stevie. 'Just the baby.'

Ryan looked surprised.

'How come?' he said.
'Because it was mine.'

Sixty-one

For long moments the room was silent, as if the awful truth of Stevie's words were slowly sinking in. It was Kiernan who broke the silence.

'You sold your baby?' he said. 'Sold it to be used in a fucking film like that?'

'What the hell was I supposed to do?' she snarled, wiping tears away. 'I had no money. I couldn't look after the kid. I needed money.'

'For drugs?' Kiernan said.

'Yeah, for drugs. I had to have them. Right?' she rasped.

'So you sold your own fucking child just so you could pay for shit to stick in your arms?' he said derisively.

'Don't come over all sanctimonious with me. You fucking people are all the same. You sit in your nice cosy houses, living your nice cosy lives, looking down on people like me.'

'What the hell are we supposed to do? Use you as role models? Do you want sympathy?'

'I don't need your fucking sympathy,' she hissed. 'You don't know what it's like on the streets. When you've got nowhere to go but an empty house, no one to care for you, no way of making money. No future.'

'You threw your own fucking future down the drain when you started taking that shit,' Kiernan said.

'And your sister didn't? Why do you think she started? Why do you think she ran away from home in the first place?'

'You don't know why' Kiernan said.

'I lived with her, remember? I talked to her. You wanted to find her.' She smiled bitterly. 'And what were you going to do when you did? Take her back to her loving family? How do you know she would even go with you?'

Kiernan didn't answer.

'Who did you sell the child to?' Ryan wanted to know.

'Two guys. I forget their names' she said.

'Try and remember' he said, his gaze on her unwavering.

'I can't' she protested.

'Who set it up?'

'Ray did. When he found out I was pregnant he went mad.

He knocked me about.' She shrugged. 'Still, it was my own fault. I forgot to take my pill.'

'I thought you lot used condoms with punters' Ryan said.

'It wasn't a punter's baby, it was Ray's' she told him. 'He said I couldn't stay with him if I was pregnant. If I was pregnant I couldn't work, well, not for much money anyway. All I could do after the seventh month was suck cocks or do hand jobs. It wasn't bringing in enough money.'

'Whose idea was it to sell the kid when it was born?' Ryan asked.

'Ray said that he knew of some blokes who wanted a baby for a film they were making. He said he'd done business with them before. I needed money, too, for my stuff.' She rubbed her arm self-consciously, as if to wipe away the track marks.

'So Howells set up the sale with these blokes?' Ryan continued.

She nodded.

'One thousand quid,' she told him.

'What were their names?' the private detective pressed her.

'I told you, I can't remember.'

'Think,' Ryan said, puffing on his cigarette.

She wiped her eyes again.

'Clayton or something like that,' she mumbled. 'Clayton and . . . Neville.' She nodded. 'That was one of them. Neville. Don Neville.' She looked pleased with herself.

'Don Neville,' Ryan murmured, writing the name on a piece of paper. 'It'll do for a start. So Ray Howells supplied the kids for Neville and Neville made the films, right?'

She nodded.

'Then I have to find Neville and Howells,' the private detective mused. 'I need your help, Stevie. You're the only one who knows what they both look like. Help me find them.'

'Are you mad?' she grunted. 'Either of them would kill me if they found out I was helping to put them away.'

'I didn't say anything about putting them away. I need to find them. I've been hired to track down the girl in that film.' He swallowed hard.

My daughter.

'The only way I can do that is by finding these men and the quickest way to do that is with your help.'

'No,' she said. 'They'd kill me.'

'You've got a choice, then. Get your shit from another dealer and risk filling yourself full of poison, risk Neville or Howells killing you or risk me doing it instead. I'll tell you now, I'm going to find them and you're going to help me. If you don't, I'll do things to you that fucking scumbag Howells never even thought of.' He held her in his cold stare. 'I'll pay you.'

'How much?'

'Two hundred when I find Howells' he told her.

'Three hundred. Half now,' she demanded.

'You're in no position to bargain, Stevie. Three hundred. But only after I've got Howells. Deal?'

'Deal' she said.

'I'll help, too,' Kiernan said.

'I don't need your help,' Ryan told him.

'You need all the fucking help you can get, especially if you have to rely on some drugged-up tart to track this scumbag down,' the Irishman said.

'Fuck off, you pig-eyed . . .' she began.

'Shut it,' snapped Kiernan. Then, to Ryan:

'My sister is out there somewhere. I've been looking for her too long now to give up. If I help you find Howells I've got a chance of finding her too.'

Ryan sat back in his chair, his fingertips pressed together, his expression blank.

'I'm going to find her, Ryan' the Irishman said. 'We might as well work together. Besides, the only way you're going to stop me is to shoot me.'

Ryan leant forward.

'All right' he said. 'You're on. But you fuck up once and I will shoot you.'

Sixty-two

'How many more times do I have to say it? We can't tell anyone.'

Joseph Finlay shifted his position in his seat and rubbed his temples with the tips of his index fingers.

'If the media even get a sniff of this they'll be all over us. I can't afford that kind of exposure, Kim. You have to understand that. I've been rushing around for the last two days raising the money and the banks are beginning to wonder why.'

'All I understand is that my daughter has been kidnapped' Kim said angrily. 'She could be dead by now for all we know.'

'And you think going to the papers is going to get her back? I was told that no one was to be told, especially not the police. Do you want them to kill her? Because that's what they'll do.'

'What are we supposed to do? Sit around waiting for someone to arrive and tell us they've found her body?' Kim blurted.

'Ryan will find her. Have faith in the man; he was your husband, after all. I thought you believed in him,' Finlay said, a note of scorn in his voice. 'He's supposed to be good at his job. He'll find her.'

'How much longer before the ransom deadline is up?' Kim asked.

'There is no deadline as yet. They said they'd ring again to give me more instructions.'

Finlay clasped his hands across his stomach, squeezing his fingers together.

He hadn't heard from Neville for more than twenty-four hours now.

What was the bastard playing at?

More to the point, he hadn't heard from Ryan either.

He pulled himself to his feet and crossed to the drinks cabinet, where he poured himself a large Scotch and downed most of it in one swallow. He tipped more into another glass, added a splash of soda and handed it to Kim. She merely shook her head and put the glass on the coffee table beside her.

'We can't hide forever, Joe,' she said quietly. 'People are going to start asking where Kelly is.'

'Like who?' he demanded.

'The people who live around here. Her school. Her friends.'

'She's only been gone two days. She's on her school holidays. If anyone asks, tell them she's gone to stay with relatives' he said, dismissively.

'Just like that?' Kim said acidly.

'Well, what the hell do you expect me to say?' he snapped. 'I told you, we can't tell anyone. For Kelly's sake.'

'And for yours.'

'What's that supposed to mean?'

'You said you couldn't afford that kind of exposure. You couldn't afford it. Whose life is in danger here, Joe? Yours or Kelly's? What damage could it do to you?'

'It would damage my reputation, my standing amongst my colleagues. I don't want every detail of my fucking life dredged up and plastered across every stinking tabloid newspaper in the country. Can you even begin to imagine what that would do to my business?'

'That's all that matters to you, isn't it? Your business. As long as you're not embarrassed or inconvenienced you couldn't give a damn about Kelly.'

'That's not true, Kim, and you know it.'

'Do I? I thought I knew you but now I'm not so sure.'

'Meaning?'

'She's my daughter, Joe. I just want her back.'

'She's my daughter, too,' he said none too convincingly.

'But you want her back for different reasons. You want her back so you don't have to worry about newspapers prying into your business. What's so important that you need to hide from them anyway, Joe? What's your big secret?' She looked at him accusingly and saw his expression change fleetingly to one of concern.

She couldn't know of his connections with Neville.

'There are no secrets,' he lied.

'And when it's over and we do get her back, please God. What then? What if Nick finds her and brings her back? Do you think you can just sweep it under the carpet? What do you plan on saying to Kelly? "I know you've been kidnapped but if you could just keep quiet about it things will be much better"?' There was anger in her voice and something else which sounded like contempt. 'You think she's going to get over it that easily? God alone knows what it will do to her, even if she gets through it alive. We don't know what the bastards who've got her have done to her.'

I could tell you, thought Finlay, gritting his teeth.

'This business isn't just going to go away, Joe, no matter how much you want it to,' she reminded him.

'Perhaps you should be thinking about getting her back first before you start deciding how psychologically scarred she's going to be,' Finlay said, a touch of sarcasm in his voice. 'And whether we do get her back is down to Ryan, so you'd better hope he's as good at his job as he thinks he is.'

She glared at him, her eyes filled with anger.

Or hatred?

An image of her ex-husband flashed into her mind. She found her thoughts turning to him, to the awful truth he'd told her about his illness. His death.

Six months.

She shuddered.

Her daughter and her ex-husband.

It seemed just a matter of time before they were both dead.

And she had no way of knowing which of them would be the first.

Kim glanced across to the other side of the room and the photo of Kelly smiled back at her.

Sixty-three

The child had been dead for nearly twenty-four hours.

The body was rigid, most of the fingers and toes already rigored; some of the extremities were beginning to blacken. The flesh looked waxen and bloodless. The eyes were closed, as if in sleep, but one lid was slightly open revealing the dull, lifeless eye beneath.

Don Neville looked down at the body indifferently.

'We'll have to get rid of it' Edward Caton offered, his gaze also drawn to the body. 'It's going to start to smell in this fucking weather.' He wiped a hand across his face and wiped the sweat off on his jeans.

'Do you want us to take care of it?' said Neville, turning away to face the third occupant of the room. 'Or will you handle it?'

The third figure nodded.

'You'll do it?' Caton echoed.

The figure nodded again.

Both men smiled.

'You could try the Thames this time,' Caton chuckled, looking down at the body again. He wrinkled his nose.

He crossed to the window and pushed it open, allowing in something approximating fresh air which drifted in from Carnaby Street. It was preferable to the stench of human putrefaction, though.

The flat was above a large shop which had, at one time, sold martial arts equipment. There were entrances both in Carnaby Street itself and also through a rear door in Ganton Street. It was that door through which Neville, Caton and the third occupant of the room had entered less than an hour ago.

The flat itself was divided into four rooms, all of them small. A sitting-room, a kitchen, a bathroom and what had once been a bedroom. There was still a bed in it, or a mattress at least, stained and damp. The sitting-room was furnished with two wooden chairs and a table. The windows had been boarded up, several slats pulled free to allow light into the derelict dwelling. In the kitchen the sink was cracked and brown. It smelled of cat's piss and damp. There was a three-year-old calendar hanging on one wall, the pages curling and faded.

The heat inside the flat was almost overpowering, unrelieved by Caton opening the one window that hadn't been boarded up. The glass was filthy, caked thickly enough with filth to prevent anyone seeing inside.

The dying rays of the sun glinted on shop windows below, reflecting off them in a blood red haze. Carnaby Street itself was empty now. Gone were the shoppers, the tourists and the curious who thronged it during business hours. As Caton glanced out he saw only two young men walking along, laughing as they chatted.

'I want it out of here as soon as possible,' Neville said. 'If anyone comes up here they're going to wonder what the fucking smell is.'

'Who's going to come up here?' Caton wanted to know. 'How could they get in?'

'Same way we did. Break in,' Neville told him.

He watched as a spider scuttled across the floor, climbed over one tiny, outstretched, rigored hand then ran on to disappear into the shadows. Caton made a move to stamp on it.

'Leave it,' said Neville. 'It's bad luck to kill a spider.'

Caton chuckled.

Neville wandered into the bedroom. The other two followed him as he stood by the mattress, looking down.

'We'll get rid of the body, then call Finlay again,' he said.

'How long you going to give him to come up with the money?' Caton wanted to know.

'Forty-eight hours, tops,' Neville said. He knelt beside the mattress, pulling something from his jeans pocket. The other two saw that it was a flick-knife. He pressed the release catch on the blade and the familiar swish-click sound filled the room as the steel was released, springing upright at his touch. He turned the blade over in his hand, looking down at the mattress.

Tied to it by three lengths of thick hemp was Kelly.

There was masking tape across her mouth and, but for a sheet draped over her, she was naked. Her eyes were swollen and puffy from constant weeping.

'Your fucking old man had better pay up,' said Neville, pressing the blade against her cheek. 'Otherwise he's going to be getting another tape through the post. And this time he'll be able to see what we do to you with this fucking knife.'

Kelly tried to turn her head away but Neville held her chin.
Caton smiled.
The third occupant of the room looked on indifferently.

Sixty-four

'That's it, there' said Stevie Collins, pointing towards the large, red-bricked building in Ossulston Street. 'That's the hostel.'

Ryan lit up a cigarette and dangled it out of his side window, gazing intently at the building Stevie had indicated.

Three storeys tall, almost Victorian in appearance, it had been given a paint job and a new roof but it still looked dirty and forbidding.

'How long were you there?' Ryan wanted to know.

'Three months. That was the longest time any of us were allowed to stay. It's a short-stay hostel. Three months and you're out' she explained.

'How many kids are there in there?' Ryan asked, sucking on his cigarette.

'There are usually about sixty or seventy, perhaps more. All of us were about the same age, fifteen up to about twenty-five.'

'Is that where you met Jo?' Kiernan asked.

Stevie nodded.

Ryan stroked his chin thoughtfully, his gaze never leaving the building. He watched as two or three people left. All of them were young. They wandered down the street into the Euston Road, two of them disappearing into a small cafe on the corner. He waited a moment longer then reached across to the glove compartment of the Sapphire, pulling out his camera. He raised it and clicked off four shots of the hostel before replacing it.

'Who runs it?' Ryan asked. 'Who should I speak to there?'

'I think her name was Emma something-or-other. Emma Powell, that's it,' Stevie said, smiling, pleased with herself.

'What are you going to do?' Kiernan wanted to know.

'I'm going to speak to this Miss Powell to find out what she can tell me.' He looked at Stevie. 'Did she ever see Howells?'

'He used to hang around the hostel a lot, but I don't think she knew him,' Stevie said.

'What do you mean, he used to hang around a lot?' Ryan enquired.

'He knew the girls and the blokes coming out of the hostel had nowhere to go. He knew they'd have no money or friends. He used to talk to us, tell us he could find us somewhere to live, get us work.'

'And you believed him?' Kiernan said indignantly.

'So did your fucking sister,' Stevie hissed. 'That was how we met him. Jo and I were having a cup of coffee in a cafe near here one day and Ray came in and started chatting to us. He said he knew we lived at the hostel. He asked us what we were going to do when we left. He said he could help us.'

'Considerate bastard, isn't he?' chided Kiernan.

'Did you know of any other girls who went to work for him?' Ryan said.

'He told us that lots of girls had left the hostel and gone with him, that he'd helped them,' she informed him. 'We needed someone to rely on, somewhere to go-'

'Someone to get your fucking drugs for you,' Kiernan interjected.

'Fuck off,' snapped Stevie. She looked at Ryan: 'Can't you tell him to shut up?'

'Let her speak, Kiernan,' the private detective said, his eyes still on the entrance to the hostel. Two young girls went in.

The Irishman sat back in his seat, gazing out of the side window.

'Anyway,' Stevie continued, 'when Jo and I left the hostel we went to find Ray. He'd given us an address.'

'And he got you into prostitution and porn movies,' Ryan said flatly, sucking on his cigarette.

Stevie nodded.

'At least it was money,' she added as an afterthought.

'And I bet he took most of that, didn't he?' Ryan said.

'He said he was entitled to it for finding us work. You know, like a sort of agent's fee.'

Kiernan laughed mockingly.

'Regular little entrepreneur, wasn't he?' he said.

'Did Neville ever get mixed up in this? Did he ever hang around here?' asked Ryan.

Stevie shook her head.

'Ray used to pick up the kids who left the hostel. He was like the middle-man. Besides, Neville had nothing to do with Ray's everyday business.'

'Selling drugs and running a stable of pros,' Ryan said. He dropped his cigarette end and started up the car.

'What the hell are you doing? I thought you were going to talk to the woman who runs the place?' said Kiernan.

'I am, but later,' Ryan told him. 'And while I do that you two can find Howells.'

'How the fuck are we supposed to do that?' Kiernan said.

'Stevie knows where he hangs out,' Ryan reminded him, pulling away. 'Check everywhere he might be hiding. You'll find him somewhere. Even the biggest turds float sometimes. He'll turn up.'

'What do we do if we find him?' Kiernan asked.

'Ring me. I'll give you instructions where you can get hold of me.' As they passed the hostel he slowed down slightly, peering towards the building once again. Then he sped off.

'Do you think Howells is supplying the kids for Neville's videos?' Kiernan wondered aloud.

Ryan inhaled, held the breath then let it out slowly.

'I wouldn't bet against it,' he said quietly. 'Where do you want me to drop you off?'

Sixty-five

Charles Thornton sat behind his desk watching the bubbles in the Perrier water rise to the top of the glass. It was an expensive glass and Thornton handled it with the care it deserved, holding it delicately between his thumb and forefinger by the stem.

Seated on the Chesterfield opposite sat Frank Price and James Houghton. They too held glasses, although Price was more concerned with the papers spread out on his briefcase. That, in turn, was propped on his lap like a makeshift table; he was running one index finger down a column of figures, apparently lost in thought.

Houghton, a year or two older, pulled at his tie, feeling the heat despite the air-conditioning inside the luxury apartment. He was a big man; his body looked as if it had been poured into his dark blue suit.

Over at the far side of the room stood Phillip Alexander, arms folded, gazing out of the large picture window onto Craven Hill Mews. He could see Thornton's Mercedes parked below; his driver, Colin Moran, stood beside the impressive vehicle smoking. Alexander envied him. He was dying for a smoke but Thornton wouldn't allow it inside the apartment. He took a sip of his ice-cold beer, careful to replace the glass on the coaster provided.

'Well, Frank, what do you say?' Thornton asked. 'What do we do about Finlay? I've given him nearly two weeks, like I said I would, and I've heard nothing from him. I've called the bastard and he hasn't even had the fucking decency to return my calls.'

'The decision is yours in the end, Charlie. I'm only your accountant,' Price said.

'So can I afford to buy him out?' Thornton wanted to know.

'Well, you're not short of money, Charlie, you don't need me to tell you that, but the problem is, you can't buy him out if he won't sell.'

'I offered him whatever he wanted for that fucking place in Cavendish Square,' hissed Thornton. 'He still wasn't interested.'

'If he won't move, we'll have to move him,' Houghton offered.

'Yeah, I know that, Jim, but it's not that easy,' Thornton said, taking a sip of his mineral water.

'Can't he have an accident?' Alexander interjected.

The other men laughed.

'If he goes for a walk under a bus, that leaves me free to move in on the building, but Finlay's a powerful bloke and I don't mean in the same sense as myself.' He smiled self-satisfactorily. 'The only reason I've stayed friendly with him for so long is for his contacts.'

'Fuck his contacts,' said Houghton. 'If he takes a dive under the number 14, who's going to know it's got anything to do with you?'

'No, no, you're missing the point,' said Thornton.

'Killing him isn't a problem, but he's made things easy over the last few years. He's smoothed the way, if you like.'

'So find someone else to take his place,' Price said. 'Buy another property developer.'

The other men laughed.

'How much do I stand to make if I take over that building, Frank?' Thornton wanted to know.

'On these projected figures, and remember I can only make an educated guess, nothing's concrete' the accountant reminded him, 'you stand to make two million or more in the first eighteen months. Pre-tax.'

'Tax? What the fuck's that?' said Thornton, grinning.

The sound of laughter filled the room.

'So that settles it then, right?' Houghton said. 'Finlay's history. When do you want him taken out?'

'I'll give him a couple more days,' Thornton said.

'Why? He's fucked you around long enough already,' Houghton said.

'I'll speak to him again, see what he says. If he still says no then you can get rid of him. Right?' Thornton raised his glass and his men followed suit. The gang boss was smiling. 'Cheers.'

Sixty-six

The place looked horribly familiar to Kiernan.

Maxims in Dean Street boasted a MALE AND FEMALE BED SHOW on its hoardings. He knew different; he'd been inside the place during his search for Jo. They waited until there were six people downstairs before the 'show' began. He'd sat there one day himself for more than an hour as two or three people had drifted in and out, finally tiring of the wait and the oppressive atmosphere of the place. He doubted if Maxims ever put on a show; he doubted six people would be stupid enough to sit for long enough in the grubby shithole to witness it.

Now, as he stood outside, he grabbed Stevie by the arm and pulled her back.

'What are we doing here?' he said.

'Ryan said to check out all the places Ray used to go, didn't he?' she said. 'He used to be friendly with the manager of this place. He could be here.' She looked at him and smiled, mockingly. 'Why, too shy to go in?'

He pushed her gently, following her inside.

'Hello, Jed, is Dickie about?' she said happily, smiling at the doorman who sat behind a small counter reading a newspaper. The doorman looked suspiciously at Kiernan; for a moment the young Irishman wondered if he might have recognised him from his earlier visit. He reasoned to himself it was highly unlikely, and even if he did, so what?

Stevie leant on the counter gazing at the doorman, who finally managed to look at her and force a thin smile.

'We haven't seen you here for a while,' he said. The words were spoken slowly and, it seemed, with effort. It was the kind of voice Kiernan usually associated with pissheads or half-wits. Looking at the doorman he was inclined to think it was the latter.

'Can you get Dickie for me?' she said.

'Dickie ain't here,' she was told.

'When will he be back?'

'In about three months, unless he gets time off for good behaviour.'

'Shit,' murmured Stevie.

'What did you want him for, anyway?' the doorman enquired.

'I wondered if he'd seen Ray lately. You know, Ray Howells.'

'Your pimp?' He laughed to himself. 'No, he ain't been in either.' He looked at Kiernan again. 'Who's that, your boyfriend?'

'No, I'm her father,' said Kiernan scornfully.

'What?' the doorman said menacingly, taking a step towards Kiernan. 'How long you been a fucking comedian?'

'About as long as you've been stopping buses with your head,' Kiernan replied, making for the door. 'Come on,' he said to Stevie, 'let's get out of here. It'll be feeding-time soon.'

He led the way back out onto the baking pavement, wiping his face with his handkerchief.

Stevie slipped off her light jacket and slung it over her shoulder, sweat forming rings beneath her arms, darkening the red T-shirt she wore. She pulled the sleeves down as she saw a policeman wandering past.

'Afraid he'll see your little tattoos?' said Kiernan acidly, jabbing at her arms.

'Fuck off,' she snapped.

'Where to now?' he said. 'What other exotic places did Howells frequent?'

'There's an amusement arcade just off Leicester Square,' she told him. 'We'll try there.'

'How do you know he hasn't left London altogether?' asked Kiernan as they headed towards Shaftesbury Avenue.

'He wouldn't,' Stevie assured him. 'This sort of thing's happened loads of times before. He'll be around somewhere, just laying low until things blow over.'

'Did you get Jo hooked on drugs or was it Howells?' asked Kiernan, looking down at her, as they crossed the main road.

'It was her own choice,' Stevie told him. 'No one forced her.'

'Bollocks.'

Stevie ignored him, gazing straight ahead.

'Was it heroin?' he continued.

'I don't know what she was on,' Stevie said wearily. 'Come on, we go down here,' she added, turning right into Chinatown. 'It's her life, you know. Did it ever strike you she might be perfectly happy doing what she's doing? Why did she run away in the first place? If she was that happy at home, she wouldn't have come here, would she?' She reached into her handbag and took out a packet of Silk Cut, stopping to light one up. 'Did you ever think she might not want her big brother to rescue her? Why couldn't you just leave her alone?'

'Because I care about her,' Kiernan said quietly.

'Well, maybe she doesn't care about you,' Stevie said, looking at him.

'What the hell do you know about caring?' Kiernan snapped. 'I doubt if anyone would want to find you, would they?'

She didn't answer, merely puffed on her cigarette and looked over his shoulder.

'Why did you run away in the first place?' he pressed.

'It's none of your business.'

'Whatever kind of life you left behind must have been better than this.'

Stevie laughed bitterly.

'No,' she said, her voice quivering. 'There are worse ways to live, believe me.'

She wiped her eye hurriedly with the back of her hand, anxious to hide the tears. She smudged her thick mascara and it left a dark mark on her cheek. 'Shit,' she murmured, moving to a shop window to check her reflection. She tried to rub the mark away with her fingers but it only spread more.

Kiernan nudged her, handing her his handkerchief.

'Here,' he said.

She took it, wet one tip with her tongue and wiped away the mark. Then she pushed the linen square back into his hand.

'We'd better get on,' she said, moving down the narrow alley towards Charing Cross Road.

'So?' he said quizzically, catching up with her, 'what was so bad that you had to run away?'

'I told you, it's none of your business,' she said, angry with herself for showing emotion.

'I was just trying to help,' he said. 'If you don't want to talk about it. . .'

'I don't,' she said with an air of finality, turning right and striding ahead through the crowds. Kiernan, bulkier, had to step into the street, avoiding oncoming taxis, in order to find the room to speed up and reach her side. By the time he had done so, they were at the doors of the Hippodrome.

Sixty-seven

Nick Ryan wiped sweat from his forehead and gazed at the pad in front of him. On it were written three names: Emma Powell Don Neville Raymond Howells

He drew a bracket around Howells' and Neville's names and added a question mark.

Howells dealt in child pornography, that much he knew from speaking to the assistant in the sex shop the other day. He also ran a stable of very young prostitutes.

Stevie said that he had enticed several former residents of the Ossulston Street hostel to work for him, including her and Kiernan's sister. He also knew that those same youngsters were supplied for porno videos made by Neville.

How then did Kelly come to be in a video which could have been made by . . .

By whom?

Kelly had been kidnapped.

Why had she been kidnapped?

Because Finlay had money.

But why use her in such a vile way, in such a monstrous video?

No reason. No link.

'Shit' he snapped, bringing his hand down hard on the desk top.

No link.

And yet.. .

There was something nagging at the back of his mind. Stuck there like the last few chords of a song which stayed, unwanted, in the brain.

Howells promised the homeless kids who left the hostel somewhere to go, Ryan thought. Told them they could rely on him.

When you're homeless you take help from anyone.

Homeless.

Runaways.

No one cared about them.

So no one would miss them.

Ryan stroked his chin, feeling how hot his skin was.

No families.

No one to trace them.

Nobody gave a shit about kids who slept rough on the streets of London or any other big city.

Nobody but Raymond Howells and Don Neville?

Ryan smiled thinly.

HOMELESS. He wrote the word on the other edge of the pad, drumming the fingers of his free hand on the wood.

Homeless.

Untraceable.

The private detective reached for the phone, punching out digits with the end of his pen. He kept looking at his pad as he listened to the ringing.

Homeless and living rough.

The phone was picked up at the other end.

'New Scotland Yard' said the voice. 'Can I help you?'

'I'd like to speak to Detective Constable Peter Trent, please,' Ryan said, still gazing at his pad.

The line went dead for a moment, only the hiss of static burbling away in his ear. Then he heard a different ringing tone.

He waited.

Something in the back of his mind . . .

And waited.

'Come on,' he murmured.

'Hello,' the voice at the other end finally said.

'DC Trent, please,' Ryan said.

'Who's calling?' the voice asked.

'Just tell him it's a friend,' Ryan said cryptically.

There was a moment of silence on the other end then Ryan heard movement, muffled voices; the taker of the call had obviously put his hand over the mouthpiece.

A moment later he heard a familiar voice.

'DC Trent. Who's this, please?'

Ryan smiled.

'You took your fucking time, didn't you?' he said.

'Who is this?'

'A blast from the past' Ryan said, grinning.

Give it another six months and it could be a rave from the grave, he thought, his smile fading.

'Jesus Christ' said Trent.

'Not quite, but then you never were very good with voices, were you, Pete?'

'Nick Ryan?'

'Is there another one?'

'What the fuck do you want?' Trent chuckled.

'Your help, Pete' the private detective told him.

'A rich and famous private detective wants my help? I'm honoured' Trent joked.

'Just shut up and listen, will you?'

'That's no way to talk to your old partner, is it? Getting touchy in your old age?' chided Trent.

'How many years did we work together? Six?'

'It seemed like longer' Trent told him, laughing.

'If you don't shut up it'll be six years before this fucking conversation ends' Ryan told him. 'Just listen to me. This case you're working on, the one with the murdered kids, the runaways. What kind of progress are you making?'

Trent sighed.

'You know I can't talk about that, Nick. What the hell's wrong with you?'

'I need some information, Pete. It could be important to both of us.'

'What are you working on?'

'That's not important at the moment. What is important is that you get me some information.'

'Wait a minute' Trent said. 'I'm transferring this call to my office.'

Ryan heard a click and a buzz and waited a moment longer until he heard the phone picked up again.

'I couldn't talk,' Trent told him.

'Yeah, that's the problem with New Scotland Yard,

isn't it? Bloody place is always swarming with coppers. Now listen, Pete, this case you're on. According to the papers, you haven't got fuck all to go on, apart from the fact that all the kids were runaways, right?'

'What did you ring for? To tell me something I already know?' Trent muttered. 'Because if you did . . .'

'I need their names,' the private detective said flatly.

'What?' Trent blurted, incredulous.

'I need the names of the six murdered kids.'

'No way, Nick. I can't give out information like that. You know the rules.'

'Fuck the rules.'

'What do you know? How are you tied in with this case?'

'I might not be, I don't know. But I have to have the names of those kids.' His tone softened a little. 'Look, if I find out anything I'll tip you off. Perhaps if you crack the case instead of Baxter they'll promote you. Then you can have the fucking job I should have had.'

'I won't have any job at all if someone finds out I disclosed information to an outsider,' Trent told him.

'I'm not an outsider, Pete.'

'You are now. You have been since you resigned.'

'And you know why I resigned.'

'It doesn't make any difference why, Nick. I still can't give you that information.'

'We were partners,' Ryan reminded him. 'More than that, we were friends.'

'Don't try to give me the loyalty bullshit, Nick.'

'There's something else too, Pete. You owe me and you know what I'm talking about.'

There was a heavy silence on the other end.

'If it wasn't for me you'd be dead now,' Ryan continued. 'I saved your life.'

'Look, Nick . . .'

Ryan cut him short.

'You don't need reminding, do you, Pete?' The private detective continued acidly. 'Four years ago in Chinatown? That little shit we were after for carving up a Triad leader, the one who came at you with a meat cleaver. The one you never even saw. The one who would have split you in half if I hadn't stepped in. Remember?'

'Yeah,' rasped Trent, 'I remember.'

'You owe me, Pete. You said it at the time. Well, now I'm calling in that favour. Give me the names of those six kids.'

'You bastard,' hissed Trent angrily. 'You were always a shithouse, Nick, but

'The names, Pete,' Ryan interrupted.

There was another long silence at the end of the phone. Ryan pressed the receiver to his ear, wondering for a moment if Trent had hung up on him. When the policeman spoke again his voice was low.

'Give me thirty minutes,' he said. 'I'll call you back.'

Sixty-eight

The profusion of sounds inside the amusement arcade combined to form a deafening cacophony. Music blared from speakers mounted high on the walls; the constant buzz of chatter, the electronic burblings of the machines and the periodic rattle of change all combined to create an unearthly din.

The Crystal Rooms in New Coventry Street were busy. Vince Kiernan found himself checking out the faces as he followed Stevie through the maze of fruit machines and electronic games.

Most of the occupants of the arcade were in their late teens or early twenties; some were much younger. Their faces were lit by the multi-coloured lights which flashed so brilliantly as they played. Their eyes seemed blank; the only signs of life were the flickering colours that danced endlessly before them.

Had Jo spent her spare time in a place like this, he wondered?

He bumped into two young lads, barely eighteen, playing one of the electronic games. The first of them, a youth with pitted skin and a dirty Dead Kennedy's T-shirt, shot him an angry glance. TOO DRUNK TO FUCK his T-shirt proclaimed.

Kiernan held the youngster's glassy stare for a moment before looking briefly at his companion, a girl about a year younger whose hair needed washing. She also looked at Kiernan angrily, moving closer to the youth.

The young Irishman moved on, seeing that Stevie was heading for a change booth up ahead.

The woman inside, intent on her magazine, gave her only a cursory glance as she approached.

There was a large, black man dressed in jeans and a polo shirt leaning against the side of the booth. He stepped forward as he saw Stevie approaching.

She smiled up at him but received no response. He merely looked her up and down; he did the same to Kiernan.

'Do you know Ray Howells?' Stevie said, forced to raise her voice over the music.

Neither the large man nor the woman in the booth spoke.

Kiernan stepped forward.

'Ray Howells,' he repeated irritably. 'Do you know him?'

'I heard what she said' the large man told him.

'So do you know him?' the Irishman continued.

'Are you friends of his?' the woman in the booth asked, eyeing them both suspiciously.

'I've been looking for him all over. He usually spends some time in here' Stevie explained.

Kiernan stepped forward again but Stevie held out a hand to push him back.

'Your friend's a little eager, isn't he?' said the woman in the booth, glancing at Kiernan.

'Have you seen him?' Stevie asked.

'Who's asking for him?' the black man wanted to know.

'My name's Stevie Collins. If he comes in, ask him to get in touch with me, will you? I work with him. He'll know where to reach me. Tell him it's important.'

She took a piece of paper from her handbag and scribbled her name on it, pushing it across the counter to the woman in the booth. She took it and looked at it.

'Thanks' said Stevie, turning and tugging at Kiernan's sleeve in an effort to make him follow her.

The woman in the booth waited until they were out of sight, then turned to the large black man. He shrugged.

She screwed the piece of paper up into a ball and tossed it into the rubbish-bin beside her.

Stevie emerged out onto the pavement outside and turned angrily towards Kiernan.

'I told you I'd handle this,' she said. 'What the hell were you doing, sticking your nose in?'

'They knew more than they were letting on' snarled Kiernan.

'And they might have told us if they hadn't thought you were a fucking copper,' she said, walking away from him.

Kiernan grabbed her arm and spun her round,

ignoring the three or four passers-by who watched the little fracas.

'What makes you so sure they thought I was a copper?' he demanded.

'Because you were too pushy' she told him, shaking free of his grip. 'Just leave it to me next time.'

'I've left it to you so far and we're no nearer to finding

Howells.'

'So look for him your fucking self. Perhaps you think you know these streets better than I do.'

He shook his head.

'I've only walked them. You've worked them.'

'Then leave it to me to find him. If we don't find Howells, you've no chance of finding Jo. Perhaps you'd better think about that before you go sticking your oar in next time.'

They glared at each other, the temperature around them matching their blazing tempers.

'Lead on, then,' Kiernan said acidly. 'Let's see where your expert knowledge takes us next.'

Stevie shook her head and spun round, walking back towards Charing Cross Road.

'No wonder Jo ran away from home if she had you going on at her all the time,' she said.

'I wasn't the reason she left,' Kiernan snapped.

'You surprise me.'

'And I'm the only one who's cared enough to come looking for her. I don't see anyone searching for you.'

'I wouldn't want them to.' She rounded on him. 'Especially if they were like you. If I knew you were looking for me I think I'd have left for another fucking planet.'

She pushed her way through the crowd, turning left then left again into Leicester Square tube station.

'Where are we going now?' Kiernan asked, following her down the stairs.

'He used to hang out in a snooker hall in Pentonville Road. We'll try there. We can get a tube to King's Cross from here, then walk.'

'Great' murmured the Irishman.

'You want to find her, don't you?' Stevie snapped. 'You want your little sister back?'

'And you want Howells?'

'Fucking right I do.'

'You don't care about Jo, do you?'

'Why should I? She's your sister. All I care about is getting the money Ryan promised me. You want your sister, I want the money and the only way we're going to get what we want is by working together. Like it or not and believe me, I hate it as much as you.'

'I doubt it,' Kiernan snapped.

'Fuck off,' she rasped.

They headed for the ticket machines.

Sixty-nine

Ryan looked at his watch, then at the clock on the wall, to verify that both timepieces showed the same configuration.

They did.

He paced the office, puffing agitatedly on a cigarette, his gaze constantly drawn to the phone.

He paused by the video in the corner of the office; the tape was still propped on top of it. That tape.

Thoughts of Kelly flooded into his mind, swiftly followed, he was alarmed to discover, by the images on

the tape. He blinked hard, as if to wipe them away. He wanted her to stay in his mind as the happy, smiling young girl he knew and loved so well, not the perverted plaything of the two scumbags in the film.

Ryan felt a twinge of pain in his chest. This time, instead of subsiding after a moment or two, it grew more intense. So much so that he was forced to sit down. After a minute he clambered to his feet and crossed to his desk, sliding open one drawer, taking out a small bottle of white fluid and the spoon alongside it. Controlling his shaking hands, he poured first one, then two measures of morphine, swallowing it quickly, sucking on his cigarette to banish the flavour. And, sure enough, the pain began to subside. He replaced the bottle in the drawer and closed it, shutting away the cure as easily as the morphine had shut away his pain.

Until the next time, anyway.

He turned again and looked at the video, trying not to think of Kelly strapped to that bed but unable to banish the thoughts. Perhaps somewhere inside him he wanted to cling to them, repugnant though they might be. Yet in that revulsion was one of his reasons for carrying on.

The desire to catch up with the men who had subjected his daughter to such obscenities was growing.

It was swelling inside him as surely as the cancer. His desire for revenge was becoming almost intolerable. Christ, he wanted them to suffer as she had suffered.

And he wanted them to end his suffering.

They wouldn't hand her back without a fight. That had always been his hope. He didn't want her handed back; he wanted to be forced to take her from them. To confront them. To precipitate the violence that would end his life before the disease inside him ate him away.

What if her kidnappers didn't want to fight?

What if they handed his daughter back willingly?

Ryan would not let them. He would make them fight.

Make them release him from his agony.

He sought' something in death he had never had in life.

He sought honour.

Ryan's philosophical musings were interrupted by the ringing of the phone.

He waited a moment or two, glanced at his watch then picked up the receiver.

'Ryan Investigations' he said.

'Just shut up and listen' Trent told him angrily. 'Have you got a pen there?'

Ryan smiled, reaching for a biro and a pad on his desk.

'Go ahead, Pete' he said.

'The names of the kids you want are as follows: Alison Cole. Matthew Jarvis. Carla Sexton. Claire Cottrell. John Molloy and . . .'

'Wait a minute. Spell Cottrell' said the private detective, writing furiously.

Trent sucked in an angry breath and did so.

'Got it. And the last one?' Ryan enquired.

'Maria Jenkins. Got that?'

'Yes, thanks for your help, Pete.'

'All right, Nick. Now, listen! You get anything on this case, anything at all, I want it. You come to me first, understand? I don't want you messing it about.'

And the DC slammed the phone down.

Ryan replaced the receiver, pulled the sheet of paper from the pad and folded it, slipping it into his pocket. He lit up another cigarette and headed out of the office.

He guessed it would take him about thirty minutes to drive to Ossulston Street hostel.

Seventy

The King's Cross Snooker Club in Pentonville Road stood next door to the Scala Cinema. Both buildings looked as if they badly needed renovating.

The sign hanging over the door of the club showed a black, a white and a red ball; the paint was peeling away from all three. As Kiernan pushed open the black doors that marked the entrance to the club, more paint fell away in tiny, cinder-like flakes.

He and Stevie found themselves at the bottom of a long narrow stairwell which led up to a cramped landing. The wooden steps creaked protestingly as the two newcomers climbed. A single unshaded bulb lit the stairwell, casting thick shadows. Kiernan glanced up at it, seeing motes of dust floating in the dull glow it gave off. In places on the wall, mostly in felt-tip pen, phone numbers and occasionally names had been written, some of them faded.

'What's that?' Kiernan asked. 'The local Yellow Pages?'

Stevie ignored him and kept climbing.

'Where's your number?' the Irishman added.

She glared at him and shook her head.

'How do I know you're not protecting him?' he asked, looking back at her. 'We could be trekking round London for days trying to find the bastard.'

'Why should I protect him?' she demanded. 'He ran off with my money. Besides, I can think of better things to do than wander round London with you.'

They reached the landing and were confronted by a small glass-fronted booth that looked like a cinema cash desk. Inside, a heavy-set man seemed to have been wedged. He ran appraising eyes over them both, his gaze lingering for a moment on Stevie.

'Two, please' said Kiernan.

'Are you a member?' the man asked. He smoothed down one side of his thin moustache.

'No, I just want a couple of games,' Kiernan said, smiling.

Moustache smiled too.

'Five quid an hour,' he said. He looked at Stevie again. 'But, er, no women, I'm afraid. Sorry, love.'

She sighed irritably.

'That's the rules, I'm afraid.' Moustache told her apologetically. 'If it was up to me, I'd let you in, but it's not up to me so I can't.'

Stevie pulled Kiernan to one side and lowered her voice.

'You can't go in there on your own,' she said. 'If Ray's in there you wouldn't recognize him, anyway. We might as well go.'

'I'll recognize him if you describe him for me,' Kiernan told her.

'Five quid an hour, mate,' Moustache reminded him.

Kiernan dug in his pocket and pushed a ten-pound note across the desk.

He received a small yellow ticket in return.

'What does Howells look like?' Kiernan demanded.

Stevie looked at Moustache, who was pushing the money into a drawer, then turned back to Kiernan.

'He's about five ten, slim. He usually wears a track suit and trainers. He's got hair to his collar but it's shaved at the sides over his ears. He wears a gold earring in his left ear.'

'Is that it?'

'What else do you want to know?' she said, exasperated. 'His shoe size?'

'Keep your voice down' Kiernan said, holding her gaze. 'Now, where will I meet you when I come out of here?'

'There's a cafe over the road; you'll see it as soon as you come out. I'll wait there for you.'

He nodded and turned to go inside.

'Kiernan, what are you going to do if he's in there?' she asked.

'I'll give it an hour. If he's not in here, I'll come and meet you. If he is here, or if he does arrive, I'll keep my eye on him, make sure he doesn't leave.'

'And how do you propose to do that?'

'Let me worry about that,' Kiernan told her and turned away, pushing open the door that led through into the snooker hall itself.

Stevie retreated down the stairs, glancing at her watch.

It was 3.05 p.m.

Seventy-one

Nick Ryan stood at the bottom of the short flight of steps and looked up at the entrance to Ossulston Street Hostel. He took the cigarette from his mouth, grinding it out under his foot, then made his way towards the door.

As he reached it he found his way blocked by a slim girl with dark hair and a sallow complexion. She looked at him quizzically as she opened the door to let him in.

He nodded a greeting to her, glancing down to see that she was barefoot.

Suzi Gray pushed a hand through her hair and studied the private detective with her cold grey eyes.

'I wonder if you could help me' he said.

'That depends what you want,' she told him.

Ryan looked more intently at her, realizing that she was obviously considerably younger than her appearance. There were lines around her cheeks and eyes that really had no right to be present in one so young.

'I'm looking for someone called Emma Powell,' he announced. 'She runs the place, doesn't she?'

'Are you with the police?' Suzi wanted to know.

Ryan grinned.

'Why, do I look like a copper?'

She didn't answer.

'As a matter of fact, I'm looking for someone,' he told her. 'I'm looking for my son, Roger. Roger Grant. Do you know him?'

Suzi shook her head.

'Well, I had a letter from him saying he'd been staying here, and mentioning this Miss Powell. I'd like to see her if l can.'

'So go and see her,' Suzi said.

'Is she free?'

'I just live here,' Suzi told him. 'I'm not her secretary. I can take you to her office, though.'

'You're so kind,' Ryan said, with a hint of sarcasm.

He followed Suzi as she turned and headed back up the corridor, leading him up a flight of steps to the first floor.

As they walked he glanced around him, peering into open

doors, spotting other residents of the hostel. They were all young. He doubted if any of them were older than twenty-five. In one room two youths sat on a bed talking and smoking. In another he saw a young girl reading. She glanced across at him as he passed and smiled thinly.

A fat girl in an out-of-date punk outfit passed them in the corridor and Suzi spoke to her. The girl looked at Ryan, then disappeared.

'Here' Suzi said, indicating a door with a frosted glass panel. 'This is Emma's office.'

She turned and walked away.

'Thanks for your help,' Ryan said, knocking hard.

A voice from inside told him to come in and he obeyed, stepping into the small, warm office, closing the door behind him.

Emma Powell looked bemused as she saw him and put down her pen, ignoring the work she'd been doing.

'Can I help you?' she said.

'I was hoping you might be able to help me. Miss Powell. It is Miss Powell, isn't it? Emma Powell?' Ryan said.

She nodded.

'Have we met?' she asked.

'No,' he said, smiling. He crossed to a chair in front of her desk. 'My name is Grant,' he lied, extending a hand. 'Stuart Grant.' She shook the offered hand and invited him to sit down.

'I'm looking for my son,' he told her as convincingly as he could. 'I have reason to believe he spent some time here.'

'And what was his name?' she asked.

'Roger Grant. He was sixteen. He's been missing for more than eight months now.'

'And what makes you think he stayed here, Mr Grant?'

'He wrote to me to tell me where he was up until about two months ago. He mentioned this place. He mentioned you, too. That's how I knew where to come.' Ryan rubbed his forehead in mock concern, pleased with his own charade. He rarely looked at Emma who was constantly studying him, making her own appraisals.

'I don't recall the name, Mr Grant. I can't remember your son. Are you sure you have the right hostel?'

'Definitely. Mind you, I can understand you not remembering

individual faces. You must see hundreds during the course of a year.'

'Yes, I do.'

'It's a pity you can't do more for them.'

'Meaning what?'

'Well, throwing them back on the streets again after three months doesn't help much, does it?'

'I don't throw them back on the street as you put it, Mr Grant. I have no choice. This hostel is a short-stay hostel. No one is allowed to stay here for longer than three months. If you're looking for someone to blame, blame the government.'

Touchy.

'So you say you can't remember my son?' he continued. 'You keep files, don't you? You could check and see if he stayed here.'

'I told you, his name doesn't ring a bell,' Emma said defensively.

'You also told me that you see hundreds of runaways a year. I can understand you not remembering every single one. Perhaps if you checked . . .'

'I'm very busy, Mr Grant,' she said.

'Too busy to check for one name?'

'Look, my files are private. Besides which, I have no proof of who you are. You could be anyone who's wandered in off the streets. I'm supposed to protect the youngsters who live here. They're in my care. They trust me. I can't pull out a file just because a total stranger walks in, claiming his son once spent some time here. How do I know you're Roger's father? You haven't even shown me any identification.'

Ryan smiled to himself.

Very efficient.

'No, you're quite right,' he said. 'I'm sorry for being so rude. It's just that I'm worried. I've been looking for a long time; this is virtually my last resort.'

She eyed him suspiciously across the desk, turning her pen over and over in her hand.

'My son mentioned a man called Raymond Howells in one of his letters,' he lied. 'Do you know anyone of that name? My son said this man used to come into the hostel sometimes.'

Ryan watched for any sign of recognition in her eyes but he saw only steely defiance.

'The only people who come into this hostel, Mr Grant, are the residents and myself and my staff. Unless this Mr Howells was a resident here at the same time as your son, I don't know what you're talking about.'

'My son said he was a drug pusher,' Ryan said flatly.

'This is ridiculous,' Emma said indignantly.

'My son said he used to try and bribe the young girls here into working for him. He was a pimp, too, you see,' Ryan continued, still watching for some reaction.

All she did was look at him blankly.

'Howells, how shall I put it, secured the services of several boys and girls who lived here. He enticed them into working the streets for him. How much do you know about that?'

'I don't know anything about that at all,' she said. 'All I do know is I'm beginning to doubt you are who you say you are, Mr Grant, and if you don't leave here soon I'll have to call the police.'

'I'm here to make honest enquiries about my son,' he continued. 'I want to find him and all you can do is question my motives.'

Ryan watched Emma's face intently.

'He also mentioned someone called Don Neville' the private detective added.

A flicker.

He saw her swallow hard.

'Mr Grant, I think you ought to go,' she told him. 'I don't remember your son. I don't think I can help you. Now, unless you show me some identification, I'm going to have to ask you to leave. If you won't leave I'll call the police.'

She moved her hand towards the phone and rested it on the receiver.

Ryan didn't move.

Seventy-two

The only light inside the snooker club seemed to be coming from the huge overhead rectangular devices which were suspended a few feet above each table. The lamps gave off a dull glow, enough to light the table and about a foot or so around it. Each table looked like a little island of luminescence in a sea of gloom.

Kiernan could see figures moving around the tables, could hear the clack of a snooker ball on ball. There were low mumblings every now and then, but apart from that the place was relatively silent.

There was a counter on a raised platform to his left which served hot drinks, canned drinks and spirits.

Two or three men sat alone around the makeshift bar. One watched him intently as he ordered an orange juice. His gaze moved swiftly from face to darkened face, but as far as he could tell there was no sign of Raymond Howells as yet.

There were twelve tables in the first floor room but only three were occupied, the games being played in virtual silence. A single rotary fan turned in the centre of the ceiling, the whoosh of the blades sounding like a muffled helicopter rotor. The fan did little to alleviate the stifling heat. As the barman returned and pushed Kiernan's orange juice towards him, beads of perspiration on the other man's forearm glistened in the dull light behind the bar.

On the walls of the room hung posters of snooker players both old and new. Joe Davis. Jimmy White. Ray Reardon. Alex Higgins.

'I played him once, you know.'

The voice startled the young Irishman. When he turned, a man a few years older than himself was nodding towards the picture of Alex Higgins.

'He played an exhibition match here and I played him,' the man explained. 'Bloody near beat him, too.'

Kiernan nodded and sipped at his drink, his eyes still roving.

Every now and then he glanced at the door, as if expecting Howells to walk in.

What if the bastard had changed his appearance somehow?

What if the description Stevie had given him was wrong?

He sipped at his drink and tried to push the thoughts from his mind.

She thought her watch had stopped. It seemed that every time Stevie Collins looked at the timepiece the hands were in the same position. She raised it to her ear and heard the ticking. It wasn't her watch at fault. It was as if time itself had frozen.

She shifted position on the plastic chair, gazing out of the cafe window across the street at the snooker club, hardly lowering her watchful stare even to sip at her 7UP.

Perhaps Howells was already inside.

She looked at her watch and saw that it was 3.23.

There were only three other people in the cafe. An old woman was sipping at a cup of tea and two men were chatting, the sports page of a newspaper laid out before them.

A middle-aged woman with large thighs and very bad varicose veins mopped tables and collected dirty cups. She passed Stevie twice, glancing at her quizzically.

The young girl sipped her drink and kept her eyes on the entrance to the club.

A number of men passed by but none that she recognized.

She scratched absent-mindedly at one of the track marks on her arm, picking a scab free and tossing it into the ashtray where a number of butts already lay. She lit another cigarette and glanced again at her watch.

3.26.

'Fancy a game?'

Kiernan looked at the man on his left and exhaled wearily.

'I said, do you fancy a game?' the man repeated, nodding towards the tables. 'We can have a fiver on it to make it more interesting, if you like.'

'Yeah, okay,' Kiernan said, putting down his drink.

He went and selected a cue from the rack. The other man opened up a small wooden box and took out two halves of a cue which he began screwing together.

'This used to belong to my old man' he announced. 'He was a fucking good player. It was the only thing the old bastard ever gave me in his life, but it's a good cue.'

Kiernan nodded and began racking the balls up.

'My name's Courtney, by the way. Tim Courtney,' the man

announced.

'Vince Kiernan.'

'I haven't seen you in here before. You're not local, are you?' Courtney said.

'No. I came in looking for someone, as a matter of fact.'

But there's no sign of the bastard yet.

'Well, this'll pass the time while you're waiting, won't it?' Courtney exclaimed. 'Let's see your money.'

'What?'

'A fiver, we said.' He dug out a five-pound note and put it on the next table. Kiernan did the same. 'You break,' Courtney said, chalking his cue.

Kiernan took a final look at the door and made his first shot.

As the cue ball came to a stop near the top cushion he stepped back. One of the other men at the bar was watching him. Kiernan tried to ignore him.

Where the hell was Howells?

She froze, the glass mid-way between her lips and the table.

Peering through the window of the cafe, Stevie was certain.

Raymond Howells tossed a cigarette butt away, then made his way into the entrance of the snooker club.

There were two other men with him. One she recognised, a thick-necked individual with a multicoloured shirt flapping open to reveal his torso. His black skin looked like polished ebony in the blazing sunlight. Carl Masters stood a couple of inches taller than Howells. The other man, whom she didn't recognise, was slightly shorter and wearing a football shirt, red and blue stripes with the word Tulip on it. There was a dark stain down his back.

She watched the three of them disappear into the doorway. Her breath came in gasps.

Stevie looked round frantically.

She had to warn Kiernan.

But how?

Even if there was a phone in the cafe she didn't know the number of the snooker hall and . . .

A phone.

Ryan had told them to call him if they found Howells. She had his number written on a piece of paper in her purse. She quickly rummaged through it, finding the scrap. She noticed there were two numbers on it; one was his car-phone.

Stevie got to her feet and hurried across to the counter.

'Is there a phone in here?' she asked the large woman with the varicose veins.

'Not in here, love,' the woman told her. 'There's one in the pub over there.' She nodded towards the building facing the cafe.

Stevie turned and ran towards the pub.

'They'll be shut now. They're a bit old-fashioned over there,' the woman called after her.

Stevie didn't hear.

It wasn't until she reached the pub that she found it was, indeed, closed.

Seventy-three

'I told you before, Mr Grant' said Emma Powell irritably. 'I have the welfare of the youngsters in my care to consider. I can't allow anyone to look through my files.'

'It's the welfare of my son that I'm worried about' the private detective said, satisfied with his own insincerity. He didn't think she suspected anything untoward. A worried parent was bound to be a little irrational, weren't they?

Experience had taught him that much.

'So you don't know anyone by the name of Howells or Neville?' he persisted.

'No.'

'If you won't allow me to see your files, would you mind if I spoke to some of the other youngsters who are staying here?' he asked.

'You say your son was here two months ago, perhaps longer' she said. 'It's unlikely any of the residents at the hostel now would have been here at the time your son supposedly was. I would appreciate it if you just left, Mr Grant. There are other hostels where you can check.'

'Well, I hope they're more helpful than you've been,' said Ryan, with suitably melodramatic indignation. He got to his feet and looked down at her. 'I've read in the papers of that series of murders of runaways, Miss Powell. I just hope my son isn't next.'

'Goodbye, Mr Grant' Emma said flatly.

He turned and headed for the door, slamming it behind him in mock anger.

Emma stared at the closed door for a moment, the vein on her temple pulsing angrily. As she heard his footsteps receding away down the corridor, she sat back in her chair and exhaled deeply.

What she didn't realize was that Ryan had turned right instead of left out of her office when he left. Instead of heading towards the steps which would lead him to the ground floor and out, he had darted off the other way, past two or three closed doors.

He had spotted the fire alarm further up the corridor before he'd entered; now he looked quickly back and forth to ensure the corridor was empty and, with a powerful blow, drove his hand against the glass of the alarm.

The impact was enough to shatter it. The strident ringing of alarm bells filled the building.

Ryan stepped back, inside one of the doors, hoping there was no one inside.

He was lucky.

As the bells continued to shatter the stillness he eased the door open a fraction, just enough to see Emma Powell's office.

It was only a second before she came hurtling out, heading straight for the stairs, shouting words he couldn't quite make out. Others were hurrying from the other rooms, too. With the clanging bells ringing in their ears, their only thought was to reach the safety of the street.

Ryan slipped across the corridor and into Emma Powell's office. Beneath him and around him he could hear the sound of running feet; of shouting, too.

He knew he would have to work fast.

He slid open the top drawer of the filing cabinet behind Emma's desk, simultaneously digging into his pocket for a piece of paper. On it were written the names of the six runaways murdered in the last few months. He looked at the first name.

ALISON COLE

It matched the name on one of the files.

He checked the next one:

CLAIRE COTTRELL

That also matched.

MATTHEW JARVIS

Check.

He slid open the second drawer.

It was then that he heard movement outside the door.

Seventy-four

Stevie tugged frantically at the pub doors but found they were locked.

She gasped in disappointment and began hammering on them, not stopping until a face appeared from within. The man looked angrily at her, raised his watch and tapped the face.

'We're closed,' he said, his voice muffled by the glass.

'I have to use your phone,' she called back. 'Please, it's an emergency.'

'We're closed,' the man repeated.

1 heard you the first time, you fucking idiot.

Stevie banged on the door again, her face contorted by anger and frustration.

'Please' she shouted. Passers-by gaped at her. 'Open up. I have to use the phone now. Please.'

Anxious to prevent her shattering the glass in the door, the landlord reluctantly set about unfastening it. Stevie stood back a pace, hearing bolts being pulled back. As the door was finally opened a fraction she barged in, nearly knocking the man over.

'What the fuck are you doing?' he snarled. 'I told you, we're closed.'

'I've got to use your phone. Please.'

He regarded her silently for a moment, then jabbed a finger towards a corner of the bar. She saw the pay-phone and scurried across to it, picking up the receiver, feeding coins into the machine. She stabbed out the numbers frantically and waited.

As the ringing continued she tried to control her breathing.

'Pick it up,' she said under her breath.

She heard a click, then the answer machine in Ryan's office cut in.

'Shit,' she hissed and pulled down hard on the cradle. She pulled the piece of paper from her bag and tried the car-phone number.

It rang twice then a metallic voice announced;

'The vodaphone number you have reached is not in use. Please try again.'

She slammed the receiver down, found more change and

tried again.

First the office.

Nothing.

Then the car-phone.

No answer.

'Where are you?' she gasped exasperatedly.

'Right,' said the landlord, advancing on her. 'That's enough. Come on, out.' He hooked a thumb towards the door.

'No, please' she protested. 'I have to make this call. Please.'

'I'll give you five minutes,' he said with finality. 'Then you're out. Got it?'

She nodded and dialled again.

He was just as she'd described him.

Vince Kiernan looked up as he heard the club door open and he saw Raymond Howells walk in, flanked by a black man and a man in a football shirt.

Howells was wearing a loose fitting T-shirt and track suit bottoms which bore the England team's crest. He was thinner than Kiernan had imagined. The unusual thing about him, he noticed, was how big his hands were, disproportionately large for his frame. His hair was indeed shaved over his ears, making it look as if he had a pointed head.

The gold earring dangled from his left ear. Kiernan noticed that it was in the shape of a sword.

For a while the young Irishman stood by the table, his gaze rivetted on Howells as he moved across to the bar with his companions.

So this was the man he'd waited so long to find? The man who might know the whereabouts of his sister. This pimp, this pusher, this ponce. Kiernan closed his fists around the cue until his knuckles turned white, gripping the wooden shaft like a club. His first instinct was to take the cue and smash it across Howells' head. To shatter the wood then use the sharp points on him, drive them beneath his flesh. Pierce his body with them until he told him where Jo was, until he admitted how he had abused her and got her hooked on drugs and . . .

He knew he could not do that.

Not yet.

All he could do was stand helplessly by, not quite sure what to do. Helpless in his rage.

'Your shot' said Courtney, nodding towards the table.

When Kiernan didn't answer, his companion saw where his gaze was directed.

Howells was laughing and joking with the barman and with the two men.

'Do you know him?' Courtney asked.

Kiernan shook his head.

'I thought he was the one you were waiting for. You've been staring at him ever since he walked in,' Courtney said.

The young Irishman tore his gaze away from the pimp.

'Do you know who he is?' Courtney continued as Kiernan tried to line up his shot.

'He just looked familiar that's all,' said Kiernan, trying to dismiss his obvious interest.

Courtney looked on, unimpressed. He glanced across at Howells, then at Kiernan again.

Who the fuck was this guy?

Undercover copper, maybe?

Courtney leant against the next table, watching the young Irishman.

Wondering.

Seventy-five

As Ryan heard the door handle turn he dropped down behind Emma Powell's desk, one of the files still gripped in his hand, the sound of the fire alarm drumming in his ears.

The door opened a fraction and he was vaguely aware of someone peering in, presumably to check that the office was empty. A second later the door was closed and he heard footsteps echoing away down the corridor.

He got to his feet, perspiration beading on his forehead as he shoved one file back into the drawer and looked for the next one.

It would only be a matter of time before they discovered that there was no fire; but, as he found the file, he knew he only needed moments.

Ryan grabbed it and looked at the name, checking it against the list he had.

MARIA JENKINS

He remembered the name from the newspaper articles he'd read. She'd been the most recent of the runaways to die.

He worked swiftly and efficiently, blotting out the strident ringing of the alarm bells, concentrating only on the files in front of him.

JOHN MOLLOY

That name, too, was on his list.

As was the last one.

CARLA SEXTON.

'Jesus,' he murmured under his breath, slamming the drawers shut. As he turned away from the cabinet, a thought struck him. He pulled open the top drawer and ran his finger along the manilla files.

It was there.

STEPHANIE COLLINS

He licked his lips.

Stevie.

From the second drawer he found the other file.

JOSEPHINE KIERNAN.

Ryan slotted both files back into place, then headed for the door, slipping out into the corridor and heading down the stairs.

As he reached the ground floor he saw figures still dashing in and out of rooms. Some were heading out of the main door, where he could see a dozen or more of them gathered.

Ryan glanced to his left and right and saw that one of the rooms was empty. He slipped inside and crossed to the window, sliding it upwards far enough to enable him to crawl through. He hauled himself over the sill and dropped the two or three feet to the ground. He found himself in a narrow alleyway that ran alongside the hostel. Moving unhurriedly, he walked along it and emerged into Ossulston Street itself. To his right he could see the group of hostel residents gathered on the pavement.

By now they would have figured out there was no fire. That didn't matter to him. He'd seen what he wanted to see.

Every single runaway killed in the last few months had spent some time in the hostel.

There were dozens of them all over London; it had to be more than a coincidence that this one home should have been temporary shelter to all six victims.

He headed back to his car and slid behind the wheel.

Emma Powell saw him as the Sapphire pulled away. Her eyes narrowed in anger. She knew what he'd done, realized that he had probably managed to get a look at the files she had been at pains to keep from him.

She hurried back into the building, up the stairs to her office. The filing cabinets were still open; one of the files stuck up out of place in an otherwise immaculately kept arrangement.

It was the file belonging to Stevie Collins.

If the mysterious Mr Grant was looking for his son, she reasoned, why was he so interested in Stevie's file?

As the alarm bells were shut off and peace descended again Emma picked up her phone, ensuring first that the office door was closed.

In fact, before she dialled, she locked it.

This was one call she didn't want anyone walking in on.

Seventy-six

'Come on, for Christ's sake.'

Stevie Collins pressed the phone more tightly to her ear, listening to the constant ringing from the car-phone.

She finally slammed her fingers down on the cradle.

'You've got one more minute, then you're out,' the pub landlord reminded her, leaning against the bar.

'All right, all right,' she said exasperatedly, dialling again, this time to Ryan's office.

As soon as she heard the answer machine begin she hung up.

'Where the hell are you?' she breathed.

She tried the car-phone again. Then the office.

'Come on, for fuck's sake,' the landlord said irritably. 'If you're not off that phone in thirty seconds I'm chucking you out.'

'Look, this call is an emergency,' she said.

'Yeah, they always are,' he said, unimpressed.

She waited a second or two then pressed the digits again, glancing across the street towards the snooker hall.

She wondered what Kiernan was doing inside there. How long Howells would stay.

There was no answer from Ryan's car-phone, just that infernal metallic voice telling her the number was not available at present.

She tried the office and got the machine again.

Stevie was beginning to realize that it was too late.

Her fingers were hurting from pressing the digits so often but she kept trying, knowing deep down that time had virtually run out.

Courtney sent the black ball into the centre pocket and stood back triumphantly.

'Game to me' he said, grinning. 'And my tenner too, I think.' He scooped up the two five-pound notes from the next table and pocketed them.

Kiernan looked across the room at the table on the far side where Howells and his companions were racking up balls for their own game.

At least if they were playing, he thought, it would keep

Howells in one place; perhaps long enough to alert Ryan.

Kiernan knew he had no choice but to watch Howells until the bastard moved, until he left the snooker club. Even if it meant stopping there until late at night he knew he had to stay on his tail. Now he'd found him he didn't intend letting him slip away.

He just hoped Stevie had seen the pimp enter and had called Ryan.

When the club door opened he turned, hoping to see the private detective. To his disappointment it was the man with the moustache from the cash desk outside. He got himself a can of cold drink from behind the bar and retreated back out of the room.

Kiernan licked his lips and tasted sweat.

Just hold on. Stay with Howells.

'Do you fancy another frame?' Kiernan asked. 'Make it a tenner each this time?'

Courtney smiled and nodded.

'Why not? I'll take your money if you want me to. Set the balls up, I'm going to have a piss.'

As his companion disappeared, Kiernan began fishing the balls out of the pockets and placing them in position.

His eyes were drawn hypnotically towards Howells but he kept his head low, anxious that the pimp shouldn't spot him.

Just keep playing, you fucker. I'm not letting you out of my sight.

With the balls set up, he waited for Courtney to return.

Waited and watched.

At last.

The phone rang almost as soon as he picked it up and Ryan flicked it on, reaching for the handset.

'Ryan.'

'Who's that?' he said, disorientated.

'It's Stevie. Where the hell have you been? I've been trying for ages.'

'All right, take it easy,' he said, noticing the urgency in her voice.

'We've found him,' she blurted. 'Howells. We've found him.'

Ryan sat up in his seat; even the stab of pain in his chest was forgotten as the news sank in.

'Where are you?' he wanted to know.
'I'm in a pub . . .'
He heard a series of high-pitched beeps.
'Oh, Jesus Christ,' he heard her say.
'Stevie.'
'Howells is . . .'
The line went dead.
She'd run out of change.

Seventy-seven

'Right, that's it' said the landlord, advancing towards her. 'Out. I said five minutes. You've made your call, now shift your arse.'

'I ran out of fucking change,' Stevie blurted. 'Please, I've got to complete this call. It's a matter of life and death. Just ten pence, that's all I want.'

He shook his head, dug in his pocket and found a twenty-pence piece.

'Here' he said, tossing it to her. 'Have a party.'

Stevie caught it with one hand and immediately pushed it into the phone, dialling frantically.

Try as he might, Kiernan could not keep his mind on the game and he found himself behind once again.

Courtney moved slowly but purposefully around the table potting balls, murmuring approvingly to himself in the process.

Kiernan's attention was focused equally on his opponent and on Howells who was standing watching as his colleague in the football shirt potted balls.

Without realizing it, the young Irishman was staring at Howells.

The pimp noticed.

For interminable seconds across the dimly lit hall they gazed at each other. Then Howells turned to his black companion and said something. He too looked across at Kiernan and nodded. Howells leant closer to speak again.

What if they'd realized who he was? Kiernan thought in a moment of blind panic.

How could they know?

The black man put down his cue and began walking across the hall towards Kiernan.

Now what?

Kiernan felt his heart thudding madly against his ribs as he drew nearer.

'Your shot' said Courtney, but Kiernan seemed uninterested in the game any longer.

The man was still advancing.

'Come on' Courtney pressed.

Then he saw that the Irishman was staring at Howells.

'Do you fancy that fucking geezer or what?' he asked, scornfully. 'You've been watching him ever since he came in.'

The black man was a matter of yards away now.

Kiernan moved around the table, gripping the cue, ready to use it as a weapon if necessary.

'Do you know him or not?' Courtney persisted, prodding Kiernan in the back. 'Is he the one you came in here to meet? Because if he is, then go and play with him. 1 wanted a decent game.'

The black man was at the far end of the table now, his eyes fixing the Irishman in an unyielding stare.

'Either take the fucking shot or let's call it a day here and now' Courtney said. 'I'll take your tenner and . . .'

Kiernan turned and glared at his opponent.

The black man passed by, giving Kiernan a cursory glance. He headed towards the toilets.

Kiernan let out a sigh of audible relief and bent down to take his shot. He put a red into one of the top pockets, looking round as he got up, stealing a glance at Howells then towards the toilets.

He wondered how long it would be before the black man emerged.

She kept one eye on the rapidly disappearing units as she spoke to Ryan.

They clicked away with alarming speed.

'Howells is in a snooker club in the Pentonville Road,' Stevie said, noticing that the units had already flickered down to sixteen. She knew she had to speak fast. 'It's right next door to the Scala Cinema.'

'Where's Kieran?' Ryan wanted to know.

'He's in there, too. He's keeping an eye on Howells.'

Twelve units left.

'He's got a couple of mates with him, Ryan.'

'Do you know them?'

'One of them. A big black guy called Masters.'

Eight units to go.

'Do you know where this bloody club is?' Stevie said.

Six units.

'Yeah, you just hang on. I'll be there in ten minutes.'

He hung up.

Seventy-eight

She saw the Sapphire approaching, saw Ryan glancing agitatedly left and right looking for somewhere to park. There was a barrier of traffic cones across the road opposite and Stevie ran over, dodging between the other cars, pulling two or three of the cones aside.

Ryan shot across the street, cutting in front of the other traffic. A chorus of hooters greeted his manoeuvre but the private detective ignored them, stepping on the brake and bringing the car to a skidding halt. The engine was still running as he slid out from behind the wheel. Only as he clambered out did he turn it off and pull the keys from the ignition.

'How long's Howells been in there?' he asked, striding towards the snooker club.

'About half an hour,' Stevie said, having to run to keep up with him.

'You're sure it's him?'

'Positive.'

As they passed the front entrance of the Scala Cinema a tall, skinny youth with a faded black T-shirt pushed through the door and pointed at Ryan's car.

'You can't park that there,' he said.

'Fuck off,' Ryan hissed, glaring at the youth, who hesitated then stepped back inside the cinema.

Ryan's shirt was flapping as he walked; he was careful to ensure it didn't blow open wide enough to reveal the holster around his waist. Nestled in it was the 9mm Automatic.

He reached the door of the club and almost sprinted up the wooden steps. Stevie struggled to keep up.

'You say he's got two mates with him?' he said.

'I only recognized one of them, though. I've seen him around a few times . . .' She allowed the sentence to trail off, realizing Ryan wasn't listening.

They had reached the top of the stairs now and Ryan moved straight towards the door.

'Hold on, mate,' said the man with the moustache, pulling himself out of his cash desk and blocking the private detective's path. 'I've got to see your membership. You can't just go walking in there and you,' he looked at Stevie, 'I've told you once there's no women allowed, right?'

Ryan looked straight at the man, his eyes blazing.

'Your membership . . .' Moustache said.

'Here's my fucking membership' snapped Ryan, pulling the Automatic from its holster.

He pressed it up under the other man's chin, forcing him back against the door and then through it.

It swung back on its hinges and Ryan, Moustache and Stevie all stumbled in.

Kiernan looked up, a smile flickering briefly on his lips as he saw the private detective.

Everyone else froze.

Ryan pushed Moustache away and the big man stumbled and fell against the bar.

'Fuck,' hissed Raymond Howells. 'The Law.'

Then he saw Stevie.

'There he is,' she shouted to Ryan, pointing at the pimp.

Howells yelled in anger and hurled his cue at Ryan, making him duck. As he did, Moustache suddenly decided to be a hero.

The big man flung himself at Ryan, crashing into him, knocking him against the door. The gun fell from his hand but Stevie snatched it up, watching as Ryan drove a flailing arm out, catching Moustache in the face.

Howells saw his chance.

'Let's get out of here,' he shouted and he and his two companions bolted for the door.

Kiernan stepped in front of them, twisting the snooker cue in his hand, gripping the thinner end.

He swung the cue like a club, the heavy end smacking hard into the face of the black man.

It connected with such force that the cue snapped, leaving the Irishman clutching the thick end.

Masters went down like a stone, clutching his face, blood pouring through his fingers from his broken nose.

'You cunt,' roared the other man, hurling himself at Kiernan.

They crashed against one of the tables, rolling over it, scattering the balls.

Kiernan felt the cue slip from his hand. Strong fingers gripped his throat as the man in the football shirt lifted his head a few inches and slammed it back against the slate bed of the table.

Kiernan thought he was going to black out from the impact, but he reached out frantically for something to defend himself with and his hand closed over one of the snooker balls.

Using all his strength he brought the ball up and smashed it into the temple of his assailant.

The man fell backwards, cracking his head on the overhead lamp, which began to swing crazily.

Kiernan rolled off the table and drove a kick into the ribs of his fallen attacker, smiling as he heard the crack of breaking bone.

Ryan grabbed Moustache by the front of the shirt and headbutted him, catching him above the right eye, splitting the soft skin.

The big man fell back, blood pouring down his face.

'Ryan,' Kiernan bellowed, pointing at Howells who had almost reached the door.

The pimp tried to side-step the private detective's lunge but failed and both of them fell to the floor, Ryan recovering first, driving a fist into the face of his opponent.

The blow split Howells' bottom lip and blood burst from the fleshy flap. Ryan scraped his knuckles on the other man's teeth but kept a firm hold on him, gripping his T-shirt, hauling him to his feet.

Kiernan turned to see the black man rising, one hand still covering his face. He was teetering uncertainly and the Irishman took advantage of his plight, kicking him hard between the legs. The man howled in pain and went down again, rolling over to lie beside his companion in the football shirt who was gasping for breath, clutching his side in an effort to relieve the pain of his cracked ribs.

Stevie handed Ryan his gun and he jammed the Automatic into Howells' face, pushing him out of the door towards the stairs.

Kiernan sprinted across to join them, looking back at the three fallen men.

As they reached the top of the stairs Howells tried to squirm free of Ryan's grip.

'You're going down those stairs, you little ponce,' Ryan

hissed, pressing the barrel hard against the pimp's cheek. 'You either walk down or you go down head first, it makes no fucking odds to me. Got it?'

'You can't fucking do this,' Howells snarled defiantly.

'And who's going to stop me?' the private detective snapped.

'You fucking grassed me up, you slag,' Howells shouted at Stevie.

'Just walk, shithead,' Ryan said, pushing him towards the stairs, keeping a firm grip on his T-shirt. 'Save the conversation for later.'

'I'm saying fuck-all to you,' Howells told him. 'I want my solicitor.'

'Just walk, while you still can.' The private detective glanced at Kiernan. 'Keep your eye on the top of the stairs. Just make sure none of this half-wit's mates decide to try and rescue him.'

Kiernan nodded, moving slowly down the steps behind them, his eyes fixed on the door.

Only when they reached the pavement did he move up alongside Ryan.

They walked to the car.

'You drive,' Ryan said to Kiernan, pushing Howells into the back seat and climbing in after him. He tossed the ignition key to the Irishman, who started the car.

Stevie slid into the passenger seat.

'Where to?' Kiernan wanted to know.

'Just drive,' Ryan told him. 'I want to talk to our friend, Mr Howells.'

Seventy-nine

'Who the fuck are you, anyway? If you're a copper, you'll never make anything stick. What are you going to do? Use that fucking slag as a witness? Was she the one who grassed in the first place?'

Raymond Howells spat out the words, the vein in his temple throbbing madly. He looked alternately at Ryan and Stevie, saving his most venomous words and looks for the girl. She sat with one arm draped over the back of the passenger seat, looking at him.

'You fucking bitch,' he rasped.

'Why don't you shut up?' said Ryan wearily.

'You'll never make anything stick, you . . .'

'I'll stick your head through that fucking window if you don't shut it.'

'Tell me who you are. If you ain't with the Law, then who sent you?' Howells went on. 'You won't get away with this. I've got friends, you know, you . . .'

Ryan shot out a hand and gripped Howells' T-shirt, pulling him across the back seat so that his face was only an inch or two away.

'That's enough,' he hissed. 'Now shut your mouth and listen, for a change. I want you to answer some questions. If you do, I'll let you go. If not,' he drew the Automatic and shoved it hard into Howell's groin. 'If not, I'm going to blow your bollocks off. Got it? I tried to keep it as simple as I could, you fucking half-wit. Now you listen to me. Do you know a man called Don Neville?'

Some of Howell's bravado disappeared as he felt the gun crushing against his testicles. He swallowed hard, trying to look unconcerned.

'Maybe,' he said warily.

Ryan pressed the gun harder against his groin.

'Either you do or you don't,' he snapped. 'Now, unless you want a nine-millimetre vasectomy, you'd better tell me. Do you know Don Neville?'

'Yeah, I know him. Who told you? That slag?' He jabbed an accusatory finger towards Stevie.

'You worked with him,' Ryan said. The words were a statement, not a question. 'Supplied him with girls and boys to make his videos, didn't you?'

'Look, I'm not saying anything until you tell me who you are,' Howells said.

'What difference does it make?' Ryan snapped.

'I want to know who you are.'

'I'm the bloke who's holding a gun against your bollocks. Good enough? Now, how long have you been working with Neville?'

'Why don't you just ask her? She'll tell you,' Howells said angrily.

'I'm asking you, scumbag. How long have you been working with Neville?'

'I'm not saying. I don't work with him, anyway. Yeah, I did supply some kids for his videos. She was one of them. She never fucking complained when she got paid for getting fucked up the arse by three blokes, though, did you?' His anger was again directed at Stevie. 'It was good enough to get you what you really wanted, wasn't it? The shit to stick in your fucking arms.'

'I never saw that money anyway, you bastard. You took it' Stevie said angrily. 'Just like you took the last lot I gave you.'

'So Stevie was in Neville's videos, right?' Ryan interrupted. 'What about a girl called Jo? An Irish girl. Do you remember her?'

Kiernan's ears pricked up as he drove.

'Why should I remember some mick tart?' he wanted to know.

Kiernan glanced at him in the rear-view mirror.

'She was my fucking sister, you bastard,' he snarled. 'If you've hurt her, I'll kill you.'

'I haven't touched her,' Howells said indifferently.

'When did you last see her?' Kiernan asked.

'A couple of days ago' Howells told him. 'Who cares?'

'Was she okay?'

'What am I? A fucking doctor? She was walking about. What more do you want?'

'Kiernan, head for Brompton cemetery' Ryan said, spotting a road sign.

'Why the fuck are you taking me there?' Howells asked.

'Who said we were?' Ryan asked.

'Then where are you taking me?' the pimp demanded.

'Just somewhere quiet so we can have a chat' Ryan said, looking deeply into Howells' eyes. 'And believe me, you are going to talk to me, sunshine.'

Eighty

Her mind was spinning. Images and thoughts tumbled through it. Kim Finlay found she was unable to concentrate on anything for more than a few seconds, unable to focus. She gazed blankly at the TV screen but saw nothing; the images made little or no sense. In fact, if someone had sneaked into the room and removed the set Kim probably wouldn't have noticed. The images were inside her head.

Kelly.

Ryan.

The thought that she could lose her daughter and her first husband so close together was almost intolerable, too horrific to contemplate. Yet it was a thought she found herself confronted with time and time again as she sat motionless on the sofa.

Ryan was dying. That much was certain.

The shock of that was bad enough, but to know that her only daughter might also soon be dead, by violent means, was more than she could take.

Ryan had not contacted them since he'd begun his search for Kelly. She told herself it was because he wanted to wait until he'd found her safe and well before he announced the news. Perhaps he'd even turn up at the house with her. The other side of her mind, the side that insisted on confronting her with logic, told her he had not been in contact because he had no information. Why tell them his search had been fruitless when the absence of communication was testament to that?

Kim exhaled deeply and rubbed her face with both hands, feeling totally numb.

Finlay sat across the room from her, slumped in an armchair, a drink in his hand. He'd drunk a lot that evening; a little too much for Kim's liking, but she could understand. He was under as much stress as she was. But when she looked at him and saw that his expression, too, was blank, she might have expected the images tumbling through his mind to be the same as those which plagued hers.

They were not.

Joseph Finlay was thinking about Kelly, but he was also

thinking about Don Neville and Edward Caton.

And the tape.

That tape.

Ryan had that tape. But who was to say Neville hadn't made copies? Who was to say that, after all this was over, he wouldn't still sell it? More to the point, what guarantee did Finlay have that, when he paid the ransom as he must surely do, Kelly would be released safely?

He had seen what had been done to her on that tape.

What state of mind could he expect to find her in?

If Neville had succeeded once with blackmail, what was to prevent him trying it again?

Secrets.

They filled his mind. Tormented him.

He got to his feet and wandered out of the room, heading for the lavatory.

When the phone rang, Kim picked it up.

It could be Ryan, ringing to say that he'd found Kim, that she was safe and he was bringing her home.

It wasn't.

'I want to speak to Joseph Finlay,' the voice said briskly.

She knew instinctively that this voice belonged to the man who held her daughter.

'Who is this?' she asked, her voice quivering.

'Is Finlay there?'

'He's just popped out. He'll only be a second.'

'If you're trying to keep me talking so the police can get a trace on this line you're wasting your time, Mrs Finlay,' Neville said. 'And if there are police listening in, you're putting your daughter's life at risk. I told your fucking husband he wasn't to contact the police.'

'No one's listening and we haven't been to the police,' Kim said quickly. 'I swear it.'

'You tell your husband I'll ring back.'

'You'd better not hurt my daughter, you bastard,' Kim said defiantly.

Neville chuckled.

'Perhaps you'd better ask your husband why this happened, Mrs Finlay,' Neville said and hung up.

Kim sat there for a long moment, the phone still pressed to

her head, only the drone of a dial tone in her ear.

She still had the receiver in her hand when Finlay walked back into the room.

'Who was that?' he asked anxiously.

She dropped the phone back onto the cradle.

'The man's who's got Kelly,' she said flatly. 'He's ringing back. He wanted to speak to you.'

'What about?' Finlay demanded, his brow furrowing.

'I don't know, Joe. You'd probably have more idea than me.'

'What the hell is that supposed to mean?'

'He said I should ask you why Kelly was kidnapped. Why would he say that? Why would you know?'

'The bastard's playing games with you, Kim. It's not enough for that kind to realize the misery they cause, they have to hear it too. They enjoy it.'

'Who are they, Joe?'

'How the bloody hell should I know?' Finlay snapped with undue defensiveness. 'I told you, that kind of person, they . . . it's a game to them. A psychological game.' He picked up his drink and drained what was left in the glass, wiping his mouth with the back of his hand. 'If Ryan got his bloody finger out and found some leads this could all be over with.'

'Don't blame Nick,' she said irritably.

The phone rang again.

This time Finlay picked it up, his hand shaking.

'Yes,' he barked.

'Just listen to me, Finlay,' said Neville. 'This has gone on long enough. I'm sick of waiting for the fucking money. I want it by midnight tomorrow night, got that?'

'And Kelly . . .'

'Just shut up and listen. You pay up and you get the kid back. Bring the money to Forty-three Carnaby Street tomorrow night. We'll make the exchange then. Midnight. If you're one minute late then the kid is dead. And don't forget, come alone. If I so much as suspect you've got someone with you the deal's off and you can use some of that fucking money to go towards your daughter's funeral. Understand?'

Finlay swallowed hard.

'Understand?' Neville hissed.

'Yes, you bastard, I understand.'

'Midnight tomorrow night and we'll complete this little bit of business.' Neville chuckled. 'Don't forget what I told you. Come alone. If I see anyone else but you I'll do my magic trick for you.'

'What are you talking about?'

'I'll turn your fucking daughter into dog meat.'

He hung up.

Eighty-one

The noise of the crowd was deafening, even at that distance. Coupled with the rattle of passing tube trains the spot in Brompton cemetery where Kiernan stopped the car was anything but peaceful.

It was ideal.

The floodlights of Chelsea Football Club's Stamford Bridge stadium shone brightly, illuminating the dusky sky, while thousands of supporters roared encouragement.

As Ryan stepped out of the car the roar seemed to diminish; he assumed one of the visiting Liverpool players had the ball. But his thoughts were not of football as he moved away from the car and motioned for Howells to follow him.

Kiernan and Stevie were already out of the Sapphire and standing close by, watching as the pimp eased himself uneasily out of the vehicle and glared at each of them in turn, his most venomous look reserved for Stevie. Some of Howells' bravado had disappeared, however. His eyes still darted back and forth angrily but there was fear behind them.

'Why the fuck have you brought me here?' he said.

'I want you to tell me about Neville' Ryan said calmly. He lit up a cigarette and drew hard on it.

'I told you all I'm going to tell you,' the pimp said.

'Yeah, so you said,' Ryan reminded him. He took a step forward so that he was barely a foot away from the pimp, who recoiled slightly. 'Now I want to know when was the last time you saw him?'

'I haven't seen him for months.'

'When was the last time you supplied him with kids for one of his videos?' Ryan persisted.

'I told you, I haven't seen him,' Howells insisted.

The movement was so swift it took Kiernan and Stevie by surprise.

Ryan swung the Automatic upwards and slammed it into the side of Howells' head, opening a cut on his temple. As the pimp went down heavily, Ryan grabbed him by the T-shirt with one hand, sliding the 9mm into his belt at the same time.

Using two hands he raised Howells up and slammed the back

of his head against the back door of the car.

There was a dull thud. The pimp moaned; his head felt as if it were about to burst.

'How long since you saw Neville?' Ryan snapped.

There was a series of loud roars from the direction of Stamford Bridge.

'I haven't seen him,' burbled Howells, blood running down his face.

Ryan pulled open the rear door and jammed Howells' left hand between the frame and the chassis.

Kiernan, realizing what he was about to do, looked at the private detective in astonishment.

'How much did he pay you for the kids?' Ryan snapped.

'He didn't pay me...'

Ryan kicked the door.

It crashed shut, crushing Howells' hand, bones splintering under the impact. Two knuckles were pulped; the fingers bent into bloodied lumps.

Howells screamed in agony.

He tried to pull his hand away, but Ryan held it there and glared into his eyes. They were filled with tears and bulging madly.

'Talk to me, you cunt' he hissed angrily at the pimp. 'How much did he pay you to supply the kids?'

Howells didn't answer. The pain from his pulverized left hand seemed to have crept up his arm until it felt as if the entire limb was on fire. The appendage was numb; only the pain made him aware it was still attached to his wrist. He tried to pull away but Ryan kept a firm grip on him, twisting him round so that he was staring into his face.

'You got kids from the Ossulston Street hostel, didn't you?' the private detective snarled.

Howells opened his mouth to speak but no words would come out, only sobs of pain.

Ryan slammed the door on his hand again.

Howells' caterwaul of agony was swallowed by a massive roar from the Chelsea fans.

The pimp's hand now looked as if it had been dipped in blood. Kiernan could see pieces of shattered bone sticking through the pulped mess of lacerated flesh.

'You got kids from the hostel, didn't you?' Ryan snarled.

Howells was sobbing now, tears of pain rolling down his cheeks.

'Didn't you?' bellowed Ryan, kicking the door shut again.

As the door shut for the third time on his crushed hand, it looked as if Howells was going to pass out. Ryan grabbed him, slapping his face hard to keep him conscious, denying him the oblivion of a blackout.

'Didn't you?' he repeated.

'Yes,' Howells screamed, blood from his pulped hand running down the side of the car.

Ryan looked across at Kiernan and Stevie and saw the Irishman nod imperceptibly.

'How much did Neville pay you for the kids you supplied him with?' the private detective continued.

Howells was slumped on one side, his hand dangling uselessly by his thigh, blood oozing from several lacerations.

'How much?' Ryan persisted.

'I can't tell you,' Howells wailed.

Ryan shut his right hand in the door.

As he dragged it open the pimp fell face down on the earth, his body motionless.

'Get up, you fucker,' snarled Ryan, placing one foot perilously close to the injured left hand.

Howells didn't move.

Ryan kicked him hard in the side.

The pimp rolled over; his body was racked by sobs.

'Please,' he blubbered.

'Please what?' Ryan hissed. 'Please don't hurt you? Don't hurt you the way you hurt those kids you sold to Neville?'

'I didn't know what he was going to do to them, I fucking swear it,' Howells cried.

'Liar,' said Ryan and stamped on his shattered left hand. He kept his foot there, twisting the heel, not letting Howells get up.

There was another roar from Stamford Bridge.

'Ryan, for Christ's sake,' Kiernan said, stepping forward.

The private detective glared at his companion.

'What?' he snarled. 'Didn't you want me to hurt him? Remember, Kiernan, this is the bastard who used your sister. She could be dead because of this piece of shit.'

Dead, like my daughter.

'How much did he pay you?' Ryan demanded.

'A hundred for each one,' Howells whimpered, both his hands now little more than crimson lumps.

'When was the last time you saw Neville?' Ryan continued.

'I'm not sure,' Howells sobbed..

Ryan brought his foot crashing down on the pimp's outstretched left hand with such force the nail of his middle finger came off.

'When?' Ryan shouted.

'About three months ago' Howells screamed.

'Fucking liar. When?'

'Three months ago! Jesus fucking Christ, I swear it,' Howells said, the pain now intolerable.

'Where?' Ryan demanded.

'I can't remember, honest to God. If I could, I'd tell you. I haven't seen him for three months at least. I've told you all I know, I fucking swear it.'

'Where does he make the videos?' Kiernan interjected.

'I don't know that either,' Howells blubbered. 'I just got him the kids. On the last film he said he didn't need me. He'd found somebody else to get them for him, he said. I haven't seen the cunt since.'

Ryan looked at Kiernan, bemused.

Someone else to get the kids for him.

'Who was getting him the kids?' the private detective asked.

'He didn't tell me.'

Ryan stepped back. The pimp was curled up in a foetal position, rocking himself gently, his pulped hands held out like bloodied trophies.

'How long is it since you worked for Neville?' Ryan said to Stevie.

'About three months,' she confirmed.

'So the bastard's telling the truth. Maybe Neville's was getting the kids from someone else. What we've got to find out is who.'

He held out his hand towards Kiernan.

'Give me the car keys,' he said.

'What about him?' Kiernan said, nodding towards Howells.

'He's told us all he knows' Ryan said with certainty. 'He's served his purpose.'

The private detective drew the Automatic from his belt and aimed it at Howells who, even through his pain, looked up in terror, trying to drag himself backwards on what were little more than pulverized bleeding stumps.

'You can't' he sobbed. 'Please.'

'I don't think you'll be missed' Ryan snarled. 'What's one less piece of dog shit on the pavement?'

He pulled the trigger.

The hammer slammed down on an empty chamber.

Three things happened simultaneously.

There was a massive roar from Stamford Bridge that seemed to fill the night.

Raymond Howells filled his pants.

Then he fainted.

He lay still on the earth.

Kiernan exhaled deeply.

'When did you take the magazine out?' the Irishman asked.

'As I got out of the car' Ryan said, sliding behind the steering wheel.

He glanced round to see Stevie going through the pockets of the unconscious Howells. She scurried back to the car brandishing a couple of twenty-pound notes, which she stuffed into her handbag.

'At least I got some of my money back,' she said cheerfully.

Ryan looked blankly at her then started the engine, guiding the car along the cemetery's narrow tarmac tracks until he reached the main gate.

As he waited to turn left into Fulham Road he glanced first one way, then the other. He caught sight of some slicks of Howells' blood on the rear door. He ignored it and drove on, heading back into the West End.

Eighty-two

The suite Charles Thornton used as offices consisted of four rooms situated over The Emperor Club in Dover Street. It was the largest of the casinos Thornton owned; it was especially close to his heart because it was the first such establishment he had ever purchased. It seemed an eternity since he'd taken over the licence from the previous owner, albeit with a campaign of intimidation the Krays would have been proud of. But the club was his and now he sat in the opulent splendour of the largest room, the one he used as his personal office, sipping a glass of mineral water and gazing across the room at a huge panoramic painting depicting the Circus Maximus. Thornton smiled to himself. His admiration for the Roman way of life, the power and the organization, had prompted him to name the club after the ancient civilization's leaders. He saw himself as something of a modern-day Caesar, conquering where necessary, consolidating, bargaining and generally ruling the largest underworld empire in London. Most of what he dealt with was legitimate; to the outside world Charles Thornton represented the face, and an acceptable one too, of successful business.

Now this successful businessman, who had personally been responsible for at least three killings and indirectly responsible for many more, sat brushing specks of dust from his polished desk, glancing now and then at his own reflection in the gleaming sheen.

'Are you sure I can't get you a drink?' he said, smiling.

Joseph Finlay shifted in his seat and shook his head.

'I told you, Charles' he said. 'This isn't really a social call.'

Thornton smiled again.

'Well, if it's that important, perhaps we'd better get on with things.'

Finlay looked round to see Phillip Alexander standing by the door.

'I wanted to talk in private,' Finlay said.

'I trust the people who work for me, Joe. You can speak in front of Phil.'

'In private,' Finlay said, unimpressed.

Thornton's smile faded. He looked at Alexander and nodded

towards the door.

'Just wait outside for a bit, Phil,' he said and the other man left.

Finlay waited until he heard the door close before he spoke.

'I need something from you, Charles. It's important.' He swallowed hard.

Thornton raised his eyebrows quizzically.

'I guessed it must be for you to come here,' he said.

'I don't know how to say this.' He lowered his gaze momentarily. 'I want someone . . . taken care of. I need you to . . . dispose of someone for me, or however you put it in your business.'

'My business. What's that supposed to mean?'

'You know bloody well what I mean. All this . . .' He made a sweeping gesture, designed to encompass the entire room. 'You didn't get it by using your business acumen, did you?'

Thornton regarded him coldly.

'You're a crook, Charles. A gangster. Let's not beat around the bush. We've known each other too long for that.'

'Yeah, let's not beat around the bush' Thornton echoed angrily. 'You call me a gangster, a crook. What does that make you? Don't try to come across all fucking virginal with me, Finlay. You're dirtier than 1 am. It's just that you try to hide behind your credentials, behind your nice cosy little family.' He glared at the property developer. 'Like the man said, Finlay, we're just part of the same hypocrisy.'

'I want someone lolled' Finlay said flatly. 'A hit. I'm willing to pay for it.'

'Well, well, well' Thornton said sardonically. 'Mr Upstanding Himself.'

'I said I'd pay. Will you do it?'

'Why is it so important to you?'

'I can't say. Listen, Thornton, you're the only one who can help me now. Either you'll do it or you won't but I'll pay you whatever you want.'

Thornton could hear the desperation in the other man's voice. He considered him carefully.

'Who's the bunny?' he wanted to know. 'Who's giving you so much grief you want them hit?' He emphasized the word scornfully.

'There are three of them.'

'Three? Jesus, what have you been up to, Joey boy?'

'This is no joke. Will you do it or not?'

Thornton stroked a hand over his hair and sat back in his seat.

'It's going to cost you, Finlay' he said slowly.

'I told you, I don't care how much I have to pay. Money's no object.'

'And money's not what I want. You're right, it's going to cost you but not cash.' He tapped the desk top gently. 'I want that building in Cavendish Square. The one you've been sitting on all this fucking time. That's my price, Finlay.'

'You can have it' he said unhesitatingly.

Thornton narrowed his eyes, suspicious of the other man.

Two weeks ago you'd have shit glass rather than sold me that building. Why the change of heart?' he wanted to know.

'I told you, I need you to do this job for me and I don't care what it takes. If it's going to cost me the building, that's fair enough.'

'Write it down,' said Thornton, pushing a piece of paper and pen towards the other man.

'What are you talking about?'

'Put it in writing that the building is mine. I want it on paper. We'll get it done properly later, but I want assurances from you.'

Finlay hesitated.

'Do it, Joe,' Thornton insisted. 'Just something simple will do. I, Joseph Finlay, hereby declare that as of today's date,' he looked at his wristwatch to verify what it was, 'agree to sell Number Seven Cavendish Square to Charles Thornton. This agreement to be effective as of noon today.' He checked his watch again. 'That's in about ten minutes' time.'

Finlay gripped the pen until the tip of his finger hurt but then he began to write. Finally he handed the paper to Thornton.

'Sign it,' Thornton told him, pushing it back.

He did so.

'Satisfied?' Finlay said irritably.

Thornton smiled and nodded.

'The building's yours. Will you do the job for me?' Finlay persisted.

Thornton got to his feet, taking the piece of paper with him.

He crossed to a small wall safe which he proceeded to open, placing the folded paper inside.

He took out something Finlay couldn't see until he laid it on the desk before him.

The metal glinted under the lights.

'Ruger .45 revolver' said Thornton. 'You can load those in it.' He tossed a box of shells onto the desk beside the pistol.

'What the hell are you talking about?' Finlay said, suddenly anxious.

'I'm not sanctioning a hit on your behalf, Finlay. You want the fucking job done, do it yourself.'

'We made a deal' Finlay said angrily.

'You should know not to trust me, Joe. After all, I'm a gangster according to you.' His smile vanished rapidly. 'But I've got better things to do than send my men chasing around blowing away some arseholes who've upset you. What do you think this is, the fucking Godfather?' He glared at Finlay. 'Now get out. Our meeting's over.'

'You bastard' hissed Finlay, reaching for the gun.

He gripped it and pointed it at Thornton, who merely shook his head.

'Get out of here, Joe, or I'll stick that gun so far up your arse you'll be able to load it through your nose' he hissed. Then he shouted, 'Phil.'

The door opened and Alexander entered.

'Make sure Mr Finlay leaves the building, will you, Phil?' Thornton said.

Finlay picked up the gun and ammo and dropped them into his jacket pockets.

'You don't want to be walking around the streets like that, you know, Joe' he said, grinning.

Finlay glared at him.

'I ought to kill you,' he hissed.

'I wouldn't recommend you try. By the way, who are you going to kill?'

'What fucking business is it of yours?' snarled Finlay.

'They might be friends of mine,' Thornton said, grinning.

'Their names are Neville and Caton.'

Thornton frowned and shot a glance at Alexander. He merely shrugged.

What the fuck was going on here?

'And the third one?' Thornton asked, his smile replaced by a look of bemusement.

'He's a private detective,' said Finlay. 'His name's Ryan.'

Eighty-three

'I can't see what good this is going to do,' Stevie said.

Ryan tapped gently on the steering wheel, waiting for the lights to turn green.

The private detective didn't answer at first; his attention was drawn to the young woman driving the car in the next lane. It was an XR3i, with its top down. The woman was wearing a pair of denim shorts and a halter-neck top that barely restrained her breasts. She brushed the hair away from her face, re-adjusting her Ray-Bans. Then she glanced in Ryan's direction and realized he was looking at her.

He smiled. She smiled back.

Sit on this, Ryan thought.

While you still can.

He closed his eyes tightly for a second. When he opened them again the girl had gone. The lights were green and someone behind was banging their hooter. He drove on, trying to ignore the pain in his chest. He'd taken a double dose of morphine that morning but he still felt discomfort.

Was the end coming more quickly than he'd expected?

He gripped the wheel tightly, catching a brief glimpse of his haggard reflection in the rear-view mirror.

'I said, I can't see what good this is going to do' Stevie repeated.

'I heard you,' he said, the words almost lost as the car entered the Euston Road underpass. The sound of so much traffic reverberated around them; the stink of exhaust fumes became even stronger. Only when the car eventually emerged into daylight again did Ryan speak.

'I want you to have a look at the files in Emma Powell's office,' he told her, 'to see if you recognise any of the kids there. She's got pictures of most of them in the files.'

'And how the hell are we going to get into her office? She's not going to invite us in and make us a cup of tea while we look, is she?'

'Did she always keep the files locked away?'

'How the hell do I know?'

'You stayed at the bloody place; you must know how she ran

it.'

'I wasn't really interested in how the place was run. It was somewhere to live, that was it. I didn't give two fucks about how it was run.'

'More interested in the charming Mr Howells, were you?'

'You're starting to sound like Kiernan, now. He never stops digging at me. It's my fucking life and I can do what I like with it.'

'It makes no odds to me at all what you do with your life, Stevie. I just need your help. I'm paying for your fucking help, in fact.'

'Yeah, that reminds me. You owe me money. You said you'd pay me when we found Howells. Well, we found him. I helped you find him. You owe me.'

'You'll get it, don't worry,' Ryan snapped. 'It's not going to break your back to do one more thing for me. I'll give you another hundred quid if you're that fucking desperate.'

She took a comb from her handbag and began running it through her hair.

'What are you going to spend it on when you get it?' Ryan asked. 'Drugs?'

'Is it important? Why the hell are you and Kiernan always preaching? Have a look at yourself in the mirror before you start trying to run my life for me.'

'How well did you know Kiernan's sister?' Ryan asked.

'We were friends. We used to work the same beat, we had the same punters.'

'And the same pimp,' he said. 'Where do you think she could have gone?'

'London's a big place, Ryan, you don't need me to tell you that.' Stevie shrugged. 'Paddington. The Strand. Any of the other meat racks. It's difficult to say. I reckon he'll be lucky if he finds her, though. I mean, it's like trying to find a needle in a haystack, isn't it? Besides, I don't think he's realised she might not want to go home even if he does find her. She must have left home for a reason to begin with.'

'And you? Why did you leave?' the private detective wanted to know.

Stevie swallowed hard and turned her head to look out of the window.

'I was pregnant,' she said flatly.

'Did your parents want you to get rid of the baby?'

'My father did. My mother didn't know, or didn't care either way.'

'So you left?'

She nodded.

'My father gave me the money for the abortion. He didn't want me to have it, you see.' She smiled bitterly. 'He didn't want anyone to find out it was his.'

When Ryan glanced at her, he saw that there were tears in her eyes.

'That's right, I was being fucked by my own father,' she said, looking at him. 'It started when I was eleven. I got pregnant when I was fifteen. He tried to blame it on someone else, but I knew it was his. I left home just before my sixteenth birthday and came to London. Two days after I arrived I had a miscarriage.' She shrugged involuntarily. 'I've never seen so much blood. The hospital said I was lucky I didn't die.' She looked down at her hands. 'Put it down to experience, eh?' There was contempt in her voice.

He swung the car into Ossulston Street, looking for a parking space close to the hostel.

Stevie glanced towards the building, seeing no movement on the steps that led up to the main door.

Ryan drove past once, still looking for somewhere to park.

'Ryan, look,' Stevie said suddenly, jabbing his arm.

He followed her pointing finger.

Emma Powell had emerged from the hostel. She looked to her right and left and then set off down the street towards Euston Road.

'She looks like she's in a hurry,' Ryan mused, observing her short, agitated steps. Every few yards she would break into a run.

Ryan turned the car in the middle of the street, narrowly avoiding an Astra parked on his left, and headed off down the thoroughfare.

'What are you doing?' Stevie asked.

'I want to know where she's going,' he said, his eyes never leaving Emma as she hurried along.

'What about the files?'

'They can wait.'

As they waited, Emma looked at her watch and quickened her step.

'Do you think she's late for an appointment?' Ryan said.

A pedestrian moved to step in front of his car and Ryan blasted a warning on the hooter, not wanting to lose sight of Emma.

She headed down Euston Road.

'What if she's just going to get a sandwich?' Stevie asked.

'Then I'll have been wasting my fucking time following her, won't I?' Ryan replied.

Emma was finally turning into the gateway that led to the main entrance of St Pancras Station.

Ryan raised his eyebrows in surprise and guided the car up the ramp in front of the station, ignoring the taxi that was almost on his rear bumper. The private detective kept his eyes on Emma.

'What the hell is she doing?' he murmured.

Heading for the entrance, she was checking her watch again.

She broke into a slight run when she saw the person she had come to meet.

The man was leaning against the red brickwork of the station facade. As he caught sight of Emma he smiled broadly and walked towards her.

Ryan watched as they embraced, holding each other before kissing passionately.

'Well, well,' he said, smiling. 'I wonder who the boyfriend is?'

Stevie gazed intently at Emma and her companion as they stood close, arms around one another.

'And during work hours, too,' Ryan said with mock reproach.

Stevie was still staring at the couple, her eyes unblinking. He lit up a cigarette.

'Do you know that geezer?' he asked.

Stevie nodded.

'That's Don Neville.'

Eighty-four

There was a steady stream of people moving both into and out of St Pancras and Neville guided Emma away from the irregular procession, pulling her closer to him. She kissed his cheek and he smiled at her, tilting her head up and looking into her eyes.

'What's wrong?' he asked, smiling. 'Why were you so anxious to see me?'

'Are you complaining?' she said.

He shook his head and snaked an arm around her waist.

'Let's go in and get a drink,' he suggested.

'I can't stop, Don,' she told him. 'I've got to get back to the hostel. I had to speak to you, though.'

'What's on your mind? I know you well enough after ten months to know that something's bothering you. What is it?'

She sighed.

'There was someone round at the hostel,' she told him. 'He said he was looking for his son. I forget his name. He wanted to check my files, everything.'

'Did you let him?'

'Of course I didn't.'

'So what's your problem?'

'He was asking questions, Don. He asked if I knew Ray Howells.'

'So what? So he's heard Howells' name. A lot of people know the little prick. That's no big deal.'

'What if he was a policeman?'

'If he'd been with the law, he'd have looked through your fucking files whether you wanted him to or not. And even if he had looked, so what? What would he have found?'

'There are files on the six kids who've been killed.'

'So what? That doesn't necessarily link you to them. Let the law come looking and asking questions if they want to.'

'That's easy for you to say; you're not the one who'd have to face them. I'm not sure I could, either.'

'What does that mean, Emma?'

'It means I've had enough, Don. I can't do it any more. I can't carry on giving you the names of kids leaving the hostel. I can't carry on sorting out the ones with no families so you can use them in your films. I want out.'

Neville eyed her suspiciously for a moment.

'It's only a matter of time before the police pick up a lead and then they'll find you. They'll find both of us. And then what?'

'You're asking me to stop making the films, is that it?' he said sharply. 'You're asking me to stop selling them, to give up all the money it brings in?'

'You've killed six. How many more will there be?'

'What is this? An attack of conscience?' He laughed bitterly. 'It's a little late for that, isn't it, Emma? A bit late to try and get out? You're in as deep as me,' he snapped, grabbing her wrist and pulling her closer. 'You supplied us with the names of the kids from your hostel. You gave us those kids. And don't tell me different. You knew what my business was. You agreed to help. You got rid of that dead baby for me, don't forget that, too. You're as much a part of this as me or Eddie Caton.' He released her wrist. There were white marks where the pressure of his grip had caused indentations. Emma rubbed the marks gently and looked at Neville.

'I won't go to jail, Don,' she said quietly. 'I can't.'

'No one's going to jail,' he told her. 'Because no one's going to get caught. Understand?'

She lowered her head but Neville held her chin gently and looked into her eyes.

'No one is going to jail,' he repeated.

She touched his hand gently.

'You love me, don't you?' he asked.

She nodded.

'Then trust me.'

He pulled her to him and kissed her again, their bodies pressed tightly together.

What the fuck do I do?

Ryan sat helplessly in the car, one hand unconsciously brushing against the butt of the Automatic. How easy it would be to haul Neville into the car now, to force him to lead the way to Kelly.

'Are you sure that's him?' Ryan asked, his eyes never leaving the couple.

'Positive,' Stevie confirmed. 'He always wore his hair in a pony-tail. I'd recognize him anywhere.'

Ryan chewed his bottom lip thoughtfully.

What the fuck do I do?

The car-phone rang and Ryan snatched it up.

'Yeah,' he barked.

'Ryan, it's Kiernan,' said the voice at the other end.

'What do you want?' the private detective snapped. 'I've got Neville standing in front of me right now.'

'Jesus Christ. What are you going to do?'

'I wish I knew. What's so important?'

'You told me to stay here and monitor the phone until you got back, right?'

'I know what I told you to do,' Ryan snapped. 'Get to the point.'

'There was a phone call a few minutes ago from some guy called Finlay. Joseph Finlay. Fie said he had to speak to you urgently.'

'What did he say?' Ryan demanded.

'I didn't take the message myself, it's on the answering machine.'

'Where the fuck were you? That's what I left you in my office for, to take the calls.'

'Even 1 have to piss, Ryan,' Kiernan said angrily. 'The fucking message is here, anyway. I think you should hear it. Finlay mentioned Kelly.'

Ryan hung up and immediately started the engine, guiding the Sapphire out of the station car park and back towards Euston Road.

'What the hell are you doing, Ryan?' Stevie said, watching Neville and Emma disappear through the rear window. 'I thought you wanted to talk to Neville.'

'I'll talk to him,' he said quietly, glancing into the rear-view mirror at the man with the ponytail. For now, all he was concerned with was getting back to his office.

He had to hear the message.

Eighty-five

'Ryan. Ryan, if you're there pick up the phone. All right, listen. This is Joseph Finlay. I know where Kelly is. The kidnappers rang me. I've got to give them the money tonight. I need your help. I'll be at your office by eleven-thirty. Ring me at my office if you need to, you know the number.'

Ryan pressed the 'Review' button on the machine and sat staring blankly at it as the tape rewound. He pressed 'Play' and listened for the third time.

Kiernan sat on one edge of the desk; Stevie was perched on the end of the sofa. Neither of them spoke. The Irishman was watching Ryan's face. Stevie puffed agitatedly on a cigarette.

'It's over' Ryan said finally, getting to his feet.

'What's over?' Kiernan asked.

'Our little working relationship,' said the private detective, pouring himself a drink. 'This menage a trois.' He smiled humourlessly. 'You, me and Stevie. It's finished. I don't need you any more. You can go.'

'As easy as that?' said Kiernan.

'As easy as that,' Ryan told him, downing a large measure of whisky.

'Bollocks,' snapped the Irishman. 'I came looking for my sister and I'm going to find her. You said that if we found Howells he might lead us to Neville, and if we found Neville we' might find my sister. Well, I'm not giving up now. I've come too far for that. I'm not going home without her. I'm not leaving, Ryan. I'll come with you tonight if I have to. Anything.'

'Very touching,' said the private detective, taking another large swallow. 'What about you, Stevie?'

She shrugged.

'I agreed to stay until you found Howells,' she said. 'You said you'd pay me if I helped you find him. I helped you.' She raised her eyebrows expectantly.

'Quite right,' Ryan said, crossing to his desk. He slid open one of the drawers and took out what looked like a small strongbox. Using a tiny key on his key ring he opened the box and took out two wads of notes. He tossed first one then the other to Stevie, who caught them.

'There's a hundred and fifty in each one' he told her. 'That was the deal, wasn't it? Three hundred notes when we found Howells. It's all there. Count it, if you like.'

She pushed the money into her handbag.

'I trust you,' she said, smiling thinly.

'Never trust anyone,' Ryan said sardonically.

Stevie got to her feet and moved towards the door, hesitating when she reached it.

'Thanks for the money,' she said quietly.

'A deal's a deal,' he said.

'You're really going to walk out?' Kiernan asked. 'Just take the money and fuck off?'

'What do you expect me to do?' she protested.

'I didn't expect anything from you,' the Irishman told her scathingly. 'Three hundred quid should buy a lot of drugs. I hope you're happy.'

'I hope you find your sister,' Stevie said, one hand resting on the doorknob.

Kiernan turned his back on her.

'When you do, perhaps you should ask her what makes her happy,' she added. Then, to Ryan:

'See you around.'

And she was gone.

'Fucking slag,' rasped Kiernan.

'She did her bit,' Ryan said quietly, draining the last drops from his glass. He looked up at Kiernan. 'So you want to be a fucking hero, Kiernan?'

'I just want to find my sister, right?' he said.

'Very noble.'

'I'm sick of your fucking attitude, Ryan,' the Irishman snapped. 'I offered to help you.'

'I didn't ask, did I?'

'This isn't just for your benefit, it's for mine.'

'You don't know what you're getting yourself into. Things have changed now, Kiernan. It isn't a case of wandering around Soho or King's Cross hoping you'll spot her now, you know. You're close. And the closer you get, the more dangerous it gets. Are you ready for that?'

Kiernan nodded.

Ryan tossed him his keys.

'That cabinet over there.' He motioned to the other side of the room. 'Use the small brass key to open it.'

Kiernan did as he was instructed.

He saw the .357 lying there.

'Take it,' Ryan told him.

The Irishman reached for the pistol.

'You might need it,' Ryan said cryptically. 'Have you ever fired a gun before?'

'No.'

'Let's hope you haven't after tonight.' He fixed the Irishman in an unblinking stare. 'You could die, Kiernan.'

'Everybody dies, Ryan.'

The private detective began to laugh, a bitter hollow sound.

'Tell me about it,' he said flatly.

Eighty-six

He reached out to touch the piles of money, running his fingertips gently over the stacks of notes bound with elastic bands. Finlay swallowed hard and then closed the briefcase, snapping it shut. He exhaled deeply and turned to study his full-length reflection in the bedroom mirror. There were beads of sweat on his forehead and his skin was waxen, like a Madame Tussaud's effigy.

'Let me come with you.'

Kim was sitting on the edge of the bed, looking alternately at her husband and at the case.

Finlay shook his head.

'It's too dangerous' he said. 'Besides, they said I had to be alone.'

'They said no police, didn't they?' she insisted.

'Kim, I have to go alone,' he snapped, nervousness getting the better of him.

There was a long silence, which was broken finally by Kim. 'What if she's already dead?' Her voice was almost inaudible.

'She won't be,' Finlay told her, his assurance doing nothing to relieve her concern.

'You sound very sure of that, Joe.'

'Look, we're doing what they told us to do,' he said, agitated. 'I'm taking them the money. The police haven't been informed. We've followed their instructions. There's no reason why they should kill her. I just give them the money and they hand Kelly over to me.'

'And it's as simple as that?' she said sardonically. She was pulling distractedly at the corner of the duvet. When she looked up at him he could see the tears in her eyes.

'She'll be okay,' Finlay said, wishing he believed his own assurances.

Kim merely nodded.

He looked at his watch; his hand was shaking.

'I'd better go,' he said, picking up the briefcase. 'I've got to meet Ryan soon.'

'Don't let her get hurt, Joe, please,' Kim said, a single tear rolling down her cheek.

He paused in the bedroom doorway, thought about going back to her. Thought about kissing her. Instead, he headed out onto the landing and down the stairs.

Kim sat on the edge of the bed until she heard the front door close behind him. Then she wandered out onto the landing, crossing to the window that overlooked the driveway. She watched Finlay place the briefcase on the passenger seat and slide behind the wheel of the Jag. He started the engine then pulled away, disappearing into the night.

Kim looked at her watch.

It was 9.36 p.m.

Finlay also checked the time on the dashboard clock.

It should take him about an hour to get to Ryan's office.

As he shifted in his seat he felt the bulk of the Ruger .45 pressing against his side, secreted beneath his jacket. Kim had not known he was carrying it. He had spare shells in his pocket, should he need them.

He reached down with one hand and touched the butt of the pistol.

He had to be sure he could reach it quickly enough when the time came.

Edward Caton worked the slide on the Ithaca Automatic shotgun, chambering a round. The Deerslayer, as the weapon was affectionately nicknamed, felt comfortingly heavy in his grasp. He sat at the battered wooden table thumbing shells into the breech, working the slide every now and then.

Opposite him Don Neville was thumbing .44 calibre shells into the magazine of his Desert Eagle. When the magazine was full he slammed it into the butt of the pistol and worked the slide, flicking on the safety catch before jamming the weapon into his belt.

In the top of one boot nestled a Bowie knife. The thick curved blade glinted in the dull light as he pulled it free.

He ran a thumb over the razor-sharp edge, like a surgeon about to perform an operation. Satisfied, he slid the knife back into his boot and pulled his jeans down to cover the hilt of the blade.

He glanced at his watch.

'Do you think he'll try to fuck us over?' said Caton, putting the shotgun on the table and picking up the snub nose .38 that lay there. He began pushing bullets into the chambers.

'I wouldn't put it past him,' said Neville. 'Even though he knows we'll kill the kid if he does.' He ran a hand through his hair, pulling his pony-tail away from the back of his neck. 'I'll tell you one thing, he won't come alone.'

Caton looked at his companion quizzically.

'I know that bastard,' Neville continued. 'He thinks he's so fucking clever.' He smiled thinly.

'He wouldn't dare,' Caton said.

'If he's coming mob-handed then we'll meet him mob-handed,' Neville said. 'Get on the blower. Call Macardle and Thompson, tell them to get over here straight away. And tell them to bring shooters.' His eyes narrowed. 'I'll show that fucker.'

He looked at his watch again.

10.16.

Eighty-seven

Vince Kiernan turned the gun over in his hand, feeling the weight of the .357, seeing the office lights glint on the chrome of its frame.

It was already loaded, with six heavy grain shells pushed into the chambers.

'Have you ever killed anyone?' Kiernan asked, glancing at Ryan, who was gazing out of the office window at the lights of Charing Cross Road.

The private detective sucked hard on his cigarette and blew out a long stream of smoke.

'Yes' he said without turning round. 'But not with a gun.'

Kiernan put the pistol down and looked intently at him.

'When I was a policeman,' Ryan told him.

'I didn't know you'd been a policeman.'

'There isn't much about me you do know, is there?'

Like the fact I've got fucking cancer.

'What happened?' Kiernan asked.

'There'd been a hit-and-run accident in Camden. Some drunken bastard had ploughed into a bus queue and killed a woman and one of her kids. We tracked him down and I went in to arrest him. He ran for it. He couldn't have been much older than you. I chased him up onto the roof of the tower block where he lived.' Ryan shrugged. 'He went over the top. Twenty-five storeys, straight down.'

'You pushed him?' Kiernan asked, quietly.

'That's what the official report said.' Ryan sucked in a deep breath, wincing as he felt the pain in his chest. 'I was at the bus stop where he hit the woman and kid minutes after it happened. She was only young, twenty-two or twenty-three. The kid was pretty, too. It was difficult to tell after he'd run over her, of course. The car broke her neck and her back, fractured her skull in six places. When one of his wheels went over her arm it tore off a hand. The kid was about three. We found pieces of its brain in the treads of his tyres.'

Kiernan swallowed hard.

'So did you kill him or not?' he persisted.

'Did he fall or was he pushed?' Ryan chuckled. He looked at

Kiernan. 'He wanted to give himself up. He bottled it when he realized he had nowhere else to run. All I could see was that dead woman and kid. Then he started bleating about how it wasn't his fault. I threw the cunt over the safety rail. I watched as he fell, watched him hit the concrete.' He took a last drag on his cigarette then lit another. 'Best thing for him.'

A heavy silence descended.

Kiernan watched the private detective glance at his watch. Smoke surrounded him like a bluish mist.

The buzzer on the voice-com sounded and Ryan crossed to it.

'Yeah, who is it?' he said.

'Finlay.'

'Come up,' said Ryan and jabbed a button on the panel.

By the time Joseph Finlay had walked up the five flights of steps to Ryan's office he was sweating like a pig. As he reached the door he paused, pulling his handkerchief out of his pocket to wipe his brow. He also checked that the Ruger was hidden from view.

He found Ryan waiting for him. Even in the dull light of the office he could see how white the private detective looked. Kim hadn't been specific about the nature of Ryan's illness but he certainly looked rough.

As he glanced round the office Kiernan emerged from the kitchenette area sipping at a glass of water.

'Who the hell is he?' snapped Finlay.

'He's coming with us,' Ryan said. 'His name's Vince Kiernan.' He turned to the young Irishman. 'Kiernan, this is Joseph Finlay.'

'No way, Ryan. It was supposed to be just you and me,' Finlay said irritably.

'Well, now it's not,' Ryan told him. 'We might need all the help we can get.'

'How do you know you can trust him?' Finlay protested.

'Why shouldn't he trust me?' Kiernan snapped.

'I trust him more than I trust you. He's coming with us, so get used to it.'

'If they see anyone with me, they'll kill Kelly. You know that,' Finlay said.

'They're not going to see anyone,' Ryan hissed.

'If she dies, Ryan, I'm holding you responsible,' Finlay told him.

'Open the case,' Ryan told him.

Finlay lifted it onto the desk and flipped it open, revealing the money inside.

'Jesus, how much is there?' Kiernan said.

'One million,' Finlay told him, shutting the case again. But Ryan opened it and pulled out one of the wads, flicking through it.

'What are you doing?' Finlay asked angrily.

'Just making sure you haven't decided to be a fucking smart-arse,' Ryan told him. 'You know, a fifty at the top of each pile and a fifty at the bottom but nothing but newspaper or blank paper in between. You can bet your arse they'll check.'

'It's all there' Finlay snapped. Grabbing the money back and dropping it into the briefcase, he snapped the lid shut.

Ryan looked at his watch.

'We'd better go' he said and reached for the Automatic hanging in its shoulder holster on the back of a chair. He strapped it on, watching as Kiernan did the same.

'Remember,' Ryan said to the Irishman, 'if you do have to use that don't jerk the trigger. If you're close enough to what you're shooting at you should be able to hit it. That'll put a hole in a brick wall at fifteen feet.'

'Guns?' said Finlay with mock consternation.

'They're kidnappers,' said Ryan mockingly, 'not fucking lollipop men. You take care of the money and let me worry about the rest of it. They might not be too keen on your walking out of there, Finlay, whether you've paid them off or not.'

Kiernan fastened the strap on the shoulder holster and closed his jacket over it.

'All right?' Ryan asked.

He nodded.

Ryan winced as he felt a stab of pain. He turned away so that the others couldn't see his discomfort. He opened the desk drawer and stared down at the bottle of morphine.

He shut the drawer again, gritting his teeth against the pain.

'Come on,' he said, looking at his watch.

It was 11.16.

Eighty-eight

'The cunt isn't coming' Colin Macardle said, puffing at his roll-up, spitting a piece of tobacco onto the dusty floor. He was standing against the wall of what had once been the sitting-room in the flat above Forty-three Carnaby Street. A Viking double-barrelled shotgun was propped on his shoulder.

In the kitchen Paul Thompson was pacing back and forth in the gloomy glow cast by the paraffin lights, peering at the filthy room. He seemed fascinated by the cracked sink. A large earwig dragged itself out of the plughole and scurried across the filthy china.

A 9mm Browning Hi-Power was stuck in Thompson's belt.

He moved through into the tiny bathroom, urinating gushingly into a lavatory that had long ago ceased to contain any water. When he'd finished he peered into the bedroom beyond.

Still covered by a sheet, still tied securely to the reeking mattress lay Kelly. Her eyes were closed.

Thompson stared at her for a moment and then walked back into the living-room where the other three men were gathered.

'I think the kid's asleep,' Thompson said, sitting down on a rickety wooden chair.

'I said, he's not coming,' Macardle repeated.

Neville looked at his watch.

11.43.

'He'll be here' he said sternly.

'And we have to sit around like pricks waiting for him?' the Scot muttered.

'It's nearly time,' Neville insisted. 'He'll be here.'

'What do we do after he's delivered the money, Don?' Caton asked.

'Kill him and the kid,' Neville said flatly. Then a thin smile touched his lips. 'Perhaps we should film it.' He laughed.

The picture had been taken about two years ago. Kelly was dressed in a blue dress, her hair plaited.

Kim ran her fingers gently over the glass, over the image of her daughter. She shuddered.

Despite the warmth of the room she felt cold - the chill came from within. It seemed to grow inside her like a freezing tumour.

Like Nick's?

She found her thoughts turning to her ex-husband. Suddenly they were tumbling through her mind at dizzying speed.

Ryan.

Kelly.

The kidnapping.

The phone calls.

Kim held the photo to her breast as she might hold a sobbing child.

As she would hold Kelly.

She prayed that she might have that joy again but still the iciness grew within her, spreading through her veins like a virus.

She glanced at the clock on the mantelpiece; the seconds were ticking away as the deadline drew closer.

She tried to imagine what Finlay was doing now, but all she could think about was Kelly.

And she wept.

'We'll give you two minutes, then we'll follow,' said Ryan, looking down Carnaby Street.

It was empty at such a late hour; only a shadowy figure lay in the nest of cardboard he'd pulled around him in a shop doorway halfway down the thoroughfare.

Pieces of paper drifted on the warm breeze like strange tumbleweeds. Ryan felt like humming the theme to 'The Good, The Bad and the Ugly'.

He put a hand to his chest as he felt more pain, but he forced it away and jabbed the watch-face again, ensuring that the other two men did the same.

'Two minutes?' Finlay said, swallowing hard.

He could feel the gun jammed into his trousers digging into his side.

Kiernan also checked his watch.

Finlay set off, his pace brisk, his steps even.

Both men watched him, hidden in a doorway across the street. They saw him hesitate as he reached the main door of number forty-three. He pushed it and found it was stuck. After a light bump with his shoulder it swung open.

Finlay disappeared inside.

Other eyes had seen him enter.

'Finlay's inside,' said Edward Caton, leaning back from the window that looked out onto Carnaby Street.

'Is he alone?' Neville asked.

'I can't see anyone else,' Caton said, squinting into the gloom. He turned and smiled broadly.

'Party time' Neville said. He too was smiling.

He worked the pump action of the Ithaca.

Eighty-nine

The dust was so thick it stuck to his shoes, muffling his footsteps. Small clouds rose with each footfall as Finlay made his way slowly through what had once been a shop.

The wooden floor was littered with rubbish. Waste paper and empty tin cans were scattered everywhere, covered by a fine film of dust.

In the gloom, Finlay peered upwards. Plaster had fallen from the ceiling in a number of places, here and there in lumps. It crackled when he stepped on it; the sound reverberated within the hollow shell.

Shelves had been pulled off the wall and lay strewn around in the jigsaw of neglect. Even their metal brackets had fallen or been torn free of the wall. Several pieces of timber seemed to have dropped from the panelled ceiling.

Nearly blind in the enveloping gloom, Finlay moved as cautiously as he could but the floor was like a huge booby trap. Fie managed to remain on his feet only by shooting out a hand to steady himself against a wall. Muttering under his breath he moved on, picking up the briefcase which had fallen from his grasp. It was coated in dust, too, but he gave it only a perfunctory wipe; the dust stuck to his hand.

Ahead of him on the left was a door he assumed led to the back of the shop.

He paused before opening it, stepping through to find himself at the bottom of a narrow flight of stairs.

Dull light leaked down from the top of the steps. As he stood gazing up, Finlay saw a figure appear above him.

Edward Caton was holding the .38 on him.

'Come up' he said.

Finlay began to climb.

From the same side of Carnaby Street, invisible to any prying eyes that might be watching from the window of number Forty-three, Ryan scurried from one shop doorway to another. He beckoned Kiernan to follow him. The Irishman's heart thudded hard against his ribs.

The private detective pushed open the main door, relieved when it didn't squeak. He moved into the cloying darkness followed by Kiernan, who looked round at the neglect and decay. The place smelt of cats' piss. Or rats, he thought, scanning the floor for any signs of movement.

Picking their way over the debris, the two men moved with infinite slowness through the shop towards the far end.

There was creaking from above them. Ryan held up a hand to halt Kiernan's progress.

They stood motionless for interminable seconds, frozen like statues; they even held the breath in their lungs.

Kiernan saw Ryan slip the Automatic from its holster, then he advanced again.

There were more creaks from above, then voices. They were impossible to distinguish, even in the silence.

The door ahead was slightly ajar. The feeblest of light rays trickled through the crack like water through a split container.

The private detective moved towards the door, edging it open a fraction more, trying to hear the voices more clearly.

Kiernan watched his face intently, his heart thudding hard against his ribs.

Ryan heard Finlay's voice, then another man's, and another's.

There was laughter. Muted, bitter.

He peered towards the ceiling.

'How many do you think?' Kiernan whispered nervously.

Ryan shrugged.

'Three, four. It's difficult to tell.'

He heard more creaking from above, louder this time and he motioned Kiernan away from the door.

Someone was coming down the stairs.

Ninety

'It didn't have to come to this, you know,' said Neville, holding the Ithaca in one hand, the barrel levelled at Finlay's chest.

'Just let me see my daughter,' said Finlay sharply.

'Get the kid, Paul,' Neville said to Thompson, his eyes never leaving Finlay.

Thompson headed for the bedroom.

'Put the money down on the table,' Neville said, nodding towards the briefcase.

'Not until I've seen Kelly,' Finlay said defiantly. He looked at Caton, who still held the .38, then back at Neville. Behind him Macardle was heading down the stairs.

'Put the case on the table' Neville said.

'No' Finlay insisted, feeling the Ruger pressing against his side.

His mind was spinning.

Even if he managed to get the gun clear in time, how the hell was he going to take out four men without them killing him first? He'd never even fired a gun before.

Thompson returned from the bedroom, clutching Kelly. She was bound and gagged; tears streamed down her face.

'Let her go,' Finlay said, his voice cracking.

'The money' Neville insisted.

Finlay dumped the briefcase heavily on the table, flipped it open and took a wad of notes out, hurling it at Neville.

'Now let her go' he shouted.

Neville picked up the money and held it beneath his nose, inhaling gently, smiling.

'Cut her loose,' he said to Thompson, who began untying the girl.

He pulled the gag from her mouth.

'Help me, please' she sobbed.

'It's going to be okay, sweetheart,' Finlay said.

'Touching, isn't it?' Neville said to Caton.

'You bastard' Finlay snarled.

Should he pull the gun now?

'Let her go' Finlay rasped.

'We'll count this first' Neville said, and laid the shotgun on the table top.

Now?

Finlay's breath was coming in gasps.

Where the hell was Ryan?

As the sound of footsteps grew louder on the other side of the door, Ryan eased the 9mm Automatic into the firing position, level with the head height of anyone who might step through the door.

Kiernan thought about drawing his own gun, but as he stepped back, he tripped and stumbled over a piece of thick wood.

Ryan shot him an angry glance.

The footsteps drew nearer.

The door opened and Macardle stepped into the shop.

For what seemed like an eternity everything froze, then Macardle opened his mouth to shout a warning.

Kiernan moved with lightning speed, grabbing the piece of wood he'd tripped on, swinging it up like a club.

He swung it with incredible force, driving it into Macardle's face. The impact shattered the bridge of his nose.

The Scot let out a low choking sound and dropped to his knees. The shotgun fell from his grasp.

Kiernan brought the lump of wood down again, this time across the top of his head.

The blow fractured his skull, almost splitting the parietal bone.

He fell forward at Kiernan's feet, arms stretched out on either side of him as if in supplication.

'Come on,' shouted Ryan and they both dashed up the stairs.

As he reached the top, he heard just three words:

'Kill the kid.'

Ninety-one

Ryan heard someone shouting, but barely realized the roars came from his own throat.

He flung himself up the last two steps and into the room, the Automatic already levelled.

In one brief split second he saw everything in the room with amazing clarity, as if his mind had become a camera, the image imprinted there fleetingly.

Immediately in front of him was Finlay, standing close to an old wooden table.

On the other side of the table he saw the man he knew as Don Neville and, beside him, Edward Caton.

To his right, in a doorway, stood Paul Thompson.

He had one arm around Kelly's throat.

It was her scream that seemed to signal the beginning of the explosion.

'Dad,' she shrieked.

Ryan spun round, firing twice, high to avoid Kelly. The first shot missed, blasted plaster from the wall, but the second struck Thompson in the face, powering into his jaw just below his lower lip. Teeth and bone were driven back by the impact and Thompson's head snapped backwards as if jerked from behind as the bullet caught him. Blood and fragments of bone sprayed Kelly, who fell forward, still screaming.

Finlay threw himself to one side, deafened by the thunderous discharge of the pistol in such a small room. The sound was eclipsed a second later as Neville swung the Ithaca up to his shoulder and fired.

The stock slammed back against the collar bone as the shotgun spat out its lethal load.

Hurtling up the steps behind Ryan, Kiernan crashed into him, knocking him to one side.

Luckily the collision took him out of the path of the shotgun's blast. The massive eruption blew a huge hole in the wall behind.

Cursing, Neville worked the slide and fired again, the second blast ripping a crater in the floor.

The sound of firearms in such a small area was monstrous;

they were all deafened by the thunderous retorts. Everything seemed to happen in slow motion.

Ryan fired again, scrambling forward on his knees.

The slide pumped back and forth, spent shell-cases flying high into the air.

Another shot blasted out part of a light socket; the next missed Caton by inches.

Caton swung the .38 round and fired back.

Kiernan howled in pain as a bullet cut through his left calf; it felt as if his leg was on fire. He rolled over, blood spilling from the wound, leaving a slick behind him.

He hauled the .357 free and fired twice, shouting in pain and fear, his bellows drowned by the massive discharge. The pistol bucked in his hand, the stock slamming against him with numbing power.

Two shots thudded into the wall beside Caton, who had not noticed Kelly scrambling out from beneath Thompson's body. She ran through the kitchen towards the bathroom.

Ryan was on his knees now, firing, his breath rasping in his lungs and throat, his mouth dry. The stench of cordite filled his nostrils.

Neville kicked the table over to give himself some cover.

The briefcase and its expensive load went flying,

money scattering everywhere as the table thudded over onto its side.

A bullet ripped through the wood and grazed Neville's cheek.

'Jesus' he shouted, rising to fire again.

'Come on,' screamed Ryan. 'Fucking kill me, you cunt.'

Finlay was crawling across the room towards the door, past the injured Kiernan who was trying to haul himself upright.

Caton fired twice with the .38.

The handgun retort was drowned by the massive blast of the shotgun.

Finlay screamed in agony as a bullet blasted off his right middle finger.

The digit was severed by the high velocity slug; he saw it skid across the floor.

Pain immediately enveloped his arm and blood poured from his hand.

Kiernan tried to steady the .357 but it pulled low.

More by luck than judgement he caught Caton in the left hip.

Travelling at over 1,450 feet a second the bullet shattered Caton's pelvis, blasting away a huge portion of bone before exiting upwards through the lowest lumbar vertebrae. A spray of blood and pulverized bone exploded with the bullet. Caton dropped like a stone, the gun falling from his hand, his body paralysed.

Kiernan tried to put another in him, but as he was aiming Neville swung the Ithaca around and fired.

The blast hit him in the chest, ripping through ribs and one lung, puncturing the fleshy bag like a balloon. Blood burst from the wound, the exit discharge carrying lumps of greyish-pink tissue with it which spattered the wall behind the Irishman. He went down in a heap, still clutching the gun.

Ryan saw him fall and fired again at the table Neville was using as cover. Pieces of wood were blasted away. One of the bullets skewed wide, taking off most of Caton's nose and a portion of the side of his head.

Kiernan was slumped against a wall, his body quivering madly. He looked down to see a dark urine stain on the front of his jeans. Blood from his wounds was flowing rapidly from his body; his left side felt as if someone had pulled it open with red hot tongs. He could see portions of shattered rib gleaming whitely amid the pulped mess of flesh and lung. When he tried to breathe it felt as if his chest were being crushed. He tried to speak but the blood, rising in his throat, only let out a liquid gurgle.

He saw Finlay pull the Ruger free of his belt and wave it aimlessly in the air, pulling the trigger to send a bullet harmlessly into the ceiling.

Neville hurled the table over again, trying to knock down Ryan, then the man with the pony-tail hurled himself towards the kitchen in pursuit of Kelly.

Ryan fell backwards, firing all the time, until the slide shot back signalling an empty magazine. He pulled another from his pocket, slammed it into the butt and worked the slide, getting off two more shots but missing with both.

He rose.

As he did Kiernan saw movement on his other side.

At the top of the stairs.

His face a bloodied mess, Macardle swayed there for precious seconds, the sawn-off shotgun levelled at Ryan.

Kiernan could only utter his warning in liquid sounds.

Macardle pulled both triggers simultaneously.

The massive blast hit Ryan in the back, destroying both kidneys, ripping a hole in his back large enough to get two hands in. He pitched forward, blood spilling from the gaping wound.

Kiernan raised the .357, so close to Macardle the muzzle was touching the Scot's leg.

The bullet blew his right kneecap off, splitting the patella and the tibia, almost severing the limb.

He crashed to the ground, facing Kiernan, looking up at him in pain, his mouth open.

Kiernan pushed the .357 into Macardle's mouth; the steel cracked his teeth. Then he fired.

The bullet took off nearly all the back of the Scot's head. Blood, brain and bone were blasted into the wooden floor as the bullet erupted from his cranium, the entire head looking as if someone had placed an explosive charge inside it. Kiernan was splashed with blood and viscera but it was hard to tell to whom it belonged. The room had been transformed into a slaughterhouse.

Deafened by gunshots, blinded by muzzle flashes and choked by cordite and smoke, the survivors smelled the stench of blood and death.

Ryan was lying face down, his spine visible through the wound in his back, tendrils of flesh hanging from the extremities like bloodied confetti.

Caton and Thompson were dead.

Kiernan felt very cold. Tears were forming in his eyes as he sat slumped against the wall. He told himself it was from the pain, but in fact there was little pain, even from the wound in his chest. Every time he tried to breathe the wind hissed through the ruptured lung. He saw Finlay holding the Ruger with one hand, his other arm hanging uselessly at his side, the middle finger blown off. The hand looked as if it had been dipped in red paint.

Kiernan looked down at what was left of Macadle's head and noticed that his eyes were open.

He had a speck of plaster on the iris of his left eye.

Kiernan wondered why something like that should attract his attention.

It was his last thought.

Finlay crawled past the dead Irishman, heading for the kitchen.

Money was scattered everywhere, great wads of it, soaked in blood.

He saw a figure in the doorway. Two figures.

Neville had hold of Kelly by the hair. In his other hand he held the Bowie knife; it was pressed against her throat.

'Finlay,' Neville rasped. 'I'm going to cut her fucking head off.'

Ninety-two

'Let her go.'

The words were gargled through blood.

Ryan felt it spilling over his lips as he struggled to force them out, holding the gun on Neville.

The private detective could hardly feel his legs but he managed to haul himself around on his side so that he was facing Neville.

'Forget it,' Neville snarled. 'She's fucking dead, anyway. Even if you shoot me I'll still have time to cut her throat.'

'Let her go,' Ryan croaked again, the gun wavering in his grip.

Neville knew he only had to wait a moment or two longer and Ryan would be dead.

Finlay took a step towards him.

'Back off' Neville said, his attention drawn to the other man.

Finlay kept coming.

'I told you,' Neville shrieked, his eyes blazing. 'I'll fucking kill her.'

Finlay raised the gun.

Ryan gritted his teeth and held the man with the ponytail in his sights. Fuck, he felt cold.

Fuck. Fuck. Fuck.

This is what you wanted.

But he had to know Kelly was safe.

Before . . .

Finlay stepped closer, the Ruger levelled.

'Last warning, cunt,' Neville snarled, spittle spilling onto his lips.

'Do it,' Ryan urged. 'Finlay, do it.'

'Now she dies,' hissed Neville.

Finlay fired twice.

He shot Ryan both times in the back. One bullet passed through the fleshy part of his side; the other cracked his collar bone as it exited.

Neville looked on, aghast, his jaw dropping.

Kelly screamed.

The shrill exaltation and the shock of what Finlay had just done made Neville lower the knife.

Kelly fell forward, free of his grip, away from the blade.

Finlay, glassy-eyed, raised the Ruger and, from less than two feet away, shot Neville.

The first bullet hit him in the stomach, puncturing his abdomen, macerating a huge portion of his lower intestine. The second struck him in the right eye, drilling the socket empty and bursting from the back of his skull like a rocket, sending blood and brain splattering up the wall in a sticky red flux. He fell backwards, the knife falling from his grasp.

'Why did you shoot my dad?' Kelly sobbed, crawling across to the body of Ryan- 'Why?'

'I'm sorry, Kelly,' said Finlay, his face splashed with blood, his hand dripping crimson. He looked ashen. 'I had to.'

'Oh, Dad, no,' she sobbed over Ryan.

'I wish you hadn't seen it,' Finlay whispered, and raised the Ruger again.

He was straddling Kelly, the barrel touching the top of her head.

'I do wish you hadn't seen it,' he said again, his voice cracking.

He thumbed back the hammer.

Ryan heard the sound as if it came from a million miles away. As he opened his eyes he saw everything through a red haze.

He saw Kelly bending over him.

And Finlay straddling her, the gun pointing at her head.

He saw Neville's discarded knife lying so close.

So close.

He mouthed her name as he closed his fingers around the hilt.

Finlay pulled the trigger.

The hammer slammed down on an empty chamber.

Ryan drove the knife upwards with all the power he could muster.

The blade tore through the material of Finlay's trousers, plunging on and upwards, shearing through his scrotum, slicing one testicle in half and carving away the penis as it thudded into his stomach from below.

Finlay let out a high-pitched scream and tried to pull the blade free but Ryan kept hold of the hilt, ignoring the blood that cascaded onto his hand and face. He twisted it, driving it deeper, the churning knife slicing the other testicle free.

Propelled by a thick spurt of blood it hit the floor with a wet plop, together with a portion of the severed penis.

Finlay was still shrieking as he fell back, finally allowed to fall as Ryan released the knife.

Blood was spreading out in a massive pool around him; some of it lapped against Ryan as he lay in a foetal position on the floor.

The screams diminished slowly. Now Ryan could hear another sound.

It was the high-pitched, strident wail of sirens.

Coming closer.

Kelly was bent over his body now, crying uncontrollably.

'Oh, Dad, please,' she sobbed.

He raised one bloodied hand and touched her cheek. Tears filling his eyes.

'I love you,' she wept.

He couldn't speak the words but he mouthed them, his lips curling upwards.

'No,' Kelly shouted helplessly. 'Don't die.'

She shook him, as if to bully him into clinging onto life.

The sirens were drawing nearer.

Kelly touched his face, her body trembling.

'I love you, Dad,' she whispered.

Nick Ryan was smiling.